Windswept Hearts

by

Robynn Gabel

Robynn Gabel

ISBN-13: 978-1-941446-25-6
Edited by Chryse Wymer
Cover Design by Rachel Olson No Sweat Graphics

Original publication by © Robynn Gabel June 6, 2012
BookRix GmbH & Co. KG Einsteinstraße 28 81675 Munich Germany

Second publication by © Robynn Gabel
Tri-Swan Press, LLC February 21, 2016
3 Sunshine Dr., Lander WY 82520

2

Acknowledgment and Thanks

They say it takes a village to raise a child. The same could be said about writing a book. The best thing I ever did was get the courage to become a member on BookRix. There I met a big network of people who read, commented, directed, edited and gave advice. I have so many to thank; Lazarus, Patrick, Cav, Carolann and Val. Special thanks also to my friends, Viola, Dan and Jane.

Formatting is a foreign language, as well as blogs and websites. My grateful thanks goes to Richter Indy Publishing in helping me navigate those cyber worlds in the first edition. A big thank you goes to Gwen Steel for formatting the second edition.

My family was especially patient, and my husband, Darrell, could probably recite this book word for word.

The one I owe the greatest gratitude to, the lady who became my friend, hero and mentor, is my editor, Chryse Wymer. Without her patience, talent for drama and extensive knowledge of grammar, this would be a typical, mediocre story.

Book Cover Art

Thank you to No Sweat Graphics, for the beautiful cover set-up. If you need a cover for your e-book, please feel free to contact Rachel A. Olson at:

https://www.facebook.com/NoSweatGraphics .

Robynn Gabel

Dedication

This book is dedicated to a true romantic,

my husband, Darrell Gabel.

Robynn Gabel

Table of Contents

Robynn Gabel

Chapter 1 – Beginnings

What happens if you break a deathbed promise? Anna mused, the pull of the Corvette's engine infusing her with a sense of daring.

The car growled over the music, happily consuming miles, bringing her closer to a decision she didn't want to make. Checking the mirror, she caught sight of the luggage behind her. A frown creased her brow. *Leave it to Wyoming weather to be so unpredictable you need to pack sweatshirts with shorts.*

The strident voice of a car horn caused her to glance over at a cocky grin beneath expensive sunglasses. For several miles, she had toyed with the driver of the yellow Mustang, speeding up when he would draw even with her.

Those who knew Anna Sanchez didn't have a clue about this side of her. She floored the gas pedal with competitive glee as the powerful Vette surged ahead, effortlessly widening the gap. Gripping the steering wheel, she felt the car attached to the road like a magnet to steel. Again checking the rearview mirror, she noticed dark shadows under her eyes and the Mustang disappearing into a little dot behind her.

A smooth, mechanical voice spoke against the growl of the engine and beat of the music, "Make a right-hand turn at next exit." Confidently, she handled the power that shot the car onto the ramp, ignoring the forty-mile-an-hour sign.

Memories popped up as a slide show on a computer screen. Anna learned to drive early on her grandfather's tractor due to a farm permit--one positive to living in the country. But in her mind, there were more negatives than positives.

Anna's hands tightened on the wheel. Her grandmother, rotund and cheerful as she bustled about the kitchen, was the complete opposite of her glacial grandfather. He sat at the head of the table during quiet meals; his stern, eagle-eyed stare watched them chat, rarely joining the small talk

She rubbed her left temple. The last two years had been nothing but funerals and endings. Only her goal of completing college kept her going. Had it only been six months since Mom's passing?

The navigation system's voice broke into her reverie. "Take a left-hand turn in one-quarter of a mile." She knew the way to the ranch; the unit was on for the illusion of company. Anna slowed the Vette, rumbling over the metal bars that created a cattle guard to keep livestock from escaping to the highway. After the narrow drive cut around a low hill, a bunkhouse came into view. From there a small path traveled down to the traditional, two-story ranch house. It had two dormer windows above a white summer porch in the front. A ridge covered in scrub pine rose behind the home.

Further down the dirt road, a weathered but well-kept barn stood guard over the sloping pasture where several horses grazed. A dark-blue sedan sat parked in front of the porch. Two boys, with the exuberant energy of youth, raced around brandishing branches in Musketeer fashion.

A young woman stood on the porch, her red-gold hair framing a welcoming smile. Two years older, Emily, her second cousin, filled the role of big sister. The Vette sighed as Anna flipped the ignition off. Jumping out of the car, she opened her arms wide, giving Emily a bear hug. Their laughter tinkled in the breeze.

"How was the drive?" She stepped back, looking Anna over.

"Fast today, but, of course, the mode of transportation does make a difference."

Emily raised an eyebrow as she gazed at the sleek sports car. "I guess so. When did you get a Corvette?"

"First of May. It probably seems extravagant for a school teacher, but it's my reward for graduating college while dealing with everything that has been going on the last few years."

"If anyone deserves it, you do. You haven't visited in forever, girl!"

Anna leaned in for another hug. "Thankfully, it's not for another funeral."

"Been tough with your mom gone, hasn't it?" Sympathy softened Emily's green eyes.

Words tumbled out, tears rising. "It's hard. I miss her so much. I'll think of something I want to tell her and suddenly remember she's gone."

Emily wrapped an arm around Anna's shoulder, murmuring "I'm so sorry." They stood for a minute, leaning on each other. Anna drew a deep breath and stepped back, brushing away tears.

One little musketeer, with his brother hot on his heels, ran around the side of the porch. Emily reached out, snagged the bedraggled twig in one hand and his arm in the other. His brother recognized her intent to grab his branch next and moved away.

Anna leaned down and grabbed them both in a warm embrace.

"Oh, my, you boys are getting big! So, John, Matthew, how old are you now?" The boy closest to her, a skinny, strawberry blond, smiled at Anna.

"I'm eight, and Matthew is six."

"Already?" Anna shook her head.

"Auntie, when I get older, can I drive your car?"

Anna grinned. "We'll see. I'll give you both a ride later." She watched as Matthew circled the car, his eyes wide.

"Well, shall we check out the house?" Anna rummaged in her small purse and brought out clanking keys on a simple metal ring.

The worn key slipped easily into the brass door handle, turning with little effort. The musty smell of old inhabitation wafted out into the spring air. As if frozen in time Anna noticed tattered house slippers lay next to her grandfather's overstuffed chair. A newspaper dated October twelfth straddled the arm of the chair as if the occupant would be back any second to resume reading.

The chair's mate, a spindly wooden rocker, had an end table beside it. Small reading glasses and a worn Bible fought for space on the table. Anna's throat tightened as she remembered her grandparents sitting here in the evening.

She walked into the kitchen where dishes sat unwashed in the sink. The refrigerator hummed endlessly; the rooster clock on the yellowed wall still ticked off the moments as it had for years. She gripped the edge of the kitchen counter, her ribs feeling like they were collapsing, crushing her racing heart.

Emily had headed down the hall to scout out the rest of the house. Anna heard the bathroom door squeak open, a familiar sound. The boys scampered up the narrow staircase to the attic bedroom where Anna and Emily had spent many nights together. She pushed off from the counter and joined Emily in the room at the end of the hall; quickly glancing around noticing clothes laying over a chair; medication sitting on the nightstand, and the unmade bed. Anna had the distinct feeling she was intruding. She sighed. It was nothing new.

"I'll need to find someplace with moving boxes in town. Are any of the churches or secondhand stores taking donations?"

Emily pursed her lips. "Yes, the Methodist church, but a lot of this we'll have to throw out."

Anna nodded as she opened the closet. Antique boxes and old albums lined the top shelf. Well-worn clothing hung limply. She moved to the nightstand, absently opening the drawer. Next to a few odds and ends, she found a small, red, leather-bound book with the word 'diary' printed in faded, gold lettering. In her hand, the rustling pages gave off a slight rose odor, her grandmother's favorite perfume. She tucked the diary gently away.

Anna heard John yell. She stepped out onto the front porch to see the boy's backside as he lay on the weathered planks, peering over the edge. "I think I hear baby kittens under here. You can see where the momma cat squeezed under the boards. Eww, it stinks too."

She walked over, noting the bare earth: evidence of an animal going to and fro under the deck flooring.

Emily poked her head out. "Leave them alone. They got a momma somewhere around here. Don't disturb them. Where's your brother?"

John jumped up. "Matthew!" he hollered, running around the side of the house.

"Want to visit our old haunt?" Anna chuckled at Emily's glare.

"You know I hate those stairs. Especially how narrow they are since I'm older and much wider."

"Race you!" Anna pushed past Emily heading to the steep staircase to the attic bedroom, the old wood squeaking loudly under her steps. The spacious attic took up the entire upper level. The top of the stairs ended at the rear of the room.

It was her favorite place in the house. The old, pine floor sported a shiny glow. Two single beds, covered in Chenille bedspreads of aged white, sat under two gabled windows. Old pictures of family long past decorated the walls. Red checkered curtains completed the Western decor. Anna gazed out the window, remembering the evening sunsets over the Wind River Mountains.

Her ribs now expanded easily to take in the musty air. Snapshots of childhood memories filled her mind. The nights they spent reading under the covers with a flashlight, Emily planning the next day's adventures and both of them giggling late into the night.

Emily's heavy footsteps thudded, her breathing labored as she got to the top of the stairway. Anna sat down on a bed, smiling.

"Gosh, girl, what a workout, and as always, you get the best bed. Think I'll crash here and take a nap."

Anna giggled, feeling young again.

"You know, I told you that you were going to marry Seth Higgins!"

Emily blushed, heaving a pillow at Anna, who gracefully ducked out of its flight path. Emily plopped down, the mattress squeaking in protest.

"Yeah, well, we'll find a knight in shining armor for you yet."

"I'm perfectly happy being single, especially after the run-in with Miles."

Emily quickly changed the subject. "What are you going to do with the ranch?"

Anna lay back, gazing at the patterns on the ceiling. She rubbed at both temples for a second. Irritation tinged her voice. "You know, just when I'd finished going through Mom's things, I got the letter saying the probate period was over. I wanted a break after graduation. Instead, I get handed a cattle ranch. I only have eight weeks before I have to start my teaching job."

A loud snort turned Anna's head. "Girl, I didn't think feeling sorry for yourself was one of the steps of the grieving process."

"Ergh," Anna growled, turning her face towards the wall. She'd come here looking for Emily's stalwart advice, grounded in country experience, but had forgotten her cousin's pragmatic side.

"You know, Emily, you have a brother to shoulder some of the responsibility should something happen to your parents. I have to handle all of it myself. It was supposed to be my mother's inheritance, not mine. And by the way, anger is one of the steps of grieving." She turned back to face her cousin, waiting.

Emily grabbed another pillow off the bed, hugging it, studying the homemade throw rug on the floor. "You're right: got to be hard to handle this, but you're not alone. We're your family too."

Anna sighed. Emily had a point. Aunt Evelyn and Uncle George was the closest thing she had to parents now. In the brief silence, the house creaked with age.

"I know, you've all been wonderful. Thank you. Just hard to believe this ended up being mine." Anna stared at the ceiling again. "I've thought about selling the herd to Herman Miller. He already has time and money invested in them. I haven't the faintest idea how to run a cattle ranch. The only contact I want with a cow is on my plate. I just need a break to think this through."

"Well, you don't have much time. You've got a herd that needs branding, vetted and moved to summer range. A cattle ranch is a business; it waits for no one."

Anna sat up, smoothing the bedspread. "By the way, how's your dad doing?"

"Grumbling about the good old days and driving Mom nuts. He healed well from the hip replacement and is moving around okay. He'd help you out with this. He grew up in the business. He could give you pointers, or advice--whatever you need."

Anna flashed an irritated glance at Emily. "Yeah, I can use all the advice I can get."

"How come you promised your mom you'd keep it?"

"I promised Mom I wouldn't sell it; I didn't say anything about leasing it or letting it sit. I wanted to make her feel better. I've no desire to move here. I'd never live in the country where it's a forty-minute drive to get anywhere remotely civilized. No malls, shopping, restaurants or coffee shops."

Emily snorted again. "There's more to life than malls and the latest fashion." She had her head cocked to the side, her green eyes serious. She reminded Anna of a bird listening for a worm. "You're the modern little city mouse, I see. I guess that makes me the country mouse."

"Oh yeah, a country mouse all right! I remember you always knew what the latest fashion was,'" Anna shot back, hefting the pillow at her for emphasis.

Emily caught the fluffy, airborne missile. "It's a heritage thing, girl." Her tone was gruff. "This is one of the original homesteads in the county, with a rich history. You grew up in the city; you don't understand roots, knowing where you come from, and the struggles to get there. You can't let it sit; the buildings need constant repair. The cattle should be your first concern right now." She shrugged irritably. "But sell if you want to. Instead of looking at this as a curse, see it for the blessing it can be. I don't think your mom would come back and haunt you if you sold it. Herman would take it in a second. You got prime grazing land, a natural spring, and Bureau of Land Management leases going way back. Uncle John worked hard to have the best. His cattle always brought top dollar. You couldn't find a better stockman."

Anna jumped up and started pacing, causing the floor boards to squeak. "I understand family history, it's just Mom's request surprised me. I thought she hated this place." Her hands swept the air in agitated punctuation. "She always seemed reluctant to come here and visit."

"Well, I'm sure that was because she thought she had let your grandfather down. Being their only child and running off with your father created some hard feelings. I know your grandfather hoped

16

she would marry a local guy and take over the ranch. But your mom was a city mouse too."

Anna sighed, stopping in front of Emily, crossing her arms. "You're probably right. Mom and Grandpa didn't talk a lot about the past. She had a good relationship with Grandma, though. It broke Mom's heart when she passed away." Brusquely she turned, "Can you help me do a walk-through and check to see if everything is working?"

"Sure. Just give me time to get back down those stairs."

Anna started in the kitchen, having noted earlier the bowed floor in front of the sink. When she turned on the faucet, it emitted an alien squeal until a rusty-brown torrent ran out. Picking up a pen and pad from the counter, she started writing. An hour later, Emily and Anna met up outside to compare lists.

"Okay, we need new flooring in the kitchen and laundry room, the porch has a hole, the outside could use some paint. I'm not getting any water running in the bathroom sink; two light switches aren't working, and every room needs a good paint job. I think the water pump needs to be checked too."

Emily nodded, still scratching down notes. "Okay, well the inside of the barn is in better condition than the house. There's fence work out in the pasture, and some shingles are missing on the barn roof. Bunkhouse is musty, needs cleaning, but is in good order. If you're thinking of selling, I have the number of someone who can come out and give you a pre-sale walk-through. Several handymen hire out at the local hardware store if you need help."

Anna nodded. "I'll start tomorrow. Any place good to eat in town?"

"So you're still planning on staying out here by yourself? You're crazy. I'm willing to hang out and help."

She shook her head. "I'm grateful, but I already owe too many people."

"Girl, you've always been hard-headed and by the way, Herman would like to go over the accounting with you. He suggested after the potluck tomorrow at church."

"You know if Herman hadn't stepped up last October to take care of the herd, I don't know what I would've done. How many head did Grandpa run?"

"Over two hundred and you need to figure the feeding, vetting, and the calves delivered this spring too. If you're planning on selling the herd, I'm sure he'll subtract it from the total cost."

"And you call me stubborn? At his age, what was Grandpa thinking to run a herd that big with no one but himself?" Anna fumed.

Emily shrugged and shook her head.

"So you didn't answer my question on places to eat."

"Well, they're having a street dance tonight in town," Emily replied. "There'll be food there. So here's a chance to get that break you wanted."

Emily's poker face didn't fool Anna. She sighed. "You're rotten. Let's go."

❀ ❀ ❀ ❀ ❀

Built around the train depot, the town of Lander hadn't changed much. A fair share of booms and busts had come and gone. Cattle ranching, farming, steel industry, mineral mining, oil and other various industries had all helped build the quaint, little town. Main Street boasted of architecture from the late 1800's. One block festooned with orange cones re-directed traffic as people milled in the street. Anna caught a glimpse of a park filled with vendor's colorful tents.

Emily parked the aging sedan in front of someone's little, cottage-style home. Getting out, Anna caught the sweet odor of the lilac's spring debut. Band music traveled softly in the warm air.

Emily proceeded to introduce Anna to different people in the crowd. *Who doesn't she know?* Anna thought, as she shook hands with friendly townsfolk dressed in jeans, which seemed to be the dress code. They ducked and jostled through the thick crowd in the little block until they spotted Emily's short and portly husband, Seth, doing a balancing act with three cups.

"How are you doing, Anna? So good to see you," Seth said, handing her a plastic cup, wet with condensation. She glanced at the soda swirling darkly around ice cubes. Seth had remembered her dislike of alcohol.

"I'm checking out the band. Richard Crowley's son is playing tonight, and I'm saying hi. Want to come along?" Emily offered.

"No, I'm going to wander around. You go on without me."

Emily nodded and disappeared into the crowd with kids and husband in tow. Anna started up the street to check out the window of a jewelry store.

Rowdy voices rang in Anna's ear as a heavyset man with a sweat-stained cowboy hat stumbled back, knocking into her. The drink fell from her hand as she started to fall until two hands clamped around her upper arms in an iron grip. She gasped at the touch. Panic pushed her heart into flight. She twisted to pull away from the imprisoning grasp. The hands immediately let go. She turned to face her rescuer.

Frowning, he asked, "You okay?"

"I'm fine." Blushing, she quickly looked away. His voice had a pleasant timbre that she instantly liked, and his hazel-eyed gaze was direct.

He veered off to the left, shouting into the milling mass, "Hey Tim, watch out. You almost ran over the little lady here." He headed in the direction of the offending subject, who raised his

19

beer in acknowledgment. Anna crossed her arms over her heaving chest. She needed to escape. Her eyes caught an opening in front of the local movie theater, and she headed there. In the little bubble of space, she watched people passing by, taking deep breaths to calm her racing heart. He hadn't been half-bad looking, but his touch brought back a face from the past. Trying to find something else to occupy her mind, she looked around until she saw Emily across the street at a food vendor's stand.

A gentle breeze brought the seasoned smell of beer-brats cooking, and her stomach reminded her six hours had passed since lunch. Joining Emily, she bought one of the plump, shiny brats. Adding a dollop of mustard, she enjoyed the satisfying pop of the tough skin as her teeth sunk in, releasing a flood of flavor.

Wiping her mouth after the last morsel, she heard Emily speak behind her.

"Hey Anna, this is Steve Johnson."

She turned around, mouth full, holding up one finger while she chewed furiously. Emily continued, "He's the son of Jack Johnson, owner of the hardware store in town. He'd know of any handymen needing work." She appeared smug at finding a workhand.

Catching Steve's bemused expression, Anna looked down, and quickly wiped her mouth again. She noticed his weathered cowboy boots sticking out from under his faded jeans. *Great, a red-necked cowboy type,* derisively skimmed across her mind. Anna glanced up, noticing his confident smile created little crinkles at the corners of his eyes. "Oh, Steve, right? Uh, thank you for your help earlier."

Emily smiled impishly. "You've already met Steve? What did he help you with?"

Anna glanced at her overly observant cousin with irritation.

Nonchalantly, Steve interjected, "Tim never looks where he's going. I'm always picking up after him." He ran his fingers through his unruly hair. "So really, it was no problem. What type of job do you need done?"

Anna spoke quickly, "I recently inherited my grandfather's property, and it needs some fixing up...possibly to sell."

He nodded. "Give me your number and I'll get back to you on our schedule. What kind of repairs?'

She opened her purse, pulling out a slip of paper to write on, relieved not to have to make eye contact. "I'll just list them for you. Also, if you know anyone who does ranch work, like fencing, I would appreciate their names." She handed him the note, looking up quickly, with a curt nod. "Again, thank you."

His lips turned up in a slight smile, but she slid her gaze to the band and stepped away, dismissing him. Behind her, she overheard him talking to Emily.

"Thanks, Emily: can always use the work. How's your dad doing?" Steve and Emily walked a little farther into the crowd, catching up with Seth and the boys, sharing neighborly information. Anna kept her distance as she followed behind, glad not to be the center of his attention. He said goodbye to Emily, glancing back at her. Staring intently for a brief second, he turned, disappearing into the throng. As the multitude began to thin, the band shifted into slower tempos and Seth's princely bow to Emily caught Anna's attention.

"Well, my darling, would you care to dance with me?" Seth extended his beefy hand towards his wife. Anna chuckled as Seth pulled Emily into a country swing. She moved gracefully, despite her portly size, around her balding little husband.

The sun disappeared over the mountains, and the lavender hues of dusk began to settle. Matthew tugged at Anna's hand. "Stay with us, Auntie. You can sleep in my room! We are going to camp outside tonight. Please." Anna smiled down at his pleading face.

"If you don't go back to the ranch tonight, we'll stay later," Emily added breathlessly, joining her. "I can take you out after church in the morning and pick up those boxes you need."

Oh, what will it hurt? Anna thought. It will be better than being all alone with the family ghosts tonight.

"Okay, sounds good. Let's find some ice cream," she said to Matthew, giving his shoulder a squeeze.

"Be on the lookout for Rob Miller. I ran into him when I visited the band. He asked about you and wanted a dance with you." A mischievous giggle escaped Emily.

Anna groaned. "For heaven's sake, Emily, I can't deal with any more cowboys tonight!"

Chapter 2 — Expectations

Steve Johnson kept his eyes closed while his mind shook off the night's slumber. The floor squeaked as something moved across it. He smiled, waiting for the stalker to pounce, a girlish giggle his only warning. His arms caught the awkward bundle as it landed on his chest.

Affectionately, he growled, "Grr," rolling to his side. The adoring, blue eyes of his sister stared at him as he kept her caged in his arms.

"Morning, pipsqueak," he said, chuckling.

Chelsea squealed, "You're faking it! You weren't sleeping!"

"You'll never know!" He started tickling her.

She squinted, laughing, gasping for air, trying to pull away from his grip, kicking wildly. When he released her, she scrambled to the other side of the bed.

"Don't forget you're supposed to watch me at the horse show today. I'm doing Model, Showmanship, and Trail. You promised!" Chelsea shook her finger at him.

As his sister scooted back to his side, he felt a pang of guilt. In the past, his drinking had created many broken promises. "Okay, pipsqueak, I wouldn't miss you falling off for nothing!"

Chelsea giggled. "I'm not going to fall off my horse."

He smiled. Corky, his sister's appaloosa, reminded him of a fat sausage on four legs. "Go help Mom; I got to get ready for work." He tousled her static-filled blond hair. She jumped on his chest, sliding to the floor, laughing at the grunt she received for her acrobatics.

A half hour later Steve walked into the kitchen. "Morning, Mom. You don't have to send Chelsea to wake me up. I had the alarm set."

The petite woman at the kitchen sink smiled at him over her shoulder. "It saves us from listening to your alarm trying to wake you up. Chelsea is much more effective."

Steve grinned, pouring himself a cup of coffee. The clamorous blast of a car horn interrupted his first sip. "Gotta go, see you later."

Jumping into the truck, he greeted his brother. "Morning, Brad."

Brad nodded stiffly, putting the truck in reverse to back up.

"So what are you doing here so early?"

Brad jerked the shifter into drive and said brusquely, "Just giving you a ride to work. So how long before you get your license back?"

"About two weeks," Steve ground out.

An invisible wall of tense silence sat between them until his brother parked next to the service entrance at the back of their father's hardware store. They'd not always been at odds with each other. Walking between the neatly stocked shelves, he remembered racing Match Box cars against his brother's cars, down the shiny aisles.

"Good morning, boys," a dark-haired beauty called from the register. Her pink lips framed snowy teeth in a beauty queen smile. "Mr. Kagen called. He needs those fence posts as soon as you can get out to him."

Steve stiffened, turning his back on the girl. It was hard enough working for his brother, but the ex-girlfriend made it almost intolerable. He noticed his coworker and friend, Mike, sauntering out of the employee lounge, a cup of steaming coffee in hand.

Steve turned back to Brad. "I have a potential repair job for a lady Emily Higgins introduced me to this weekend. She inherited the Hanson ranch, and needs help on some projects."

"Okay, Dad and I can cover the store, and Mike can drive you out there," Brad said gruffly, not looking up from the clipboard he held.

Mike headed to a pegboard, covered in notes and key rings. "Mary Beth, where are the keys to the Junk Heap?"

"Oh, didn't Brad tell you? They traded it in yesterday for a new delivery truck."

Mike groaned. "But I liked the Junk Heap! I didn't have to worry about scratches and dings!"

Laughing, Brad cut in, "No, you just liked sitting on the side of the road waiting for someone to rescue you when it broke down! Just take the silver Chevy today. It's already hooked up to the trailer."

"I need to give...." Steve searched his back pocket for the paper with the number. "Okay, I need to call Anna and see if we can go out there this afternoon for an estimate. I think we can do the morning delivery run with no problem. Let me schedule her in for one o'clock. That will give us time for lunch and still give me time to watch Chelsea after work."

"Well, let's get loaded up then." Mike took a quick sip of coffee and headed for the back with Steve right behind him.

With the delivery completed and lunch over, they headed to the Hanson Ranch.

"What's that gal going to do with the ranch? I heard it's a pretty big spread, and she's just a kid."

Steve shook his head. "I met her last Friday night, and she's no kid. Kind of stand-offish. Tim Langer about squashed her at the street dance."

"Well, folks from the big city are more reserved. She's from Denver, isn't she?"

Steve shrugged. "I don't know."

Mike smiled wickedly. "You should ask her out! Just think: you could marry into a cattle ranch!"

"I don't think so, dirtbag."

As they turned onto the gravel road and rounded the hill, Mike's eyes grew wide. A sleek, plum-colored sports car sat in front of the ranch house. "There's something you don't see at many ranches."

Steve had to agree, staring with envy at the Corvette with its unusual color and aerodynamic lines. "Yeah, she's got some seriously good taste in rides."

"I'd like to take it for a spin."

"You and me both, man."

"What year is it? Do you know?"

"It's a C5 model with older chrome wheels, so it has to be somewhere between a 1997 or 1999."

As Mike came to a stop, Steve grabbed a clipboard and jumped out for a closer look. He glanced up as the owner came around the side of the porch where she'd been working. He had to stifle his urge to laugh.

She was quite a sight, not the well-groomed city girl he'd met at the street dance. He remembered her startled, blues eyes staring at him when he had caught her, and then her coolness as she pulled away from him. Right now he was facing a whole different creature.

❀ ❀ ❀ ❀ ❀

Listening to the meadow lark's morning trill, Anna poured a cup of coffee. She sat down at the kitchen table and started turning the frail pages of a photo album. A musty old-paper odor rose from cracked and faded pictures reflecting a black-and-white world. Precious few were the photos of her grandfather's childhood years. One showed him padded in many layers, standing next to a snowdrift that towered above him and the porch. His graduation picture showed a proud, young man leaning against an outdated truck. All moments caught in time but never talked about or shared.

Abruptly, she closed the album, pushing it away and putting her head in her hands. *The only father figure I had in my life, and he was a workaholic.* She remembered the disappointment in his eyes when she'd fail at things he tried to teach her about the ranch. Anna craved a grandfather that looked at her with pride, hugged and cuddled with her. Instead, she got one who hardly ever spoke, except to correct her.

Pushing away from the table, she decided to take a break from the cleaning and the past. Fresh air would be good, and the lilacs needed trimming. As she stepped onto the porch, a musky odor caused her to catch her breath. Moving over to the large hole in the porch, she peered in, seeing nothing but cobwebs and dark dirt below. *Where's it coming from?* She would have the handyman check for broken pipes. Though she never saw the stray cat, the food scraps she left out disappeared every day. She would have to get the kittens out before the repairs were done.

Gathering up gardening tools, she headed for the side of the house. The drone of a motor and crunch of gravel alerted Anna to

27

an approaching vehicle. She backed out from under the lilac bush, aware of how ungainly it must have looked to any onlookers. The sign on the side of the silver truck door announced the arrival of help. Catching sight of Steve as he admired the car, she called out, "Hello."

He looked up, a rakish smile crinkling the edges of his hazel eyes. "Uh, hi there. Remember me, Steve, from Johnson's Hardware?"

"Yes, I do." Anna nervously rubbed her dirty hands against her jeans before shaking the hand he held out.

He looked back at the car. "I'll bet it's got a three-fifty cubic inch engine, with over three hundred horsepower. What's the fastest you've had it up to?"

It was Anna's turn to smile, her eyes lighting with excitement. "You're right. It's a 1998 Coupe and on the straight away, would you believe one twenty-five?"

Steve shot an appreciative glance at her, and then looked quickly down at the clipboard, his voice catching, shoulders shaking a little. "That's awesome! Well, you need us to look at the porch, kitchen floor…uh." He avoided eye contact, the smile now a full blown grin as if he was trying to suppress a laugh as he looked towards the front door.

A slight frown creased Anna's forehead. He hadn't been so jovial at the street dance, and she couldn't figure out what he found so amusing about her car. "Why don't you start with the kitchen first?" she said, heading for the door. Another tall man joined them and as she glanced at his tanned face, she found him silently laughing too.

Anna didn't even wait for an introduction, hurriedly leading them into the house. As they walked past an antique mirror on the wall, she felt lean fingers gently grab her shoulders, turning her face to it while Steve, chuckling, said in her ear, "Ma'am, you might want to spruce up."

She tensed first at his touch, and then at the picture of herself framed there. Cobwebs, leaves, and unknown debris was scattered through her mussed, brunette tresses. It was as if she had used her hair to dust under the porch. A quick "OH" escaped as she made a dash down the hall. Over her shoulder, she called out to them to make themselves at home in the kitchen. Anna heard subdued snorts of laughter behind her.

In the quiet of the bathroom, Anna quickly brushed all traces of the lilac bush adventure out of her thick hair, knowing the bright red blush was going to take some time to leave her face.

Of all people, why did it have to be him to see me like that? Smoothing and tucking, she took a big breath, gathering what was left of her pride and trying to slow her pounding heart.

"Thank you so much," she said calmly to the two men, as they eyed the dilapidated floor.

Steve looked up with an impish smile. "No problem, ma'am. This is Mike Tanner, and he'll be working with me. We have to replace this floor. It is all rotted, and no telling what is under it. I'm assuming there isn't a basement?"

Anna quickly slipped into a business-like tone. "You're correct: no basement, but you can get into the crawl space out back."

Mike produced a stunning, white smile against his darkly tanned face and extended a work calloused hand. "Nice to meet you, Anna."

She noticed his gentle grip as she shook it.

Steve retracted the tape measure, putting it on the counter, knocking over a stack of letters perched there. He bent down to retrieve them, staring at the corner of a large white envelope with the return address of the Colorado Bureau of Corrections and Parole boldly stamped there.

Anna quickly crossed the small kitchen, taking the mail from him, noting that his brows pulled together slightly as he stared at her. *I bet he's dying to ask me what it's all about.* She shoved the worrisome envelope in a kitchen drawer.

"Well, let's see what we have in the laundry room, shall we?" Steve's tone was light, his face devoid of any emotion.

Mike followed Steve into the laundry room, glancing back, giving her another smile. She observed he walked with a solid, sure step; while Steve was lithe in his movements.

They pulled out the washing machine, and again, dry, slivered wood could be seen between the patches of worn linoleum.

"I'm afraid you have more flooring problems," Mike noted. "Are you staying here?"

"Yes, I am."

"We can work around your schedule. I'll have to turn off the water and the electricity here and there," Mike continued.

"That's fine. If need be, I can always stay with my cousin."

They all moved on to the bathroom. She watched as Mike opened the sink cabinet, crouching down, tapping on the old pipes.

Steve worked to loosen the light plate. He looked at her briefly. "So, you don't want to be a rancher?"

"No, I don't. When I get this place fixed up, I'm probably going to put it up for sale."

"That's too bad," he said softly. "You know this is one of the last original homesteads in the area? Been in your family for how long now?"

Anna shrugged, looking away. How did she explain there was no attachment to the ranch? It held no meaning or pride as it had for her grandfather and mother. It was a burden, bringing back unsettling memories.

Steve changed the subject. "Your light switch needs wiring work; you noted another one out. Which room?"

She gestured towards the bedroom at the end of the hall, now devoid of any personal items of her grandparents', the bed and mattress looking old and stripped, the walls dingy.

He glanced around the room, and then removed the light switch plate. "You know, I helped out Herman this spring. You have some wonderful grazing land and a robust herd of Angus."

"And thank heavens there is some soft ground for when you fall off your horse too," Mike said behind her.

Steve shot him an irritable look. "Yeah, that's what happens when Corky hasn't been ridden all winter. He had a little spring fever and felt like bucking. Stupid horse."

Smiling, she decided not to pry further. "You know, I could use some help again next week if you are interested. Herman is arranging a branding crew so we can get the calves ready to push out on to the summer range."

His eyes crinkled with his grin. "Yeah, that'd be great. I like working cattle. It'll give Corky some exercise too. Count me in.

Her heart lurched at his smile. *Darn, he's actually good looking.*

He moved on, tapping on the walls and tracking the wiring as Mike wrote the location of studs on the clipboard.

"I know of a really good electrician in town. I'm afraid I can only do the carpentry work," Steve remarked.

Anna nodded, and then looked away, not wanting him to catch her staring at him. She noticed he was tall, having to lean his head down just a little to look into her eyes. A slight odor of clean, washed laundry hung in the air when he moved about.

Steve walked out to the porch, appraising, and measuring, and Anna followed him.

"If you need help holding the tape measure, I'd be happy to help."

31

Steve extended the metal end of the tape towards her. "I didn't mean to pry into your business. Was just curious what you might want to do with a ranch. That way I can get the rumors started right."

A hint of a smile appeared on his face as Anna turned her gaze out towards the barn. "I bet the rumors are flying."

"Well, it is a small town after all. You say the crawl space entry is at the back of the house, right?"

She nodded. Steve stepped down off the porch and started around the lilac bush to the left, on the side opposite to where Anna had been working. Before she could warn him, two things happened simultaneously. His foot sunk to the ankle in mud that was more water than dirt, and the black-and-white stray she had been feeding decided to shoot out from under the porch.

"Skunk!" he hollered as he tried to get his feet to move in the muck. Sliding, he couldn't get his footing, going down with a wet plunk. Anna's hands flew to her mouth. Mike stepped out in time to see the last of his partner's ungraceful antics. His loud laughter pealed out, helping to deepen the thunderous look that flashed across Steve's face.

"Oh, I was going to warn you about the mud!" she gasped. "Let me get you some towels." Anna ran into the house while Mike helped his partner up. She threw the towel at the mud-covered Steve and then ran around the house for the water hose. They went to work rinsing him off.

"I'm sorry. Did the cat scare you?" Anna asked. Steve gave her a hard look as Mike chuckled.

"Ma'am that was no cat. That there was a skunk!" Anna looked at him puzzled.

"Where does your septic system drain?" Steve asked suspiciously, sending Mike into another spasm of laughter.

"Septic system? What's that?" Anna queried.

32

Steve's eyebrow shot up. "Lady, it's where all your sewer water drains to, you know, like the bath water, washing machine and the toilet."

"Well, doesn't it go into the sewer pipes? Is that what you're asking?"

Steve's jaw tightened, eyebrows pulling into a thunderous cloud. "Ma'am, I think that you've some plumbing problems, right? Slow drains?"

Anna didn't like his "ma'ams" and "lady." She didn't like the feeling of being uninformed either. She prided herself on being knowledgeable.

Flipping her hair over one shoulder, she stubbornly lifted her chin. "Yes, the drains have been moving slowly, especially after I did about eight loads of laundry to catch up on all the linen in the house. Why?"

Steve's face turned an unusual shade of red. "Ma'am, if you don't mind, do you have any clean clothes I might borrow?"

"Yes, yes," she answered quickly. Tears were running down Mike's face as she ran into the house, feeling the blush of embarrassment heating her face.

She tore through the plastic bags holding her grandfather's jeans, finding a fairly new-looking pair, praying they would fit. Then she found a checkered blue, short-sleeved shirt. She put them in the bathroom and ran back out onto the porch.

Steve was finished hosing everything off, and Mike had disappeared to the back of the house to shut off the water.

"Please, come change in the bathroom," she offered while holding the screen door open. Steve still looked unhappy, walking with a squishing sound across the living room. She followed, frustrated, not knowing how this situation had gotten so out of hand.

"It's okay. I'll be out in a second." His tone was resigned.

Anxiously, Anna stepped back out to the porch. "Please, can you explain what a septic system is?"

"Sure," Mike answered pleasantly. "Unlike in the city where the pipe takes the sewage to a processing plant, rural sewage is taken by pipe to a distance from the house. There, a perforated holding tank underground allows the water to seep into the soil around it. Bacteria works to break down the solid waste, but sometimes you need to have them pumped if they haven't been active for a while. I would say by the slope of the ground, your septic system is here in the front yard. From the looks of it, it needs some help."

Again, she felt the aversion of living in the country knot her stomach. "What do I need to do?"

Mike flashed a stunning smile again. "I'll give you the number of my cousin's sewage service, and he'll come out and pump it and let you know if there is anything else you have to do. By the way, do you have many friends here?"

Anna observed he had deep-brown eyes and a bass timbre to his voice. "Oh, I know a few people. But living out here in the country limited my social contacts when I stayed here during the summer."

Mike nodded. "So you aren't afraid to stay out here all alone?"

"No, I'm a loner at heart. Being an only child taught me how to entertain myself," Anna said with a shrug. "Besides, I'm an excellent shot."

He gave a nervous chuckle, shifted his weight, and thrust his hands into his jean's pockets, looking down. "Well, if you get scared, or ever want to do anything, you can call me."

She glanced at him quizzically. He was handsome in a dark way. Thick, jet-black hair, strong features, and a trim frame revealed a hardworking lifestyle.

"Thank you. That's really sweet."

His face lit up with the excitement of hope. "Here's my phone number. Call anytime." He handed her a business card.

Inside, Anna heard the bathroom door squeak. Steve came out onto the porch looking like a farmhand, the jeans and shirt a little baggy.

"Thanks, and if you have a plastic bag, I'll take those wet clothes out of the bathtub."

Anna quickly retrieved one for him, fumbling with the opening. Steve reached for it, taking it from her. "Here, let me."

Following him to the truck, she tried again to apologize.

"It's okay. Thank you for the loan of the clothes. I have your number. I'll call you with an estimate as soon as I can. Give me a date and time on the cattle ride and I'll be out. Thank you for your business," Steve said curtly, swinging the plastic bag over the side of the truck and getting in.

Mike grinned and held out his hand. "Looking forward to working with you."

Anna took his hand into both of hers. "Thank you for coming out. I'm sorry for the inconvenience."

His deep laugh rang out. He bent close to her ear. "It was worth it just to see that look on his face!"

He swung into the driver's side, Steve scowling at him from the passenger side.

Anna watched them drive out of view, conflicting emotions stirring.

Robynn Gabel

Chapter 3 – Roundup

Anna put the breakfast dishes in the sink as the sky blushed with the first-morning kiss of the sun. Gazing out the window, she caught sight of a coyote scurrying across the ridge behind the house. She thought of her grandmother who must have looked out this window every morning for over fifty years.

Wanting to know more about the family history, she had decided to look through her Grandma Charlotte's diary. At first, it had felt invasive reading her grandmother's thoughts and feelings as she fell in love with John Hanson, a shy, hardworking rancher. But, as Anna read on, she began to see her grandfather through different eyes. She understood why her grandmother so often joked about chasing him until he gave up and married her.

Anna's grandmother also chronicled her daily life of riding horses, working with cows, cooking and cleaning. She found it hard to imagine Grandma Charlotte riding a rough, spring bronc out to round up cows.

Well, if she could do it, I can. Hopefully old Ginger won't be feeling any residues of spring fever. Anna smiled thinking of the old sorrel mare she'd ridden for the last ten summers.

Heading out to the barn to saddle up, the cool morning air helped to quicken her step. On the worn path to the barn, she stopped and turned, hearing Emily's sedan pull up to the house. Two excited little cowboys scrambled out of the car.

"Hey, Auntie, wait for us!" John called to her. It wasn't often that the two boys got to ride horses and work on a ranch.

Calling a cheery "good morning," Emily bustled off to the house to make lunch for the crew who was handling the herd.

Within half an hour, Anna's front yard filled with an assortment of cars, trucks and horse trailers. She spotted Herman Miller, a lean, athletic man with a straw cowboy hat pushed down over his cropped, graying hair. He chatted with his son, Rob, who was a younger copy of his father and three years older than Anna. During the summer, Rob used to ride the fence line, checking it and occasionally dropping by for a visit. Her grandmother always had a cool glass of lemonade waiting for him. He'd taught Anna how to do a rollback on Ginger, and read where a cow was going to head.

Anna welcomed the volunteers as they came in, visiting and catching up on the last year's happenings. Rob grabbed her in a bear hug. Uneasy, she pushed away from him.

"Hey, Anna, it's been a long time. How are you doing?" A huge grin wreathed Rob's face. He towered over Anna, a tan offsetting his blue eyes. His ornate belt buckle, won in a roping circuit, accentuated clean jeans and narrow hips. A blue shirt clung tightly to his wide shoulders.

"It's good to see you, Rob. I appreciate you coming out to help."

"I never thought I'd see you running the ranch, being such a city girl. Heard you graduated. You plan on taking a job in the area?" He took in her slim figure with a cursory glance.

"No, I got a job in Wellington, outside of Fort Collins. I'm very excited about teaching kindergarten. It was exactly what I was looking for."

"Congratulations! You needed something to go right after the year you've had. Sorry to hear about your mom." He looked over her shoulder towards the last incoming truck and trailer.

"Thank you," she answered, following his gaze, noticing the Johnson Hardware sign on the truck door. She felt a curious twist in her stomach.

"Everyone gather round, and we'll get this started up," Herman hollered. Anna excused herself and headed towards the patiently waiting Ginger.

Herman divided everyone into groups, giving each a job. The outriders would gather and push the cows down off the ridges and into the fields below. Swinging ropes, slapping thighs, whistling, and shouting encouraged the cows to move off and join-up. The rider and horse worked together to block any cow that didn't want to go in the right direction. Herd-holders would keep the waiting herd in the field bunched by quietly riding the outside perimeter, going after any cow that would try and leave, giving mothers and babies time to find each other, pairing up.

Herd-holders also took turns pushing cows into the holding corrals beside the barn. There, between the two corrals, was a corridor where riders could separate the momma cows from their calves. A chute blocked the east end of the corridor.

In the calf-holding corral, a branding fire was burning hot, and medical supplies had been neatly stacked in plastic bins, on-hand for any problems. After branding was over, the mommas and their calves were pushed out to the field down by the gate. The tired bovines were happy to pair-up and grab a few blades of grass, so only a few riders were needed to hold them. A good day's work would see the herd out to summer pasture by late afternoon.

The air filled with low calls from worried Moms to their calves as the riders started the round-up. Anna rode alongside Herman and Rob to separate the cows at the corrals. The morning flew by as Ginger and Anna worked. With a squeeze of her leg and a touch of the reins, the little mare would quietly move between the reluctant mom and her baby, pushing the calf into the branding corral. The men took turns taking down the calves for the brand, giving any medication or vaccination needed. Released calves darted away, some kicking and others bawling for their moms.

The coolness of the morn had left now, the summer heat bringing a sweat. Flies flocked to the cows, mingling with the dust. The lowing of the momma cows to their bawling calves was a strident chorus. During a pause in the work, due to an unruly cow, Anna had a chance to rest her horse.

Rob reined his muscled Quarter horse in beside her, his gaze leisurely traveling over her. "So what are you doing this summer besides settling the affairs of the ranch?" he asked congenially.

Anna wiped her brow with the back of a leather-gloved hand. She noticed the appreciative gleam in his eyes. Had she been fourteen again, she'd have been flattered by the attention. "Just cleaning and going through my grandparents' things. Hard to do; it seems so final."

Rob nodded sympathetically. A noisy clatter instantly brought their attention to a frantic mother cow, jumping and crashing over a weak board in the holding corral. Riders scrambled to pin her, but she charged through them, heading for Anna and Rob. Ginger reacted, going into a roll-back to get out of the way while Anna grabbed the horn, almost going in the opposite direction. Suddenly a chubby little appaloosa appeared in front of her, heading the cow off, turning it back towards the corral gate. Steve flashed Anna a ruffian's grin as he tipped his hat in her direction.

Straightening up in the saddle, she realized she'd been too busy to notice he'd come in from holding the rest of the herd. He seemed to have forgiven her for the embarrassment of the other day. Mike was right behind him on a leggy, rangy-looking sorrel.

With a slight pressure of the rein, she guided Ginger towards Herman. "How about we call a lunch break? That will give me some time to find a replacement board. We need to get that corral repaired right away," she hollered over the calls of irritable cows.

Herman nodded in agreement, standing in his stirrups, bellowing, "After that last calf, let's close the gates to keep them in and grab some lunch. Make it quick because we need to spell everyone in the field for lunch too."

Anna dismounted and led Ginger to a stack of old lumber alongside the barn.

"You go grab lunch. Let me fix it," Rob said behind her as she sifted through the pile.

"Thanks, Rob. I'll go up and get us both something to eat if you want to get started on it."

"That sounds like a plan." He helped her pull out a cob-webbed board.

Emily had set up in front of the barn and was handing out food and water.

"Well, girl, how's it going? My kids being any help at all?"

Anna smiled affectionately at her. "Yes, they're a great help! They're both natural riders. Thanks for bringing them."

"Yeah, they love it all right. Sometimes I worry about bringing them up in town. It seems they just learn more about life and gain more confidence working out here in the real world."

"Why did your father sell off his ranch? How come you didn't get it?" Anna asked, gathering up sandwiches and water.

"Well, because I got married and my brother Dan went off to the Army. I think Dad just figured neither one of us had any

41

interest. It was too hard to try and split it between Dan and me. It wouldn't have pulled any profit that way. Then Dad got cancer, and Mom just couldn't run it by herself. There were medical bills to consider as well. I think Dad thought when that dude ranch outfit contacted him, offering a dream price; it just seemed time to sell. But I miss it, Anna, more than you know. If it weren't for the economic ups and downs of it, I'd have loved to run Dad's spread. Just didn't have the finances for it."

Anna was thoughtful for a moment, and then she lit up with an impish smile. "You know, Seth is doing great out there on old Midnight! He's looking downright handsome!"

Emily snored. "Would you knock it off?"

Anna giggled. She'd delighted in teasing Emily about Seth since tenth grade. He had been oblivious to Emily's feelings until Prom in their senior year. She couldn't think of a better match than those two. But it was true: Seth seemed to be thoroughly enjoying himself playing cowboy.

"It looks like Rob is enjoying your company as well. That sandwich for him?" Emily now had an ornery look of her own.

"Yeah, he's just a big flirt. You know Rob. He's probably already planning how he's going to get the ranch from me. Herman made me a fair offer for the herd. I looked over Grandpa's records and even with the vetting, feed, and new heifers he bought last summer, Herman's offer will put the ranch in the black."

Emily nodded in understanding. "Girl, you just take your time. You can sell the herd anytime. But watch out for Rob. He's had his eye on you for a while, forget the ranch."

Anna flipped her ponytail back over her shoulder defiantly. "He can look all he wants. He's a big windbag." Anna never forgave him for his snub when she was fourteen and had a very embarrassing crush on him. When she finally got the courage to ask him to a movie, he had laughed, saying she was too young for him. Anna thought it was because she was too plain. Rob Miller had his pick of swooning possibilities. Popular, outgoing, wealthy and athletic, he was a huge catch.

When she came back, the corral board was in place. They sat down on the stack of wood to eat. Down at the lower end of the pile, Steve, Mike, and Emily's boys had already taken up residence. Anna tried hard to ignore the little surge her heart did at the sight of Steve.

Rob was in rare form today, trying to impress her with his manners and wit.

"So Anna, seen any good movies lately?" he said after a swig of water.

"Not really. Between finals, getting Mom's affairs in order, and graduating, I haven't been able to get out much."

"Well, let me fix that! Let's go to dinner and a movie. Don't break my heart--say you'll go with me!" He looked at her expectantly with eager, blue eyes.

She had misunderstood his question, walking right into the trap. Anna examined her sandwich with great interest, taking a long sip of water while her mind raced. What should she say? How could she turn him down? She was at a disadvantage with his helping her today. Would it be rude to say no? She couldn't go on a date with him. There was just no way.

She looked into his confident face. He was certain of victory.

"I can't, Rob. I just don't have the time to date. I've got too much here at the ranch to do. I hope you understand." She gave him her most winning smile in return.

Rob stared at the milling herd. "Well, I'm just around the corner when you're ready." He tipped his hat back, giving her an arrogant smile. "I got to check on Dad--see if he needs anything." He unfolded his frame from the boards and sauntered off.

Anna watched him leave with a bemused smile. *That went better than I thought it would. Now I can enjoy the rest of my lunch in peace.* She heard a snort at the other end of the wood pile and

43

noticed Mike looking at her while Steve's shoulders shook with laughter. *What is it with those two that they find me so amusing?* She picked up her empty water bottle and headed back to the house, giving them a good view of her stiff back.

Taking the feedbag off Ginger and leading her to the water trough, Anna waited until the horse finished before mounting. Rob was back to separating the cows, and she noted that Steve and Mike had joined him. A lively conversation was going on, an angry frown crossing Rob's face. Anna didn't have time to be curious. She was needed at the vetting chute to decide on what to do with an injured calf.

By early afternoon, the branding was done, and it was time to push the herd out to the freedom of summer pastures. Outriders opened the big gate to the Bureau of Land Management land behind the ranch and reunited momma cows and calves lazily wandered through, looking for greener grass. Anna was swiping at the annoying flies when Steve rode his chubby appaloosa up to her.

"Ever thought of putting that horse on a diet?" she said archly.

Steve flashed a good-humored smile. "Yeah, well, Corky's owner loves him a little too much. That's why I'm working him today. The sorrel Mike is riding is my horse. Hey, I have a deal I want to pass by you."

Anna looked at him for a moment, and then prompted, "Okay?"

"How would you like to earn an easy fifty bucks and get a free meal in the deal?"

She stared at him, liking the way his skin crinkled around his eyes, giving him an impish look. Coming out of her reverie, she asked cautiously, "How?"

"Well, this Sunday after the service there's a Friendship potluck. I have a bet with your pushy admirer over there that I can get you to go on a date with me. Of course, he didn't specify when or where, and I figured a potluck at church wouldn't really be a date, but would look like one. What do you think?"

Anna felt someone staring at her. Glancing to her left, she saw Rob smiling smugly at them on the outside of the herd. It is too much; she thought, a chance to rid herself of any more date offers and zing his pride all in one. Besides, there was some logic to Steve's offer.

Anna carefully crafted an irritated look to hide her delight. "I see your point, yes; we can do that. This Sunday, right?"

Steve nodded enthusiastically. "Yeah, we can sit together through the service, and the ladies of the church can really cook, so you'll get a first-class lunch."

"Yes, I know. I set up a potluck last Sunday to thank everyone in the congregation who helped when my grandfather died last fall, but I didn't see you there."

Steve shifted in his saddle uncomfortably. "I had a meeting."

"Okay, well, I accept. See you first thing Sunday morning."

For a split second, shock registered, and then an ear-splitting grin crossed his face. He reined Corky away from her, letting out a whoop that sent the cows bolting, and rode over to Rob, who looked stunned. She pushed up behind the cows, not daring to steal a glance at Rob. Maybe now he'll get the hint.

The evening grew hushed, the crickets starting their serenade. Anna helped Emily put up makeshift tables to feed the hungry crew. The mouth-watering smell of barbecue drifted on the slight breeze while donated side dishes started appearing.

"Don't know what you did to piss off Rob, but you are certainly getting some dark looks from him," Emily said casually.

Anna grinned. "Yeah, I noticed. It's because I took Steve Johnson up on his offer."

Emily looked up quickly. "What offer?"

45

"Well, old Rob there bet Steve I wouldn't go on a date with him. That was after Rob had asked me out and Steve overheard me refusing him. So Steve offered to split the winnings with me if I go to church with him and stay for the potluck this Sunday."

Emily's laughter rolled out. She finally calmed after getting some curious stares. "I can't believe you did that! You are so rotten!"

"What? It wasn't my idea! But Rob deserves it," Anna answered saucily.

Emily was still grinning as they set the last table.

Anna raised her voice, calling all to dinner. "I just want to thank you all again for your help today. Without it, we could never survive out here. Also, let's give a big hand to the ladies who brought all the extra goodies to add to this feast and Emily for all her hard work and cooking. Now dig in!"

Clapping erupted, and soon, all that could be heard was the clink of silverware and low murmurs as everyone hungrily scooped up food.

Anna caught Rob's glare and put her head down, digging into the beans on her plate, pretending not to see him. As people finished eating, she started to help clear the tables. Steve came alongside to help.

"So have you decided what you are going to do with the ranch yet?"

Anna stopped to watch as Emily separated her two wrestling boys, directing them to help with cleanup. "I have an idea or two. Know a good lawyer in town?"

Steve frowned. "Unfortunately, I do. I can give you his name and number."

"What did you need a lawyer for?"

Steve looked at her for a few seconds. "Well, there're some things I'm not proud of. Someday I'll tell you all about my dark past," he said, his tone teasing now.

Herman came up, nodding a quick hello to Steve. "Anna, you think on what we talked about. Just need to make the transfer before the end of the summer."

"Yes, I agree. Unless something comes up, I'm pretty sure I'll be selling them. I couldn't have done this without you. You've been such a terrific friend to my grandfather and me. Again, thank you." She held out her hand, and Herman shook it vigorously.

Rob was on his heels. Anna extended her hand. "Rob, thank you. I really appreciated the help today. Hope you can forgive me."

Rob averted his eyes, the flush of embarrassment creeping up his neck. He held out his hand awkwardly, and she shook it gently.

He shot a dark glare towards Steve and then followed his father to their truck.

Robynn Gabel

Chapter 4 — Connecting

Throughout the old ranch house, all the pictures were of landscapes or cowboys. Except for this one, hanging on the wall where the old Kenmore washer and dryer had sat. Anna stared at the oak-framed print. Against a backdrop of yellow wheat stalks, two sinuous black panthers glared at each other in defiance while they circled each other, creating a picture of symmetry.

A soft chime from the grandfather clock startled her back to the moment. She glanced at her watch, letting out an irritable "oh." *It's a good thing I like to drive fast and have a car that can do it,* she thought. Heading towards the front door, she paused to check her hair in an antique mirror.

What was I thinking? I should've never agreed to Steve's offer; she chided herself, hurrying to the car. Anna didn't mind attending church; it just wasn't part of her usual routine and this Sunday she was feeling pressed for time.

The Vette purred in greeting as she started it up. Once off the gravel road, she accelerated, feeling her body relax into the speed of the car. *I wonder where I got my love for speed.* Anna smiled, remembering her mother, who'd been a timid driver, hating to go fast in anything.

Coming down the hill into town the first traffic light flicked to red, and reluctantly she slowed to a stop. Rumbling up next to her was an old truck. Grinning like a silly scarecrow, a young man hanging out the passenger window gave her a thumbs-up. The driver revved the engine in challenge. She pursed her lips and shook her head, hands tightening on the steering wheel. Then she glanced quickly in the rear view mirror--and chuckled. Coyly, she looked up at the young man. The light popped green, and the truck roared off, racing ahead of her while she demurely accelerated. A flashing red light flew past her as the police car came up behind the pickup that headed to the curb in front of her. She took the left lane, smiling innocently as the driver shook his head dejectedly.

Still laughing, she pulled into the church parking lot. *It's a good thing I'm going to church; I need to pray for forgiveness!*

Anna took a big breath, noticing Rob coming up the steps as she headed to the door. He stepped up quickly to open it. She nodded to him, not looking him in the eye and went in.

Hurrying towards the chairs, she picked a couple close to the back of the church, sat down and waited.

"Good morning. How are you today?" a pleasant-timbered voice asked. She glanced up into familiar hazel eyes.

It's just a bet she told herself as Steve slid into the chair next to her. He slouched immediately with outstretched legs crossed, arms folded over his chest, settling in for the service.

Steve flashed a teasing smile. "So, been feeding any stray skunks lately?"

A hot blush rose to her cheeks. Why did he have such a knack for making her feel unsettled?

"No, I'm afraid I'm well versed now in local animal life," she said haughtily.

50

He chuckled. She shifted in her seat, leaning away from him. It's just for the service she reminded herself.

"Run into any septic systems lately?" she shot back.

His smile just broadened. "Nope, no one has been making a swimming pool out of their septic systems except you."

She flipped her hair into place, ignoring his comeback. Looking away, she crossed her legs, swinging one in irritation.

"Am I bothering you, ma'am?" Laughter was evident in his tone.

"No, I'm getting used to the locals here who seem to think they have a good handle on what humor is." She turned to him and glared.

"What? You don't find me humorous?" he chuckled out.

"No, actually, I find you rude. It is bad manners to make fun of someone who's not as fully informed as you seem to be on all subjects, Sherlock." Crossing her arms, she looked away again to watch people finding seats.

He wouldn't let up. "Well, Watson, for a city girl, you don't seem to be very informed on country life."

She turned back to him with a measured stare and said in a low, taunting tone, "You know, I think you need mirror therapy. It's something us city folk use all the time."

"Really? And what would mirror therapy help me with?"

With superior air, she replied, "Well, you go to the mirror, look in it and tell yourself, I'm not funny, I'm not funny. It should help you with the delusion of having a sense of humor."

Steve's eyes widened, and he started to retort, but the church service music interrupted. With a sigh, he gave up the battle.

Anna looked at the pulpit, suspecting her grin was similar to that of the famed Cheshire Cat.

He winked at her as his lovely tenor voice soared with the refrain of the praise music, and the surprises didn't end there. He acted the gentleman by sharing the hymnal, looking down at her with a friendly smile. From a distance, she spied Rob glancing back at them in disgruntlement. *Paying out the bet hurts probably far more than seeing me with Steve,* she thought wryly.

As the service ended, he lowered his head, speaking quietly, "I'd like you to meet my parents if you don't mind."

"Um, yeah, okay."

He gently took her elbow to navigate her towards his family before she could change her mind. *Meeting his parents wasn't part of the deal. It's not like this is a real date.* She tried to breathe, very aware of his warm touch, wondering if he could feel her tension. Steve deftly steered around tables being set up for the potluck to a small family group visiting with each other.

"Mom, Dad, this is Anna Sanchez."

A petite, blond woman with vivid blue eyes that missed nothing drew her into a light hug. "Call me Rosalyn. If I remember right, you came to services when you were younger."

"Yes, my mom always considered this her home church. It's nice to meet you."

Steve's father had rough, weathered hands and a smile that ended in the same little crinkles as his son's. "Welcome, nice to meet you."

Anna gave a quick nod. "Same here."

A little blond-haired girl stood quietly, watching. Steve pulled Anna aside. "This is my sister, Chelsea."

"You're the skunk lady that my brother was talking about, right?" she said with childish glee. Anna looked up at Steve, arching her eyebrow at him. He laughed, glancing at his sister with a finger raised to his lips.

"Honey, you don't repeat things you overhear," Rosalyn quietly chided Chelsea.

Anna bent down to look into the girl's innocent blue eyes. "Yes, I thought I had a kitty living under my porch, but it was a momma skunk. In the city, you just see stray cats."

"Now there's a good excuse," Steve interjected.

Anna glared at him as Chelsea grabbed her hand, pulling towards the food line. Anna hated to cook but still liked to eat, so she was fond of potlucks for the chance to sample new recipes.

Standing in line, she looked back to see Steve was a few feet away, a frown knitting his brows together. A black-haired beauty had moved to his side, speaking quietly to him. He looked away, and when she lightly touched his arm, he stepped back stiffly. The beautiful girl glanced in their direction, catching Anna staring. Quickly looking down at Chelsea, Anna listened intently to the little girl chatter about her horse's accomplishments.

A few seconds later, a soft voice crooned beside her, "Hi, I'm Mary Beth Hollins. Heard Steve and Mike are doing some work for you. Have you been in town long?"

Anna turned, looking into Mary Beth's limpid brown eyes.

"No, just a couple of weeks," Anna replied politely.

"Well, hope you enjoy the potluck. It's nice to meet you." She moved off with regal grace.

Anna noticed Chelsea pouting. "What's wrong, Chelsea?"

"I don't like her. She's mean," was all Chelsea would say.

Emily grinned from behind the serving table. "I see it's going well."

Anna stuck her tongue out, quickly glancing around to make sure no one saw. She noted Steve had joined the end of the line behind her, giving a little wave and a charming smile. Chelsea filled a plate, heading back to the table to save a spot for Anna.

"It's going just fine, Emily."

"I see you met Miss Hollins."

With her plate full, she stepped out of line to lean into her cousin.

"Do they get along? I noticed he didn't like talking to her."

"Oh, that's right! You wouldn't know about them. She was his high school sweetheart. They worked together at the store and were inseparable, or should I say; she wouldn't separate from him. They came back from college this spring and out of the blue, she dumped him. The rumor was she got tired of waiting for him to pop the question. I think she has her sights set on Rob Miller now." Emily's voice had dropped to almost a whisper.

Steve had caught up to Anna. "So, which one of these dishes is yours, Anna?"

"Who says city girls can cook?" she tossed back.

His grin took on a wicked curve. "So you're saying you wouldn't be a good wife for a country boy who likes meat and potatoes?"

"Oh! You're insufferable, Steve Johnson," Anna huffed.

A broad-shouldered, barrel-chested man stood behind him, a more serious looking facsimile of Steve. "So are you ever going to introduce me?"

Steve sobered, speaking quietly, "Anna, this is my older brother, Brad." She noticed neither brother made eye contact with the other.

Brad dipped his head towards her. "Nice to meet you. I heard from my dirt bag brother you have quite a righteous ride."

Anna beamed. "Yes, I do."

"Yeah, but I get a ride first, bro," Steve fired back quickly.

Heading to the table Steve growled under his breath, "Daggone-it, what's she doing there?"

Anna noticed Mary Beth sitting next to Steve's mother, their heads close together, Rosalyn listening intently. They had a familiar atmosphere between them.

"I can sit somewhere else if you need to talk to her," Anna offered.

"No, I don't need to say anything to her. Please, sit with me." He looked down at her. "Besides, ole Rob hasn't paid up. I want to make sure he knows we held up our end of the bargain."

"Okay," Anna said with a sigh. Mary Beth watched Steve pull out the chairs, a smug smile curling her lips as she met Anna's gaze. *I suppose to Mary Beth, I'm no threat: just a passing nobody in her plans,* she mused. Anna flipped her hair over her shoulder, looking away. *We'll just see how she likes a little competition.* Though not as vivacious as Mary Beth, Anna had an athletic figure and shiny, shoulder-length, brunette hair. Her blue eyes sparkled, and she had attractive, girl-next-door features. Anna never lacked for male attention.

Chelsea insisted Anna sit between her and Steve, patting the chair.

"So Rob said I cheated on the bet," Steve said between mouthfuls.

Lisa, Brad's wife, looked up. "What did you bet him?"

Anna cleared her throat. "He bet I wouldn't go on a date with Steve."

Brad's face lit up, worry lines disappearing, a boyish laugh rolling out. "Hey, bro, you so desperate that you have to make bets to get someone to date you?"

They all started talking at once, ribbing and teasing Steve. Anna took a deep breath, trying to cut off the rise of her blush. Out of the corner of her eye, she saw Mary Beth's bemused glance from across the table.

"Okay, enough, all of you." Rosalyn turned to Anna. "How can you stand being out there all by yourself, Anna? Aren't you lonely?"

"No, outside of the quiet, I'm okay. I wish I had a better cell phone signal. I leave the radio on at night to sleep."

"If I had that car of yours, I wouldn't be sleeping. I'd be out cruising. One thing the cities don't have is long stretches of nothing!" Steve's eyes gleamed in envy.

Brad leaned in closer. "He's just a gearhead. He forgets about all the wildlife you might smack into."

Before Anna could answer, Chelsea cut in, "I can always come over for a sleepover!"

"Chelsea Johnson, where are your manners?" her mother gently reprimanded.

Anna put her arm around the eager child, hugging her. "It's a good idea, but your mom is right: first we need to get to know each other, and you'll have to wait until I invite you."

Chelsea bobbed her head in an enthusiastic yes.

Jack Johnson cleared his throat. "I'm so sorry to hear about your mother passing, especially so soon after your grandfather. He was a generous and kind man, a respected servant of this church."

Anna was taken aback by the genuine care in his words. She never thought of her grandfather as a warm, outgoing man. Pulling in a deep breath, trying to dispel the constriction in her throat, a simple "Thank you" was all she could muster. Chelsea sought her hand under the table.

"Hey, Steve!" several teenagers shouted, gathering around them. He stood up, grabbing a scrawny boy around the neck with his arm, mussing his blond hair. Anna watched, her heart warmed by his genuine interest in the youngsters seeking his attention.

He turned to the others. "Don't forget youth group this evening, okay guys? See you then."

56

Anna stood, gathering plates. "You're a youth-group leader?"

"Yeah, I've been helping out for several years now. We have quite the group of youngsters. They enjoy coming and hanging out, doing service projects. If you don't mind, I need to catch Rob before he leaves. I'll be right back."

Anna helped with cleaning tables, Chelsea at her side until Steve joined them. On the way out of the church, Chelsea grabbed Anna's hand again, looking up like an eager puppy.

"When will I get to see you again?"

Anna leaned down, hugging her. "Well, have your brother bring you out sometime. We can go horseback riding if it's okay with your mom."

Excitement lit up her blue eyes. "Mom!" she hollered as she ran off.

Steve walked her to the Corvette.

"Well, that wasn't so bad, was it?" he challenged.

"No, it wasn't bad."

"We should try dinner sometime."

"Steve, I'm not interested in starting any relationships right now."

Steve reached his arm around her to grab the door handle, opening it. He leaned against the car frame, catching her between him and the open door. She felt a twinge through her stomach every time he was close. The smell of fresh laundry enveloped her.

"I can understand that, but you aren't saying we can't be friends, right?" Amusement turned his thin lips into a mischievous smile.

Anna slid into the seat, looking up, shaking her head, feigning exasperation. "No, but…."

Steve spoke quickly, "Aw, Anna, just friends. I'll see you tomorrow. Here's your share of the loot. Thanks for helping me take down Rob. He's had that coming for years." He shot her a rakish grin as he pushed off from the car, heading towards his brother.

Anna took a deep breath, her mind churning, her heart feeling like a revving car engine.

"Wait, Steve," she called.

He turned back, his eyebrows raised questioningly.

"I want to check out the Central Wyoming Corvette Club next weekend in Casper. They have an autocross and some guys in my club in Colorado told me to try it out while I was up here. Would you go with me?"

"So is this another date?" A wicked smile appeared.

"No, it's not!" she said firmly. "Just friends, remember? Just two friends, enjoying cars and the day, deal?"

He shrugged, his smile creating crinkles at the edge of his eyes. "Sounds great to me, Boss."

"Do you have a helmet? It has to be Snell rated."

"Yeah, I can scrounge one up."

"Be at my house at seven next Saturday."

He gave her a quick nod, still smiling, "We should get that floor in tomorrow. See you then." He turned and sauntered over to his brother.

Her mind raced during the half-hour drive home. *Damn Mary Beth! I was going to ask Emily to go with me. What was I thinking? My plans don't include the handyman!* She shook her head irritably. *It's done now; I'll just have to deal with it.*

At home Anna went to work immediately, slipping out of her church clothes to put on basic ranch wear: jeans, T-shirt and work boots. She hurried down to the barn to check on an injured calf. Momma Cow didn't like the attention; she protected her calf, moving between Anna and him. With an exasperated sigh, Anna tried to outmaneuver the large bovine to see if the cut was draining

58

properly. The big, liquid brown eyes of the watchful cow brought back memories of Mary Beth and her irritating superior attitude. *Well, church didn't improve my mood, especially if a cow reminds me of her!*

Laughing at the thought, she lunged to the far side of the momma, catching a glimpse of the calf's leg. It looked good; Mom and Baby soon would be free to join the herd.

Heading back up to the farmhouse, a movement along the ridge to the south caught her attention. She stopped, shielding from the noon glare to stare intently. In the shadows created by the scrub brush, it looked like a tawny body with a long, twitching tail. *No way. There is no way I saw a mountain lion, probably just a coyote.* She couldn't see anything now except the swaying of pine in the breeze. Somewhere overhead, a crow squawked a warning as Anna headed to a lunch of peanut butter and jelly sandwiches.

She bit into the soft bread, the tartness of the jam hitting her palate. Cold milk helped wash the stubborn peanut butter from the roof of her mouth. She glanced around the kitchen at the disarray of tools and sawhorses. Hopefully, this project would be done next week.

The growl of a motor warned Anna company had arrived. A few seconds later, she heard the scuffle of children fighting to knock on the door. Grabbing the handle, she swung open the door. "Boo!"

John and Matthew giggled at her. "Auntie, can we go down to the barn and ride Midnight and General?

General had been her grandfather's quarter horse. The tall Palomino was gentle, and no one knew his exact age, but he loved kids. A mare called Midnight was a short, squat mixed breed, but was quick on her feet going after a cow.

"Sure, just be careful: ride in the pasture, no going out into the canyon." Anna smiled, watching them run full blast to the barn.

"So Anna, where do we start?" Seth was wearing paint-splotched coveralls. Emily waited behind him, armed with a bucket full of paint rollers.

"Well, come on in and let's make a battle plan." She noticed the old, dilapidated truck parked in front, that in some era had been red. "I see you're driving the Cadillac. Think it will make it back into town?"

Emily snorted. "Someday, I'll be lucky, and the wheels will fall off that thing."

"Hey!" Seth retorted. "That's my first love there, woman. That truck is great."

"Yeah, for learning how to be a mechanic," Anna threw back.

Laughing, they headed into the house. Anna pointed to her grandparents' bedroom. "If you two want to start in there, go ahead. When it's painted, then we can load up the furniture in the living room."

Anna headed to a project she had been avoiding. As in the rest of the house, this room would be covered in the dust of vacancy.

The brass knob was metal-cold as she turned it slowly and stepped into the past. From the time of her mother's birth, this had been Jenny's room. The white chenille bedspread, covered with pink roses, always brought back childhood memories of her mom reading to her or looking through picture albums as they cuddled together.

Running her fingers over little, porcelain horses parading on a shelf, she remembered her mother had been horse-crazy. Flowered curtains, which hung on the window that faced west, were stained with condensation from winter storms.

A sob clawed its way up through her chest, bursting forth as she fell across the bed, hugging a pillow to her face. Not even here could she find a trace of her mother, only the smell of dusty linen.

60

Finally emptied of tears, she dusted, vacuumed the old, shag carpet, and stripped the bedding. A vibration in her back pocket announced a call from across the state.

"Hello, Carolyn, yeah, just a minute. Let me get a good signal." She ran to the front room, standing next to the window. A bright, familiar voice spoke patchily on the other end, "Hey you, miss me?"

Excited to hear from her childhood friend, Anna replied, "Of course! And yes, I'm dying for a Starbucks and thanks again for watching the house. You've no idea how that helps me out. What? You guys are going down there tonight? Oh, I wish I could go with you. I love their pizza! Well, have a slice for me." After a half hour of catching up on all the happenings back in Ft. Collins, she reluctantly hung up.

Emily went by with her arms full of drop cloth. "How's Carolyn doing?"

"Enjoying civilization," Anna sighed.

"Really, Anna, you've only been out here for a couple of weeks. Tell me: what is so bad about it?"

Anna stared at the brassy sunbeams trailing along the walls in the living room, signaling the approaching sunset. Turning to look out the window, she took in the glorious, blazing deep-orange shafts that shot out from the disappearing sun, creating a crown that sat upon the midnight-blue brow of the mountains. In Ft. Collins, buildings, and trees blocked the evening art show of sunsets.

Sighing again, she said, "It's not that bad. In fact, it's beautiful. I've just never been comfortable here. I always felt like I was the cause of the trouble between Grandpa and Mom. He certainly never did anything to dispel that feeling."

"Hansons are famous for being stoic. You have some of that too, girl. He really did love you and he was proud of you."

"Oh, really? He definitely had an odd way of showing it." Anna spun away from the window. "I want to show you something."

They stood again before the image of the two panthers. "I never noticed this before," Emily said, being careful to step around the construction of the new floor, lifting the picture to look behind it. "Hey, there's a card on the back of it."

Laying the picture facedown on the kitchen table, crowded with tools, Anna pried at the envelope taped to the back. Pulling out the card inside, she noted the flowers on the face of it, intertwined around the words, 'Happy Birthday to My Love.' Inside, under a beautiful greeting of love and devotion, her grandfather's neat scrawl met her eyes.

Don't know why you had to have this sweetheart, but here it is. Love you always.

Anna stood, shocked. In all her time with her grandparents, she'd never heard or seen a display of affection from the man she considered cold.

Two excited voices caught their attention, drawing Emily and Anna to the living room. She could see outside the open front door two horses with reins hanging loose, their heads up, ears pricked forward, alert to something. Matthew and John were pulling Seth towards the porch. "Dad, we saw a mountain lion. Up on the ridge, honestly. The horses were snorting and looking, and we saw it. Hurry up, Dad!"

Chapter 5 - The Plan

The 1969 Chevy truck's stiff suspension jolted Anna over the pothole right before she turned into the parking lot. Driving the truck was quite a different feel from being so low to the ground in her agile sports car. She turned off the engine, and it talked back with a cough and sputter. Picking up the thick folder of papers she had taken from her grandfather's file box, along with her mother's death certificate, Anna sighed. What was left of her family now lay in her hands.

A bespectacled receptionist with tidy, upswept hair and a proper hint of make-up greeted her as she walked into the coolness of the air-conditioned building.

"You're here for Mr. Brannen, concerning estate matters, correct?"

"Yes, for John Hanson and Jenny Sanchez."

The receptionist nodded, parrot-like. "Just have a seat, Miss Sanchez. He will be right with you."

She sat down on the smooth leather seat, looking at the western artwork adorning the walls. The receptionist went back to clicking away on her computer. A few minutes later, an expensive-suited man, who was well-padded, came around the corner of the hallway. He handed a folder to the receptionist. "Get these to the courthouse this afternoon, please."

A western bolo snugged at his neck with huge pieces of turquoise sitting on a small chevron of silver, in place of a tie. A smile barely raised his thick lips under the long mustache. His face was blasted with freckles; a receding hairline gave the impression of maturity. He extended a manicured, beefy hand. "Miss Sanchez, I'm Zach Brannen."

"Hi, just call me Anna, please." She retrieved her hand from his moist grip and had a desire to wipe it down her jeans.

"Follow me, please."

She noted the cloy smell of cologne floating behind him. He stopped, opening the door to a room ringed with cherry wood bookcases filled with soldiered reams of leather-bound law books. She caught the glassy eye of a buffalo's head looming on the back wall. On the opposing wall, tastefully done in taxidermy art, ducks took off in eternal flight.

Sitting in one of the overstuffed, brass-tacked chairs around the massive cherry wood conference table, she felt all the décor paled in size next to it.

He sat down at the end of the table that held a scattering of folders, a file box, law books and a cup of coffee.

"Nice to finally meet you. Please, feel free to call me Zach. I've caught up on your grandfather's estate and trust. Mr. Pembroke came out of retirement just for you and was good enough to send over his notes and files. Your grandfather was quite tidy in keeping his business records. He'd have made quite a bookkeeper had he not gone into ranching."

She smiled; he described her grandfather well. John Hanson insisted on things being orderly, clean, working and profiting at all times.

"I'm sorry we have to meet in these circumstances, Zach. Steve Johnson referred you, and I can see he didn't steer me wrong."

He bobbed his head. "I'll have to thank him. Let me guess: he's doing some repairs for you? He does excellent work. I've known Steve since he was a teenager. He's a good man."

"He's working out at the ranch, helping me to get things into shape. Whether I sell or not, things still need to be in working order."

"Now, are you aware of the market value of your grandfather's estate? I believe the inheritance insurance he had will cover the federal death tax. He left you quite well-off. Let me list all the assets." He went through the market value of farm equipment, household items, vehicles, cattle count, and finally, all checking, savings, bonds, and CDs. "So that would give you a net worth of 6.7 million by my records. Of course, this is going by the last personal financial statement he did for the bank in September."

Anna was very still for a moment, her mind reeling. She had known the ranch was worth something, but she had no idea of her grandfather's total investments.

"Now, this is in non-liquidated assets, or, your worth on paper. Mr. Pembroke mentioned that your grandfather always had about one hundred-thousand dollars in the bank to back him in the event of disease affecting the stock, equipment failure, or falling beef prices. I would suggest that you get yourself an investment broker to go over this portfolio, and get a good accountant who can tell you whether to keep things as they are in the trust for tax purposes. You do know if you sell this property there will be a large chunk of capital gains taxes to pay as well."

Zach checked his quietly buzzing cell phone. "My apologies, but I must take this. Yes, Greg, where do we stand?" Zach paused; a huge grin covered his face. "That's great news! I knew that file would come in handy." He glanced at his watch before continuing,

"I think I've enough time to evaluate your new client's case. But you'll owe me dinner for this."

His blue eyes are too small for his square-set face, raced across her mind as he talked, and she tried to grasp her new financial windfall.

Setting the phone on the table, he went on, "So, do you have anyone to advise you on how to run the ranch?"

Anna nodded weakly. She'd planned to see her uncle next, to seek his advice. She had to figure out how this was going to best suit her needs and yet help keep the promise she'd made. Staring absently at the buffalo head, her mind was a whirlwind of thoughts. Zach respectfully gave her a few moments, looking through the folder she had brought.

Emotions were rolling, all the puzzle pieces falling into place. To Grandpa John, this wasn't about wealth but good stewardship, showing his love for his family through providing well.

For Jenny, Anna's mother, keeping the ranch wasn't a matter of pride in the history of the property but redemption. In trying to clear her conscience, she sought to keep her father's dream alive through Anna's promise of taking on the ranch.

For Anna, it had been all about guilt.

Being responsible was one thing Anna had learned well in the last few years of strife. She realized her greatest strengths came from Grandpa John. They'd been so alike they couldn't connect with one another. This ranch was a living memorial to those who had gone before, their spirits tangible in its existence. It wasn't the end of her family but the next phase of it.

Anna looked at Zach, squaring her shoulders, sitting up straight and taking a deep breath. She was a Hanson, and her decision to keep the ranch made her resolve firm. It was time for planning and answers.

❁ ❁ ❁ ❁ ❁

She drove the old, green Chevy truck into the circular drive of her uncle's spacious, ranch-style home, oversized tires crunching gravel. Gathering up the manila folder on the seat that now represented not the end of things, but the beginning, Anna opened the door, the hinges squawking. Emily's dark sedan pulled in behind the truck as she started up the walkway.

"So, I see you're slumming in that old beater," Emily called out.

"Yeah, but I won't be getting any speeding tickets."

Emily chuckled as they walked together towards the front door that gleamed with beveled glass insets.

"By the way, can you believe Rob called this morning?" Anna shook her head in disbelief. "He's still bugging me to go to the movies. Steve started something. Rob can't stand to have one up on him. I don't know what to do."

"Well, sell him the ranch on the premise he can never ask you for another date!" Emily chortled.

She shoved Emily's shoulder lightly. "You're the rotten one now. No, I'm not selling the ranch just to get rid of him."

They were giggling when the front door opened, and a stocky woman greeted them with an enthusiastic smile. "So, are you two going to get in here and eat, or stand out there jawing all day? Lunch is getting cold." She enveloped Anna in a hug. She struggled to keep her face above the fleshy arms squeezing her. "You're looking well, and so much like your mother."

Anna stepped back to catch her breath, wondering if Aunt Evelyn needed new glasses. She thought she looked more like her father. Emily and Evelyn, on the other hand, resembled each other closely. Both carried every extra calorie they had ever consumed in well-filled, solid frames.

Aunt Evelyn led them into a kitchen bathed in bright light from a skylight. Her uncle rose slowly, to grab her hand and pat it.

Time had treated George well despite a lifetime of outdoor work. Ten years younger than her grandfather, he'd started his family later in life. His handshake was firm, his dark hair just barely beginning to gray at the temples. Strong facial features included a straight nose and heavy jaw. He was of medium built, and unlike his spouse, had no spare of anything.

"So how's the blood-sucking lawyer?" George asked.

Anna chuckled at her uncle's outspokenness. He was the opposite of his brother in many ways. "He was very good, Uncle. He laid things out well. My grandfather handled his affairs quite well."

George nodded.

"Come in, Seth. Emily's already here!" Evelyn called to the soft knocking on the front door. Dressed in a casual tan suit, tie loosened, and his face beet red from the outside heat, Seth walked in business-like strides. "Hi, Anna, how'd it go this morning?"

Before Anna could answer, Evelyn interrupted. "Let's eat before we get talking finances," she clucked.

The table was set plainly, giving the spotlight to the scrumptious-looking food. Golden fried chicken, snowy mountains of potatoes, homemade biscuits, and fresh-picked green beans waited to be devoured.

"From your garden, Auntie?"

"Yes, the green beans came in early this year. Not a good tomato year, though."

She appreciated a solid, home-cooked meal finishing everything on the plate. She'd been living on instant food lately, discovering she missed her mother's and aunt's ranch-style cooking.

"Heard you had a mountain lion sighting. John and I never saw any sign of them at the ranch when we were growing up. Certainly had a lot of other varmints, though. Saw a bear once."

"I still think it was a coyote," Seth mumbled around a mouthful.

"I don't want to see wildlife of any type if you don't mind. The skunk was enough." Anna chuckled.

An apple pie emerged off a side counter, looking too good to eat. Evelyn turned to George. "You could've had pie a la mode if you'd quit raiding the freezer at night."

He shifted in his seat, looking sheepish, and then mumbling, "If you'd feed me more, I wouldn't need too."

"George Hanson, you get fed plenty. Just look at the size of that piece of pie and tell me who got the biggest piece." She playfully threatened him with a spatula, receiving several snickers.

Anna cleared her throat. "Uncle George, I was wondering if you'd like to be CEO of my corporation." The immediate attention of four people focused on her.

"Emily, I have a proposition for you and Seth as well," she continued. "I was wondering if you would like to be in on this corporation."

Emily's hand fell to the table, the fork clanking against the stoneware. "You're kidding, right?"

"No, I'm not," Anna said in a business tone.

"So why does a ranch have to become a corporation? Your grandfather did just fine without forming a fancy company," Evelyn inquired, starting in on a piece of the apple pie.

"I need to form a corporation to protect the assets from single proprietor taxation. A corporation will offset losses and taxes better. I don't want to run the ranch, nor do I want to give it up." Anna paused for a moment to hold back tears.

Evelyn came to her rescue. "Well, what can I do in the company? Someone needs to keep your old coot of an uncle in line; can I be President?" Laughter erupted, and they all started asking questions. George pounded the table.

"Let Anna finish!"

She took a cleansing breath. "Uncle, I need someone to oversee the money flow. You have the most experience. Auntie, I need a Treasurer, to keep track of the books and keep the CEO in line. Sorry, I need to be President."

Snickers followed Evelyn's big, exaggerated sigh. "I guess that's better than being Secretary."

"That leaves the actual property. I need a Vice President and Secretary. Also, that ranch house is big enough for a family. Though commuting may be a challenge, I think Emily and Seth can do it if they are interested. I ask only one thing: I would like Mom's bedroom to be kept as a guest room so I can come and stay in the summer." Emily flew around the table, smearing tears into Anna's face with each bear hug.

She pushed away, grinning. "I take it you won't need time to think about this?"

Seth spoke quickly. "We have to talk this over. We have a house here in town, I have my insurance company; and Emily, you're working at the hospital. We all know how much work goes into running a ranch." Seth nervously adjusted his tie, wiping his hand across his forehead.

"Of course, take some time to consider it. We can work out all the details later. My grandfather had a working business system. The property and everything on it are paid off. There're enough savings to offset any setbacks, repairs, or herd problems. I know we won't get rich any time soon, but we can make a comfortable living."

George cleared his throat. "A ranching outfit takes some backbone and elbow grease. May have to hire some work hands to help, and the horses are getting old. I'd be happy to help you work out the details, sweetheart. I'm proud that you've decided to keep the last Hanson homestead intact. You've handled it just like your grandfather would've."

Anna felt her spirits soar with her uncle's support and treasured compliment. She grabbed her water glass, holding it up. "I propose a toast to the Windswept Ranch Corporation." Five glasses were raised to clink in agreement.

❀ ❀ ❀ ❀ ❀

Flinging the white plastic grocery bags over the side of the truck, Anna again marveled at how her grandfather had kept it in good shape. After a few more errands, she headed out of town.

It was beginning to sink in it was no longer just her grandparents' home; it had been born her ranch just a few hours ago. The corporation would soon be in working order. Meetings and decisions could be handled via phone, and it was only a five-hour drive if she was needed. With Uncle George as CEO, it would go well. She could go back to Ft. Collins; the promise to her mother fulfilled. Rounding the little hill, she looked at the ranch house with new eyes, seeing the possibilities, feeling excited.

The silver Johnson Hardware truck sat in the drive, along with a small tanker proudly advertising that it was a sewage truck. Mike held a large, flexible tube that curled around the side of the house, and a scruffy-looking young man worked on connecting it to the tank cylinder. When she drove around the tanker, she saw a black SUV sitting under the huge cottonwood that provided ample shade for cars and the ranch house.

Turning off the senior truck, it coughed its disapproval once again. She jumped out as the door of the SUV opened, and Rob unfolded his lanky frame from behind the wheel. The tanker pump went into high gear, drowning out Rob's welcome. Anna had to step up closer to hear his shouting, irritation replacing the high spirits of moments before.

"Need to talk to you," he hollered. She gathered up groceries, and Rob brusquely snatched up the rest of the bags, following her. In the kitchen, things weren't much better: the whine of a circular saw and the smell of injured wood filled the house.

71

"Let me put away the fridge items and we can go to the barn. I need to check on a calf," Anna shouted over the noise. Rob nodded. Steve finished cutting the board, shut off the saw, and looked up, a scowl appearing at the sight of Rob.

"Hello, Boss. I've got two more boards to cut, and it looks like we'll have the laundry room floor done tonight. The sub-floor was in good shape, so we won't have to do as much. When do they plan on putting in the tile?"

"Day after tomorrow if they get their other jobs done," Anna replied. He nodded.

Steve curtly said, "Hi Rob," before conversation became impossible due to the tanker pump's increasingly loud chugging. Rob and Anna escaped to the barn, happy to get away from the noise.

The calf cavorted around as they walked up. A good scab had formed over the gash on his leg. She stepped into the dark coolness of the big barn. Starting on the left side of the barn was a tack room full of bridles, bits, ropes, blankets, and saddles. Just a little past it was a corridor to the holding corral. Next were three good size stalls, and a large stack of last year's hay. Over on the right side were a small workshop, a rustic bathroom, and then an open area filled with a four-wheeler, a tractor, a maroon-colored SUV, and a harrow. On the walls hung rakes, shovels, a hand scythe, cutters and other various farm tools. All was neat, oiled and in good shape. Rob eyed the tidy barn in admiration.

"Nice set-up, quite the spread. I'm here on business. I hope it's not too soon after having lost so much of your family, but I'd like to talk to you about buying the ranch." He walked over to the hay, sitting on a bale, nudging back his cowboy hat to look at her. No smile today, no arrogance, just business.

"You know the addition of your ranch to ours makes sense. Your grandfather would have approved, especially since you're no rancher." A stiff smile stretched across his face.

Anna took a deep breath and leaned up against one of the support posts, hands in her pockets, a picture of total serenity. "Sorry, Rob, I know I'd spoken of that possibility, but I'm not selling. I've decided to keep the ranch."

A surprised frown stripped the smile from Rob's face.

"Also, let your father know he gave me more than a fair enough offer for the herd, but we're going to keep the cows after all."

Rob snorted, sitting forward, leaning elbows on his knees, clasping hands, a patient look appearing on his face as if he was about to lecture a child. "Anna Sanchez, you don't know the first thing about this business, we both know that, and how are you going to run this long distance while being a school teacher in Colorado?"

"Well Mr. Miller, even though it's none of your business, I'm forming a corporation, hiring knowledgeable people and following in my grandfather's footsteps. This ranch has survived for the last hundred years under Hanson ownership and has done just fine, thank you." The stormy look in Anna's eyes backed up her resolve.

Rob re-positioned his hat on his brow. "I'm going to offer you more than a reasonable price. You just think on it. I won't be this reasonable for long--think on that too." His voice was low with persistence.

Pushing off from the beam, she straightened, standing square, hands on her hips. "Does your dad know you're doing this?"

Rob's brow furrowed, and arrogance laced his answer. "I've investments, and my dad trusts me to make a solid deal. This is between you and me."

An icy smile encased her lips. "I see. Well, the answer, Rob, is no. I understand it'd be very profitable for you to gain this ranch since it borders yours. It would help to consolidate the BLM leases and water rights as well. But we've worked alongside each other quite well for years. We can continue to do so. It's totally up to you. But I'm not selling, and I don't see that changing anytime soon. Thanks for coming out and thank you again for your help when my family needed it most. I value your family's friendship." She held out her hand.

Rob eyed her hand, and then her face for a moment. He stood slowly, shaking his head. "It's a good deal. I'll give you a week."

She shrugged and was shocked by his next move. He grabbed her hand, pulling her close, wrapping strong arms around her. Trapped against his chest, her head was forced to tip back as his lips hungrily crashed down onto hers. Wrenching her head to the side, unable to bring her hands up to push away, she stomped with all her strength on his foot.

Her reaction caught him off guard as well, and with a grunt he released her, wincing in pain. "You know you've wanted that kiss since you were fourteen!" he growled.

"Leave!" Anna spit out. She turned, striding furiously up the path to the farmhouse. Storming through the front door, she collided with Mike, his hands full of odds and ends of wood pieces. He took a step back from the force of the run-in and the naked rage in her eyes. "Mr. Tanner, please make sure Mr. Miller departs," she said in clipped fury.

Before slamming the bathroom door shut, she caught a glimpse of Steve and Mike looking at each other in bewilderment. Hearing the roar of an engine and spraying gravel inside of the bathroom, she imagined the cloud of dust raised by a speeding, black SUV.

Gripping the sides of the sink, knuckles white, her heart pounded with heavy thuds. There was a ringing in her ears, and a sheen of sweat formed on her face. Pain lanced across her chest as she took short gasps to bring air into her lungs. It wasn't the first anxiety attack she'd ever had, but it never lessened the fear that it might end in a heart attack or worse.

She glanced in the mirror, seeing the grimace of pain--the fear in her eyes. Rummaging through a travel bag for the relaxant the doctor had prescribed, she thought frantically, *if I take it now, hopefully, it will take the edge off.* A bad attack could leave her incapacitated for the rest of the day.

When a soft knock sounded on the door, she lifted her head from her hands. She had no idea how long she'd sat there, waiting for the thudding of her heart to slow.

"Are you okay? Is there something I can do?" Steve called softly.

"I'm fine. I'll be out in a while. You can use the toilet in the barn if you need to," she said with a tremor in her voice.

A soft chuckle came from the other side of the door. "That's not what I needed. I'm worried about you. What did that jerk do to you?"

Great, just what I need. I can see the headline now. Two Guys Duke it Out at High Noon on Lander Main Street! "Really, nothing. I'm just upset. He wants to buy the ranch and wouldn't take no for an answer. Honestly, I'll be out in a minute."

"Well, okay. We're done for the day, but I'll wait around. Also, Wayne from Honey Pot Sanitation has finished cleaning the septic system and needed to know if you want him just to bill you."

Her breath came out in a huff of exasperation. *I can't even have an anxiety attack in peace.* The drug seemed to have slowed her heart rate though she had a slight shake from the adrenaline. She stood and looked in the mirror. It was good enough to face the world. Unsteadily, she made her way to the door.

Steve stepped back as the door opened. She noticed his eyes quickly searching her face.

Anna turned away. "I'll get the checkbook if you would bring him in with the bill."

"Would you like me to stay the night? I can stay in the bunkhouse," Steve said quietly.

"Very nice of you, but really, I'll be all right. I can always call Emily if I need someone."

She leaned against the kitchen counter to steady herself while she wrote ou the check, smiling at the rough-looking man as he came in. "Anything I need to know?"

Wayne shifted his weight, work-worn boots scuffing on the floor. "Um, yeah, just put in a good septic bacteria and I'll check it again this fall if you want."

"That'd be terrific. I appreciate you coming out at such short notice." Anna offered her hand; Wayne reached out slowly to take it.

"Steve and Mike, go ahead on home. I'll be okay. I appreciate your concern. I'll let you know when the tile job is scheduled. What time will you be out tomorrow?"

Steve eyed her. "We've some deliveries in the early morning, so probably around ten, if that's okay with you." She nodded; sweat trickled down her back, her heart thudding again.

They gathered their tools and headed for the door, both glancing at her, but she firmly waved them out. Standing on the porch, she watched the silver truck disappear down the road behind the sewage tanker in a cloud of dust. She dialed Emily's number shakily.

Chapter 6 – Interruptions

The meadow lark warbled a song that wound its way through Anna's waking thoughts. The pungent odor of coffee drew her into the kitchen, bright with morning light.

"How'd you sleep?" Emily asked, holding out a cup.

"Pretty good. Thank you for coming out." Anna sipped the hot coffee.

Emily shrugged. "I was happy to do it. I'm sure Rob's dad would have something to say about his behavior. By the way, guess who I ran into at the grocery store?"

"I have no idea. Who?"

"Mary Beth. She sure is interested in what you're up to."

"She needn't worry. I'm not on a boyfriend safari, just here to tie up loose ends."

Emily chuckled. "Well, you'd be doing a lot of ladies a favor if you took her down a notch or two."

Staring into her coffee, Anna didn't answer, too tired to rise to Emily's baiting.

"Hey, when I was cleaning up, I came across this envelope from the Colorado Corrections and Parole. Did Miles get out?"

She glared at the offending envelope Emily held up. "Yeah, they called a few weeks back and told me his parole hearing was coming up. I could've gone, but they said it was pretty much decided he was going to be released for fulfilling his treatment early. Supposedly he made tremendous progress and, of course, was the model prisoner with a remorseful, positive attitude."

She shifted on the kitchen chair, warming her hands on the cup. "How can they think he's cured of being a stalker when after all the counseling I've had, I still can't handle crowds, and fight anxiety attacks?"

Emily pulled out a chair, lowering her frame onto it, listening. She stirred the creamy coffee in front of her. "I don't know, but not all men are like Miles."

❀ ❀ ❀ ❀ ❀

Sweat poured down Anna's face as she pulled on the barbed wire, trying to get just a half inch more to slip over the post. Icy wind stressed the wire during winter, and the hot, summer sun caused it to stretch. Tightening and checking the fence was a year-round job. Lacking the strength to gain the extra length, she leaned up against the post, panting. *It's all Steve's fault. If he weren't always around, smelling so good and flirting, I wouldn't have to find things to do out here.*

Looking down the line, she could see more sagging barbed-wire requiring back-wrenching effort. An image of her grandfather's hefty hands encased in worn, leather gloves came to mind--showing her how to grab the pliers, twisting the wire to take up the excess, and then looping it over the post. *Pull back, Anna! Harder! Never mind. Let me have it.* The disappointment in his eyes created a feeling of failure, one that she felt even now.

Irritably, she wiped at her forehead, grabbing for the buzzing phone in a back pocket. "Hello," she answered, shifting to catch the crackling voice on the other end. "Miss Sanchez, sorry, break in...." The call ended abruptly, the signal lost. "Darn it," she grumbled, jumping onto the seat of the four-wheeler. The engine turned over, but wouldn't catch. "Oh!" She rested her head on the steering bar for a second. *Anyone who likes living out here is crazy!* Angrily, she sat up and tried again; the engine sputtered, caught and chugged along. Pulling up in front of the house, she slid off to run inside.

Steve, pounding nails into the new flooring, looked up as Anna dashed into the kitchen grabbing at the old phone hanging on the wall. "If you don't mind, I need to make a call." He nodded, standing up to stretch.

"Hi, this is Anna Sanchez. Detective Stein called? Yes, I'll hold." She stared unseeing out the kitchen window. "Yeah, Chris, everything okay? No, I'm in Wyoming right now." She listened intently; a frown pushed slim brows together. "When do you think it happened?" Her voice broke. "I can make it in about five hours. Yeah, I will be able to tell. My friend Carolyn has been watching it for me. Yes, that's still her number. Okay, I'm on my way."

Returning the receiver to the cradle, she turned to face Steve, fear clouding her eyes.

"What's wrong?"

"I've got to go; I have an emergency. Emily!"

With towel in hand, Emily came out of the bathroom. "What?"

"I've got to get back to Fort Collins. I've had a break-in at my house, and the police need me there as soon as possible. Can you help out here? I'll leave you the house keys; you need to make copies anyway. Oh, and can you have one of your boys check on the calf? I should be back in a couple of days."

Emily nodded; worry etched across her face.

"Is there anything I can do?" Steve murmured.

79

"Just finish up here, coordinate with Emily. You know who is coming for wiring and tiling--just be here for them. I'd appreciate it."

"No problem. Please, drive safe," Steve said gently.

❀ ❀ ❀ ❀ ❀

Steve wiped the dust off his hands; the last board in, the floor now even, ready to be tiled. A hammer pounded staccato beats as Mike worked in the laundry room. The porch was next on Steve's list. Stepping out, he watched the Corvette making its way slowly to the road.

Something is going on in that girl's life that she doesn't want to share. He liked Anna's confidence and grit, remembering the fire in her eyes after the run-in with Rob yesterday. Working quickly, he ripped out rotting wood. He had widened the hole to get the baby skunks out earlier; now he took all the rest of the boards off.

Steve thought a lot about Anna in the last few days. He'd watched her gracefully move from one chore to another around the house, noticing that she kept herself busy, staying out of their way. He'd seen her working on the fence several times and offered his help. She just gave him a hard smile that didn't reach her eyes and a curt "no thank you."

The door opened, and Emily nodded to him. He nodded back, watching as she stepped around the construction and took two lawn chairs off the porch, setting them out on the grass. Plopping down, she gestured to the other chair. "Sit for a minute. Take a break."

Pulling off his work gloves, stuffing them into a back pocket, he lowered himself onto the chair. "So what's going on with Anna? What's this about a break-in at her home?"

"You got any interest in her?" He was taken aback by her directness.

80

"Well, yes, I thought I was pretty transparent about that. But you know my past. I'm not sure if I'm ready for a serious relationship."

Emily's brown eyes looked into his with an intent stare, as if debating the next move while searching his soul.

"Well, I guess you need to know a few things. I'm going to trust you though it's a matter of public record but...." She paused, staring at a pile of old boards, sighing.

"Anna's always been better at being one of the boys than actually dating the boys. She's not like, tomboyish or anything; she dates, but mostly she just has lots of friends. Maybe it's because she grew up as an only child that she struggles with close relationships."

Steve watched the breeze push the waxy cottonwood's leaves into flashing gems of light. "So what was so important she had to run back to Colorado?"

Emily sighed again. "Someone broke into her home. I have a pretty good idea who. When she started college, she met up with a man named Miles. He worked in the library. He had a huge crush on her, and she politely tried to tell him she wasn't interested. At first, he was just annoying, calling, sending flowers, emailing, and then the last straw: he showed up at her apartment. She went to the police, and they didn't do much. They told her to get a restraining order, which she did. It just got worse. She left her apartment and moved back in with her mother. She kept at it, keeping records, getting witnesses. Finally, one of her friends introduced her to Chris Stein, a police detective on the force who specialized in stalking cases. Finally, she got results with his help. The only problem is Miles escalated; he was waiting for her one night. Thank heavens that detective decided to check it out when she didn't answer her phone. There was a four-hour standoff before Miles finally gave up, and was sent to jail and psychiatric treatment. She felt for a long time she was the one at fault, that

81

she'd led him on. He was just released so; I think you can figure out the rest."

Steve's serious, hazel eyes met Emily's. "Jeez Emily, what a creep. No wonder that girl doesn't want a relationship. Am I any better for her? Does she need a recovering alcoholic on top of all of this?"

Emily shrugged, and then, leaning forward, she spoke firmly, "None of us are saints; we're all sinners. You both have baggage. You'll work it out if it's meant to be. I just thought you needed to know the rest of the story. She's getting things settled here, and my husband and I will be moving out to the ranch to run it. She didn't want to give up the ranch, but her life is in Fort Collins and she doesn't plan on staying here."

Steve felt a stir of disappointment. "She's a smart girl. You and Seth will do a great job."

Standing up, Emily looked at the ragged hole in the porch. "I suppose I should let you get back to that." He felt her hand on his shoulder as she moved past him to the door. "You know you're not a bad person--you've got a problem, but don't we all? You deserve happiness. Pray and ask God if she's the one for you, and listen to where He leads you."

He rose, grabbing his gloves from his back pocket. Emily's explanation put a new light on the situation. The anger he was feeling towards a stranger surprised him. Hopefully, he'd never run into this Miles and wasn't sure what he'd do to him if he ever did. Now the only thing to do was to take Emily's suggestion.

❀ ❀ ❀ ❀ ❀

Anna gripped the steering wheel of the thrumming Vette. It hugged the road, gobbling up mountain curves, hungry for more. She'd been so close to wrapping up all the ranch needs. *This*

82

should have been my going-home trip. Had it only been three weeks ago? It seemed she had been away much longer.

Just when I'm gaining some peace, he has to come back. Damn, I wonder what he's up to this time. She drove in silence, reviewing the past.

Miles's awkwardness, social ineptitude, and unattractive features had caused her to be kind to him when she had first met him. Remembering his features contorting in a frightening sneer the night he cornered her allowed fear to jump-start her heart. Sweat broke out on her forehead, chest aching. She didn't have time for another attack.

Shakily, she dialed Detective Stein's number. "Yeah, I'm about twenty minutes out. Okay, see you there."

The traffic was fairly light on the outskirts of Ft. Collins. The busy, thriving college town draped across the foot of the Rockies. It was a crossroads for people traveling to mountain getaways and skiing. At one time a bustling rail town, housing developments now fueled its growth. People poured in from all over, greedily snapping up farmland to live in the shadow of the Rockies. The city catered to a young college crowd, and Anna loved it.

She drove straight home. It had a '50s charm, gabled roof, a single-car garage and sat in a nest of flora and fauna, looking like something out of a Thomas Kincade painting.

Guiding the car carefully into the driveway, she saw a black, unmarked police cruiser sitting at the curb, its occupant emerging. Anna hurried through the front door, stopping short in the middle of the living room with a gasp.

The crunch of glass announced the detective's entrance. At about Anna's height of 5'4, he was oblivious to his Calvin-Klein-model looks. Tousled blond hair framed a sultry, handsome face where two brilliant blue eyes gazed upon the world with intensity. Eight years older than Anna, he'd one broken marriage under his belt, and she knew he had a little crush on her. But this was a man married to his work, and any woman willing to share life with him would have to understand that. She smiled, relieved to see him. "This brings back memories, Chris."

"Not good ones, unfortunately. How are you? Do I need to give you a speeding ticket for getting here so fast?" Chris's deep voice had a smoothness that flowed over Anna, calming her.

"No, I was good this time."

Chris flipped open a little black notebook, checking the scribbles there. "He gained access by breaking out the back door window."

"And I'd been meaning to get that door replaced for that very reason." She shook her head dejectedly.

"So, can you tell if anything is missing?"

She looked around, noting black powder on any surface that the crime techs thought would have a print. Though the words 'break-in' gave the general idea of the act, it did not prepare her for the anger that could be felt in the broken lamps and pictures littering the living room along with the holes in the wall. Moving on to the second bedroom that had been her mother's room, she noted a broken TV and more holes. Shattered dishes covered the kitchen and in the bathroom, shards of a broken mirror littered the floor, sink, and toilet. Every room showed the impact of the intruder's rage.

"We need to know who all was in your house in the last month so we can rule out suspects."

She nodded, mentally inventorying belongings in each room. In the bedroom, Anna was shocked to see broken frames with treasured pictures of her mother lying on the floor, scored and trampled. She put her head in her hands, wiping at the tears, trying to block this personal assault on her life. Feeling Chris's warm hand on her shoulder, she instinctively tensed. He quickly removed it.

"I'm so sorry. You've been through so much." He frowned.

84

Through the tears, she quipped in quirky humor. "Well, what doesn't kill us makes us stronger--isn't that how it goes?"

Seeing slashes in the comforter sent chills through her. She sorted through other pictures lying on the floor.

"He took his favorite one of me." Moving to the computer desk, she checked over the items laying there, suddenly gasping.

"He took my flash drives and my address book." She'd kept all personal information off her computer, hoping to deter anyone from stalking her again. A break-in never occurred to her.

Chris followed her, writing the articles as she mentioned them.

Suddenly she dashed back to the bedroom, yanking out the drawer in the bedside stand, gasping. Her heart started knocking against her ribcage in a panic to get out, pain tearing through her chest. She collapsed on the floor. Chris was at her side immediately, kneeling, holding her.

"What is it! Are you okay?"

"He has it, he has it," she gasped.

"What, Anna? He has what?"

"My diary."

❁ ❁ ❁ ❁ ❁

Anna picked up her overnight bag and headed out the hotel door. Since Miles had all her private information, it had seemed the safest place to stay while getting things in order. She opened the door of the little silver compact. It had been her first car, a rescue from Pete's Garage, and had survived several operations done in mechanics class of high school. She used it as an everyday car, keeping the Vette in the little garage at the house for long distance road trips.

Driving through the morning traffic, she missed the power of the Vette, swerving into the drive-through for the Star Bucks she'd

85

been craving. While waiting for the order, her mind raced, fingers drumming nervously on the steering wheel. Chris had discussed future options, and they decided she would head back to Wyoming to finish up business there. When she came back to Colorado, they would revisit what to do then. It all depended on what Miles would do next. No matter where she was at, from here on out, she couldn't have any routine that Miles could use.

She settled the two coffees in the cup holders. Negotiating the traffic like a salmon going upstream, she found herself yearning for the slow pace of Wyoming traffic. But it felt good to be back in Ft. Collins; this was home. She was the queen of a little kingdom here, everything at her fingertips. With just the push of a button, she could command any service in town to do her bidding. During a stop at a red light, she made a quick call to the security company to check on their arrival time. *It's a little like closing the barn door after the horse is stolen;* she thought grimly.

Carolyn, a friend since kindergarten, waited outside of the little house. Taking the coffee Anna offered, she gave her a quick little hug. "Missed you! I can't believe you remember my favorite flavor."

"Missed you too! And of course, I remember. It was you who got me addicted to the stuff. Can't do much with no kick-start," she replied, turning the key in the deadbolt.

"Oh, Anna!" she said, looking around the littered house. "Okay, where do we begin?" Perky, blond, smart and tall, Carolyn had the heart of a lion.

Anna handed her a black trash bag wordlessly, and they started in the living room. She worked quietly, picking up the pieces of her life, listening to Carolyn's chatter until everything was back in place. The security company had arrived, working around them, wiring the house with a system loud enough to warn the entire neighborhood should the intruder come back.

Out the bedroom window, Anna caught sight of Chris's black cruiser pulling up to the curb. His soft knock on the open door

86

caused Carolyn to look up from her work of putting pictures back into frames. Anna called, "Come in, Chris."

His serious gaze scanned the now-orderly living room, the holes in the wall the only evidence left behind.

"Hi, Chris, find out anything yet?" Anna greeted him, setting her broom up against the wall.

"I've called in the help of your local neighborhood watch. An arrest warrant has gone out for Miles Rannet by the fingerprints he blatantly left all over and the fact his probation officer and therapist never saw him again after he was released. I've contacted the Sheriff's office in Wyoming and sent them the history and details of this case as well. I suggest you file a restraining order in Wyoming as soon as possible," Chris reported in a dulcet tone.

"I'll be heading back tomorrow. He doesn't know the area, and I've friends and family there."

Chris's cell phone beeped; he looked quickly at the screen. "I'll be checking in on you and giving you any updates we have." He put the phone away, his intense gaze back on Anna.

"Right now he's disappeared; we suspect with the help of his sister. We're not taking any chances, especially with the violence of this break-in."

Anna's eyes widened with apprehension. "Thank you, Chris. I'll keep you informed."

Carolyn was staring at the handsome detective, blushing when he turned his attention to her. "Nice to see you again, Carolyn, though it's sad it's under these circumstances. I suggest that you change your phone number immediately as he has information on all of Anna's friends now. Please call me if you've any concerns and watch out for yourself as well. We don't know where he may take it to this time."

"Why, yes, um, thank you. I've your number, uh, thank you," Carolyn stammered.

Chris looked at Anna again, a hint of worry behind his direct stare. "Please be careful driving back."

"I'll watch the speed--I promise."

He headed to the door, pausing to look back at her, nodded and quietly departed.

Anna noticed that Carolyn could barely contain herself until after he left. "Oh, he has the most gorgeous eyes."

❀ ❀ ❀ ❀ ❀

The road was a charcoal line fading off into the pastel blue of the sky. Anna didn't notice: she was in autopilot driving mode. Her mind busily mulled over the past as her hands gripped the steering wheel. Working through problems and careful planning was a survival technique. Pulling onto the gravel road, the farmhouse came into view, feeling like a haven now.

The front porch sported a new floor, with a sturdy rail lining it. The pine slats holding up the railing were in an artistic, fan-shaped pattern. Pausing, she took in the craftsmanship. Emily stepped out, greeting her with the standard bear hug.

"Welcome back, girl. Steve and Mike just left. Fill me in."

Anna looked at her dully. "You're all in danger. He got all my contact information this time. No one is safe. Let's go inside. I need a cup of tea."

Carrying in a duffel bag, she set it on the squat, wooden chest at the end of an antique, wrought iron bed in her mother's old bedroom. Emily followed her, plopping down on the edge of the bed.

"So how about some good news? Seth and I decided we can do this out here. We're going to rent out our home for now. Found a nice couple who are moving here and she is going to be working up at the hospital too. They won't be here until after the 4th of

July. So that gives us a couple of weeks to get moved. I'll put the boys upstairs, of course, and we'll put our furniture out here to replace the old. You don't mind if we make the front corner of the living room our computer nook, do you?

"Just put everything where you want it. It's your home now," Anna answered with a weary shrug.

"Did Chris let the Sheriff know to keep an eye out? Do they have any idea of where Miles might be?"

"They're still looking for him. All we can do is wait. I'll be damned if I'm going to live my life in fear, though. I talked to my therapist, and we both agree I'm not going to let this take one more second of my life."

Emily's head bobbed in agreement. "Honey, he'd have to go through me first to hurt you. I know you've never discussed it with Steve, so I filled him in on some of the particulars. I hope that was okay."

Anna looked at her for a second, wishing she had told Emily not to say anything, but then shrugged. "It's okay. The more people who know, the safer I'm going to be."

They both jumped at the shrill ring of the house phone.

Robynn Gabel

Chapter 7 – Race Day

Steve gritted his teeth, ignoring the mound of spaghetti on his plate.

"I don't know why you can't forgive Mary Beth. Give her another chance. She's truly sorry; she just needed some space. After all, you've been her only boyfriend since the tenth grade," his mother chided him.

He didn't look up, squishing noodles with a fork. "Mom, it's time for us to move on. She can find someone better."

Irritation shone in Rosalyn's narrowed eyes. "Son, Mary Beth has stood by your side through some tough years."

"You don't get it, Mom. She put up with my crap because she wanted a ring," he fired back.

"I can't believe you'd think that of her!"

Every Sunday, if they could, the family got together for dinner. Normally, Steve enjoyed it, but tonight his failings seem to be the unenviable center of everyone's attention.

"You decided what you're going to do about college this fall?" Brad questioned brusquely.

Jack shook his head at his son. "Let's just enjoy dinner. We can talk afterward."

The fork clattered against the China as Steve tossed it down. "No, Dad, let's just get it over with. Brad, what's your problem?"

Brad appeared not to notice when Lisa, his wife, shot him a warning glance. "I'm just worried. You've been awfully quiet lately, withdrawn since Mary Beth dumped you."

Steve grabbed the table edge, his voice low and hard. "I'll figure this out. It isn't your responsibility to herd the black sheep into place. Remember what the family counselor said: tough love, no hand holding, bro."

"Tough love," he snorted. "The only education you got out of high school was how to be an alcoholic. And there was the year of treatment that puts a toll on Dad's bank account and now two years of college on top of that. I'd let you starve out there! Mom and Dad have been too damn easy on you, and you put them through hell! I just don't want to see them go through that again."

Jack's voice rumbled with authority. "That's enough. Our finances are just fine, and we can take care of ourselves. I realize you are worried. But we need to treat each other respectfully, and Steve is right. He has to figure this out on his own. He's been sober for over a year now. Give him time."

With an audible gust, Steve let his breath out. "Sorry, Brad. I just need some space. I'm not going back to college. Dad and I talked about it. I'm not going to just live off Mom and Dad, or you. I don't plan on hanging out at the store either. I promise to have a game plan by the end of the summer, okay?" He glanced back at his father. "I'll make you proud, Dad. I promise."

Sitting at the other end of the table, Jack listened intently. He dipped his head in acknowledgment. Turning to his wife, he spoke quietly, "You've also made your point. He will work it out." She shot him an exasperated glare.

"I've nothing against Anna," Rosalyn said, "but she's going back to Fort Collins. Honestly Jack, can't you see where Mary Beth has been a terrific support for him? And we all know she's a solid Christian."

Jack shook his head. Steve slowly straightened, standing up, pushing his chair back.

"All right, Mom. I get it: you want me to marry Mary Beth. I don't want that. I want my life; I'll make my own decisions, good or bad."

Angrily she shot back, "I've seen how your decisions have affected your life, first hand. Go ahead and make a decision--in fact, make any decision--because I haven't seen any lately. Brad's right. You're just coasting through life. We're not always going to be around. Mary Beth is willing to take that journey with you. Instead, you hide out in your room and act like you're eighteen again."

Steve cut through the sudden babble of voices. "Enough!" He pushed away from the table. "I can't take this. Maybe I don't make decisions because you're always making them for me. I'll be out of here as soon as I can find a place." He stalked from the room.

"I wasn't asking you to move out," his mother called out to him.

"We need to talk, Rosalyn." Jack's tone brooked no argument.

Steve closed the door to his room with a firm shove. Wearily, he rubbed at his face. The bright computer screen filled the dark room with a haunting glow. What he wanted right now, more than anything, was a cold beer. To relax, not think and let all the tension wash away in its amber liquid.

Damn Mary Beth! Why couldn't she just let it go? There was a knock on the door and his father's gruff voice. "May I come in?"

"Yeah, Dad."

His father sat on the edge of the bed, leaning forward, elbows resting on his thighs, hands clasped together. He looked down at the floor. "I'm proud of how hard you've worked on staying sober. I know that Mary Beth is worried she hurt you and would like to make amends, but that is your business to handle. Your mother just wanted to put a good word in for her. You're right. You can't live here forever. Moving out is your choice. Just don't do it in anger."

Steve stared at the computer monitor. *I'm such a disappointment to him.* Memories of failure started a chorus of guilt he'd sought to drown in the past with alcohol.

"Son, I love you. I just wanted you to know I'm here." He stood up, the silence awkward for both of them.

"Thanks, Dad." Pain gave Steve's voice a sharp edge.

The door closed quietly. *I need to talk all right;* he thought, *but not with you, Dad.* With quick staccato beats, he began typing an email to his AA sponsor.

> Hey, Jim, I'm sorry I missed the meeting. Just need to chat. Mary Beth had Mom pitching for her tonight at dinner. I got angry, told them I'm moving out. Mom is mad, but Dad is okay with me leaving. You were right about my needing to be out on my own. Guess I was just taking it easy. I'll be honest: I could really use a beer right now. Wish I could just get drunk and not be feeling all this damn guilt.
>
> I've met a girl...

❀ ❀ ❀ ❀ ❀

A slight shuffle warned him of the pounce. Steve smiled, suddenly sitting up, catching his leaping sister, and wrestling with her as she squealed.

"Got to go, pipsqueak. I have a date with a fast car and a lovely lady."

Chelsea squinted in concentration for a moment. "Anna?"

"Of course. Who'd you think?" He reached out, giving her blond hair a playful rub.

Smugness fell over her features. "She's nicer than the other one."

Steve snorted a deep "hmpf." He knew of his sister's long-standing dislike of Mary Beth.

He ducked out the front door, avoiding his mom, sprinting to his truck, exhilarated at being able to drive again. Jerking open the old white pickup's door its rusty hinges whined noisily. Sliding in, he grabbed the ball cap hanging on the rifle rack that sported his favorite rifle, a 30/30 Winchester. Quickly cramming on the hat, he turned the key. The engine thundered, tail pipes shaking with a giant intake of breath.

The drive to get into town took about twenty minutes and from there it was another thirty minutes to get to the Hanson spread. He used the drive time to think about finding new living arrangements. Mike had offered to share his small apartment, but Steve had declined. He wanted his space; college had burned him out on roommates. His brother had been right: he was searching, worried about what the future held. What did he want to do with the rest of his life?

The turn came up, and he slowed to enter the gravel road. Anna waited on the porch. A form-fitting, white t-shirt showed a trim figure and a gently swelling bosom. It hugged her ribs to disappear at the waistline where a delicate belt sat above slight hips. Straight-legged jeans, midnight blue in newness, emphasized her long legs. A brunette ponytail hung out the back of a ball cap with a Corvette emblem. He wondered if she could look plain in anything.

Her eyes twinkled with excitement; an alluring smile graced her lips. He gazed at her, pushing away sudden thoughts of desire.

Whatever transpired in Colorado didn't seem to be haunting her today. A delivery job in Dubois had kept him from being there when she had returned on Friday. He decided to wait for her to bring up the subject if she chose too.

"Good morning," he called, sliding out of the silent truck.

"Hi! You're right on time. Jump in." He wasn't sure which he wished to look at more: the lustrous lines of the car or the nymph that tortured his thoughts. The door swung out silently as he slid into the low-slung car. Satin leather cupped his body as he stretched out his legs, gazing over the long hood of the Vette.

She slid in with ease. When they hit the main highway, she flashed a wicked smile with a look of daring in her eyes. "Ready?"

He locked the seat belt with a loud click. He nodded, a ruffian's smile answering her. She floored it, the g-force of acceleration pushing them into the deep recesses of leather, kindred spirits reveling in its power. The car hugged the road, quickly attaining legal speed.

Anna sighed, setting the cruise control. "Seems slow, doesn't it?" Her sad smile was at odds with the mirth in her eyes.

"You've no idea how I've looked forward to this." He closed his eyes, leaning back into the sports seat, feeling the thrum of the powerful engine.

A few minutes later, he opened his eyes glancing over at Anna. The nervous, aloof girl of the last few weeks was gone--in her place, a confident, girl-next-door.

"So how long have you had this car?"

"I've only owned her for about six months. But I coveted it for over a year. Held my breath the entire time, hoping no one would buy her until I had the money."

Steve leaned his head to the side, staring at the large sunglasses accentuating a little, upturned nose. "So it's she? How do you know that?"

They were coming up quickly on a sleek, black Lexus. She glanced at him with a 'watch this' gleam in her eye. With the other lane clear ahead, she stomped the gas pedal to the floor. The car responded with a powerful surge, gliding by its prey. Smoothly she steered it back into the right-hand lane. He admired how confidently she handled the car.

"Did you see how graceful that was? Did you feel her response? Only a woman can be that light on her feet." Anna tipped her head back, laughing. Steve felt the urge to run his finger down her slender neck to feel how soft it was. Her ponytail curved around to lie against the smoothness of her skin.

He struggled to find a question to divert his thoughts. "So where'd you learn about cars? I heard your dad passed when you were little."

Her eyes darkened to a stormy blue-gray. "Yeah, he was killed in a drunk-driving accident when I was only a year old."

Steve shifted in the seat, changing the subject. "So who taught you about mechanics?"

"What makes you think I know anything about mechanics?" she sassed.

"I saw you working on that old four-wheeler. Anyone who could get that thing running has to know something."

"Oh, I just picked it up hanging out at a family friend's garage. Pete runs a junkyard and car repair shop. He can make any engine sing. I also took mechanics in high school."

"You know, they just don't have a lot of hands-on anymore in the world of mechanics. It's all computer chips now," Steve pointed out.

Anna looked askance at him. "What do you mean it's all computers? The electrical maybe, but not the heart; that's still pistons, cams, valves, push rods, and crankshafts. There's still a lot of hands-on in fixing things."

Steve stared at her for a second. "You know your way around the lingo. You're right; there's some hands-on. But they don't make them like your grandfather's truck anymore. There's one I would love to work on. Back when it was simple."

"So what is it you do best, Steve? What is your passion?"

Now why couldn't someone have asked me that at dinner last night? Then maybe the conversation would have gone differently. "My mom likes to think it is a youth pastor. I'll admit I like working with teenagers. In fact, I was in college for two years training to enter the ministry. You know, you're the first to ask what I'm 'passionate' about, though." For a second, he watched the sagebrush passing in a blur, lost in thought.

He continued, "I like taking things apart and putting them back together. A hobby of mine, I guess. Mom used to hate it until she realized I'd get things working again. I know it's not much of an aspiration, but I'd like to be a mechanic."

"Why is that not a worthy calling, Mr. Johnson? In fact, I'd think you would be in high demand. I have a theory: work at doing what you love. Think about it--what are you going to spend most of your life doing? Work! It might as well be something you enjoy."

Steve looked at her, amazed at the down-home common sense. She looked over at him and then back to the road quickly.

"What?" she asked bemused.

"How is it you're so smart, lady?"

The country slid by. First, there was Sweetwater crossing where Mormons had pulled their handcarts on the path to their dreams in Utah. Then, the car slid effortlessly over a rise called Beaver Rim, through Jeffrey City, which was almost a ghost town.

The silence had a comfortable feel to it, and the thrum of the engine a lullaby. Lazily he broke it, asking, "Anna, what was your mother like?"

"She was a gentle soul, more child-like than anything. She saw everything as an entity, with a life of its own. She named her cars, took in strays, and loved the underdog. She was sweet and just wanted to get along in the world, didn't want conflict. And imaginative! She could create anything, craft-wise. When I was a teenager, I could tell her anything, but when I started college, we started to drift apart." Wistfulness softened her petite face.

Shaking his head, he replied, "I know what you mean; making that break from kid to an adult is tough. They expect you to make adult decisions, and when you do, they tell you that it is the wrong one, or you're not mature enough to make them. So, looking forward to teaching?"

"Yes, I love kids. I'm passionate about kids." Her dark lashes framed a flirtatious glance. "Ever thought about how many kids you want?"

He laughed. "I'm still a kid, but when I grow up, I'd like a couple. What about you?"

"I want to plan it. My mom always regretted her decision to run impulsively away with the first boy she fell in love with. They had to get married. It wasn't a pleasant situation, even though my mom always let me know I was the best thing that ever happened to her. They went to Fort Collins because my dad had some friends there. My dad's father, Grandpa Frank, came down a little later and partnered with Pete to open a repair shop. He helped out until he died of a heart attack; I was ten. I guess you could say I'm death on all relationships in my life," she said wryly.

Steve acted scared, putting his hands in front of his face, giving her an X sign with two fingers. "Back," he said. "Back."

She laughed a beautiful, light sound. "I'm pretty sure it has worn off by now. Besides, you aren't related to me!"

They passed a pile of rocks, smoothed by vicious winds and looking like a giant had dropped them there. He pointed, and said, "That's called Independence Rock. Passing wagon trains would stop there, and pioneers carved their initials into the rock. This whole countryside is rich in history, like the cattle barons and the infamous Cattle Kate hanging."

Anna put her sunglasses on the rim of her cap. "They hung her? Really? For what reason?"

"They accused her of being a cattle thief, but they just wanted her land."

She looked at him. "Since we seem to be doing so well in polite conversation, mind if I ask you something?"

"Anything," he answered, enjoying the way she talked with her eyes. One moment the color of a mountain lake, twinkling with humor, the next a stormy blue-gray, sparking anger. Contentment was a limpid pool of ice blue. He found himself wondering what color love would be in her expressive eyes.

Her question abruptly stopped that thread of thought. "So how did you meet Mary Beth?" He frowned at her. She shrugged her shoulder nonchalantly. "You said I could ask anything."

"We met in high school; I don't remember the actual moment. She's just always been there." He looked away, studying the sagebrush again.

"Oh, come on. You had to feel something for her. You don't date for six years and not feel something." Anna persisted.

Steve ran his hand through his hair. "Look, I'll be honest with you. We've been friends for a long time, but we also used each other. I liked the other guys being wowed that she was with me. I always called Mary Beth when I needed a date for something. She wanted the prestige of the Johnson name. In a small town, anyone who owns a business is considered rich and someone important. She kept hoping I would ask her to marry me someday. She got tired of waiting, and I'm a jerk for letting it go on for so long."

100

He could see Anna's lips pinch together in a straight line, eyes on the road. "Thank you for your honesty," she finally said.

He looked out again, surprised by her quiet answer and relieved she dropped it.

"So what does your brother do at the store?"

For the next half hour, Steve filled her in on his family and their business, interspersing it with questions on what she liked.

"Blue. I like the color blue," she said.

"Hmm, so why'd you buy a purple Corvette?"

Indignantly she shot back, "It's not purple; it's plum!"

He laughed. "Yeah, right. What does it say on the title?"

"Well, sunset purple metallic, but they are obviously color blind! It looks like we're here; do you know where the Event Center is?"

"What, I get to tell you where to go?" Steve leaned away from her, laughing as she lightly punched him.

Anna concentrated on the town traffic. "So have you ever been to an autocross?"

"Well, I know it's a low-speed course designed with cones for steep turns, slaloms, and gates. If you go off pattern, you lose your time to DNF (Did Not Finish). It's not a course about speed but about skill in racing the clock. So did I pass?" His eyes crinkled as a rakish smile appeared.

Anna gave a ladylike snort. "You know more about this than I suspected, Sherlock. You've been holding out on me."

As they turned into the Event Center, scattered across the broad parking lot sat an insurance agent's nightmare. Corvettes of all models, with numbers in tape on their sleek sides, or shoe polish on windows, were being readied. Anna picked a spot to park and jumped out, heading for the registration table.

"Hi, I'm Anna Sanchez This is Steve Johnson." A dark haired, petite woman behind the table held out her hand, and as they shook, she said, "Hi, I'm Judy. Welcome. Let's get you signed up. They'll be walking the course here pretty soon. Didn't you bring a car, Steve? We can fix that," she said invitingly.

Anna grabbed Steve's arm. "Yeah. Let's go Corvette shopping, shall we?"

His heart skipped at her touch. "Yeah, right. Someday," he growled playfully.

A trim woman with a girlish-looking ponytail moved to the table, arms full of bags of homemade cookies. "Hi, I'm Lynn. My husband will do your tech inspection when you're done here." Anna eyed the rows of homemade cookies. A quick smile lit up Lynn's face. "We take donations!"

Pulling out his wallet, Steve said, "Go ahead. Pick out a good one." He watched as she went "ooh" and "ahh" over the delicious bounty, enjoying her child-like joy in the choice.

Anna wiped away cookie crumbs as she checked the last bit of paperwork. "I signed you up to ride with me if you can stand to," she said, the dare back in her eyes. "Or you can always ride with one of the guys. The Amateurs can take passengers."

Steve looked down at her fondly. "I trusted you to get us here. I'll stay with a sure thing." He followed her out towards the course, eyeing the maze of cones. "How do you remember the pattern?"

"I think of it as a map in my head, but you also have to pay attention which way the ground cones point, so you know which side of the cone to go on."

A red ball cap with a Corvette emblem on the front, sitting atop soft brown curls, caught Steve's eye as the attractive woman approached. "Hi, I'm Mary; Judy said you were from Colorado, right? I'm going to walk the course. Want to come along?"

Anna nodded. "I would love that."

"Do you live near Golden? I've raced there several times. That's quite the track."

"Fort Collins, and yes, I've only been on that track once, but it's very intimidating. Maybe you can give me some pointers. I haven't been doing this long, still in Novice."

Steve held back. "Go for it, Anna. I think I can fend for myself around here."

"Okay, catch up with you in a few." Anna headed off with Mary, both chatting about strategies.

He wandered among all the motorized eye candy. He noticed there were a lot of Z06s, preferred for their high horsepower. He gazed longingly at the coupes and hardtops, guessing at years, and when he wasn't sure, chatting with the proud owner.

Anna came up behind him. "Oh, you've got to see this. Come over here." She caught his hand, pulling him to a white car hauler, seemingly unaware of the contact. Steve sucked in his breath as the car of his dreams materialized: a candy apple metallic red, customized, eighty-one coupe.

Shaking the owner's hand, Anna said, "Steve, this is Bob. Could we see under the hood?" Happily he obliged. Steve looked over the immaculate engine intently. "It's a four twenty-seven cubic inch with twin turbo, right?"

Bob laughed. "Yep, it can reach one-fifty mph in six seconds on a good stretch."

"Look, Steve. Look at the side pipes, and it has flared fender wells for those bigger tires," Anna chattered in excitement.

Steve eyed the scoop on the hood while she looked at the dashboard and shifter.

Anna glanced up. "You're racing with a four-speed automatic tranny, Bob?"

103

"Yeah, I usually race in the low-speed auto crosses or do a drag race now and then, and I have found the automatic shifts faster than I can."

Steve listened while they talked shop. Including him in the conversations naturally, she was adept at socializing without coming across arrogant.

Anna stepped back from the side of the '81 coupe, not seeing the person behind her. He quickly slipped his arm around her waist to stop her. She glanced up in fear, and then relaxed, smiling tentatively. His heart took flight as he felt her soft body lean into him. Steve withdrew gently, and then capturing her arm to guide her through the crowd growing around the flashy Corvette.

The roar of combined engines shook the air around them. He watched Anna shake out her brunette hair, the red highlights shimmering before she stuffed and tucked it into her helmet.

"So, you're going to trust my driving?

He flashed a daredevil smile. "Lady, I will do anything to go fast in a Vette. Besides, it passed tech inspection."

She smacked his shoulder lightly. "Ooh, you're a pain. My car is probably the most mechanically sound one here." Laughing, she slipped behind the wheel, revving the engine. Steve joined her, helmet in place.

Anna pulled up to the start line, waved in by a slender man holding a checkered flag in one hand, a radio in the other. He leaned in as she rolled down the window. "I'll wave you off as soon as that other car hits the end of the slalom."

He swung the flag down, and Steve braced as Anna accelerated across the start line, her bottom lip firmly clutched with her top teeth. He saw the first set of cones coming fast, watching as she deftly let up on the gas, swinging the wheel, tires squealing. She let the car glide into the curve, giving it gas to bring it out the other side.

He marveled at her assurance, missing cones by mere inches in the turn. She increased speed again, steering agilely, whipping it around three center cones that created the slalom. She sped into the next curve, tires squealing, rear end sliding. She punched for the long stretch, braking with concise control, spinning it around the last set of cones and feeding the racing engine one last stomp of the gas pedal as it surged across the finish line.

"Wooooo!" He laughed the adrenaline pumping through him. The only thing that would have made the run better is if he had done it himself. They looked at each other, and he noticed they had matching grins.

"Awesome. Let's go again!"

"I've got to check my time, and then it'll be my turn again. Three runs make a heat, and in each division the best time wins overall," she huffed in excitement.

Anna perused the time board, and Steve stood behind her when the sound of a coughing engine caught their attention.

"Hmm, I think that Vette is in trouble," Steve said, squinting against the bright sun.

In the backstretch, a white Corvette coasted to a stop, growling in the attempts to restart. "I'll be back," Steve called as he jogged out to the stalled car.

The hood was up, the driver and two others looking at the engine. "I noticed it seemed to lose power before quitting," Steve offered.

"I'm Gary; you're from Lander, I hear." He was friendly with a ready grin. The radio in his hand crackled, a voice questioning the delay. He answered quietly, and then turned back to Steve. "Any ideas on what it could be?"

The tall, blond driver peered at Steve. "You know, it didn't feel right coming over this morning. I'm not sure what is wrong."

"Have you had it serviced lately: plugs, wires, oil?"

"Yes, had it to the shop just the other day."

"Do you have a rag?" Steve started jiggling, prying and testing with his hand wrapped to protect against the hot engine. "Let's pull the air cleaner; sometimes they will automatically shut off if the airflow is interrupted." Lifting the cover, an innocent piece of foam stared up at him. "Well, haven't ever seen that. Wonder how it got in there?"

Gary clapped him on the back; the driver shook his hand and thanked him profusely. He headed back to the time board where Anna was waiting. She looked at Steve with pride. "Great job; you're a hero." He shook his head, saying, "Just doing my good deed for the day. Let's get you back on the track."

Five laps later, Steve was disappointed that it had sped by so quickly. He watched in satisfaction as the racers congratulated Anna on her times. She had come in second in the first heat and had won the last heat in her division.

Mary Beth couldn't have driven like that; he thought with a twinge of humor. He felt a sense of camaraderie with Anna as she mingled, talking mechanics and car facts.

"Well, we need to get on the road," she said, setting the trophy gently between the folding chairs in the space under the hatchback.

The road slid under the happily humming Vette; conversation easily flowed as they shared simple things like favorite foods, movies, music, and books. He worked to memorize her profile, the curve of her lips and the long fingers that gave her hands a beautiful, cultured look.

"So do you plan on finishing college?" she asked during a comfortable lull.

He thought for a second, and answered, "I've given that a lot of thought. But no, I think I'm going to check out some tech schools in the field of mechanics."

Anna steered gently onto the gravel road to the ranch house, the shadows long in the little valley as the sun set. "Well, we have some terrific schools in Boulder or the Loveland area if you are willing to leave Wyoming."

"Are you inviting me to visit, Anna?" he said, eyes crinkling along with his chuckle.

A faint blush crept over her cheeks, and for the first time that day she seemed flustered. "I was just telling you what I know of--it wasn't--well, I wasn't asking--oh..." She cut off the sentence and the engine simultaneously, flipping her ponytail over her shoulder with an irritated twitch.

Anna's eyes had a distant look in their depths, her body stiff, retreating into her shell. Steve stepped around the front of the car, holding out his hand. "I'm sorry. I didn't mean to ruin a perfect day. Friends?"

She hesitated, taking his hand, cautiously giving it a quick shake. "Friends. Thank you; really, I had fun. You'd better head home before it gets dark and the deer start coming out. You don't need one as a hood ornament. Will I see you Monday?"

"Yeah, I'll be here, and thanks again."

Steve drove off, cursing quietly under his breath.

Robynn Gabel

Chapter 8 – Emergency

The curry brush brought up a cloud of dust, leaving a soft swath of shiny, copper-red hair in its wake. Ginger's tail swatted at flies, her eyes half-closed in pleasure as she stood tied to the hitching rack alongside the front of the barn.

Anna's mind wandered over Saturday's autocross as she groomed the mare. Mental snapshots of Steve's hazel eyes, crinkling at the corners when he smiled, caused her stomach to do a little flip. Sighing, she leaned her head against the mare's soft neck. What was she going to do? Denial didn't work anymore. She liked being with Steve.

Grabbing a hairbrush, she brushed Ginger's tail with long, agitated strokes, stopping only to work on persistent snarls. *Yesterday went so well, and then I slipped and let him get too close. And he probably has no idea of what he did.*

The forcefully thrown curry brush landed with a loud thud in the grooming box, startling Ginger. Standing in the shade of the open barn door, hands on hips, eyes narrowed, the green summer pasture lay unnoticed before her. It wasn't that Anna didn't want a man in her life. In fact, she had a very good idea of what she wanted, but the biggest hurdle was going to be the ability to trust if she wanted more than just a surface relationship with a man.

Tires grinding gravel announced the truck's arrival. Glancing down the hill, suddenly eager to catch a glimpse of Steve, her heart pattered in excitement. The horse in the trailer questioned where he was with a loud neigh. Ginger gave a deep whinny in return.

Chelsea jumped out as Steve and Mike disembarked. While they unloaded the little Appaloosa under the cottonwood tree, Anna went back to the barn to get a saddle from the tack room. Stepping outside again, she situated a saddle pad on the horse's back and then threw the saddle over it. She grabbed the leather latigo that would hold the cinch tight, running her hand over it out of habit, checking for cracks and suppleness. By the time she finished getting Ginger to take the bit, inspected the reins and tightened the cinch once more, Chelsea and Steve had joined her down at the barn.

Shooting a quick peek in his direction, she caught him staring at her, uncertainty in his eyes, frustration plain on his tanned face.

"Corky's a fine-looking little Appy," Anna said, avoiding his gaze.

Chelsea beamed, petting the overindulged horse. "He loves me, and I love him. What are we doing today?"

"We'll be pushing Momma Cow and her calf out to the first water-hole. They can find the rest of the herd and grow fat on the grass for the summer. Also, I've packed a gourmet lunch of peanut butter and jelly sandwiches."

"I want to show you how Corky and me can open a gate together."

Anna gave Chelsea a quick squeeze. "I would love to see that."

Steve cleared his throat. "I'll be starting the painting today. How long do you think you'll be out?"

Anna kept her back to him, her heart racing, wanting to fix the awkwardness between them. "We shouldn't be longer than three hours."

"Okay, take care pipsqueak. See you later, Anna," he said, his voice soft.

"Let's head out then." She watched Chelsea swing up into the saddle with ease.

Turning, Anna observed the dejected slump to Steve's shoulders as he walked up to the house. *What am I doing?*

Turning back, she walked over to Ginger and mounted up, settling into the saddle. Chelsea was true to her word, and with Corky's patient moves, she opened the panel entrance to the holding corral. With unhurried steps, Anna and Ginger moved the momma cow and baby out onto the trail to the big pasture gate.

"So Chelsea, what grade are you going into this year?"

"Second and I'm in Mr. Thornsen's class. He's the best in the whole school."

"Hmm. Well, I hope I'll be a good teacher."

"My brother said you'd do well at your job because you love children. And he told me your eyes are the prettiest blue he's ever seen." Chelsea seemed quite pleased to pass this information on.

"Oh my! That's a nice compliment." The warmth of a blush crept up.

Momma Cow moved out leisurely, her baby following closely. When she would stop to graze, Anna would ride up closer, putting pressure on the bovine to move on.

"You like horses, right?" Chelsea's face wore a somber look.

"Why, yes. Ginger has been my horse since I was a little older than you. In the summer, I would ride her and help my Grandpa work the cows."

"You would never hurt a horse, right?"

"I wouldn't harm any animal, Chelsea. Why do you ask such a thing?"

Chelsea's words rushed out. "At Christmas time, Mary Beth was babysitting me. I was supposed to be in bed, but I was at the top of the stairs, and I saw her kiss Rob Miller, and she caught me. She threatened to hurt Corky if I ever told anyone." Tears shimmered as she leaned down to pet the little horse.

Anna clamped her teeth together for a second, concentrating on the flies swarming over the cow in front of her, trying to think of a reply.

"Chelsea, sometimes people just say silly things; they'd never really do them."

Chelsea shook her head, "Nope, she means it. She pushed our cat off the porch railing when it brushed up against her. She won't ride a horse either. She says they stink and can hurt you. I'm glad my brother doesn't like her anymore."

Anna glanced over at the little girl, wanting to give her a hug, wondering what type of person threatens animals.

The trail wound through an old hay pasture and then began to climb along the side of a ridge. A small stream ran at the bottom, around rocks and grassy flats. The path got rockier, steeper, and at one point another ridge joined to create a narrow canyon. The sure-footed horses picked their way. The cow moved quicker now, calling out, trying to connect to the herd that was out there somewhere. The calf slowed, investigating different plants, and then in a rocking run, scampered to catch up with his mom.

Scrub pine crowded alongside the trail on Anna's left, their roots encroaching into the pathway, making the going slow. She ducked under branches, sometimes having to shove the prickly bows aside to pass. Chelsea followed behind, chatting about her friend's sleepover.

Ginger brought up her head, stopping; ears pricked forward, nostrils wide as she sucked in the morning air, trying to figure out the scent. Ahead of the horses, a rock ledge with a few trees held on precariously, the rocky trail wrapped around it, disappearing.

The momma cow now sensed danger, lowing for her baby, hurrying forward. To Anna's right was the steepest part of the slope, falling off to the rocky stream bottom. Treacherous footing and large boulders made getting down to the stream from the trail inhospitable to horses and cows. Anna scanned the pathway ahead, searching the trees and ledge for whatever had caught Ginger's interest.

Ginger pranced, snorting, tugging the reins, wanting to turn around on the narrow trail.

"Whoa girl, whoa. It's okay." Anna kept her voice low, her hands firm on the reins, holding the anxious horse in place. The momma cow disappeared around the bend with her calf; Ginger tossed her head in the air, pulling at the bit. Chelsea cried out. Corky was now snorting, trying to back up.

"Chelsea, let him back up to that wide spot in the trail--it's not far. Then turn him," Anna commanded, catching a movement to her left.

"Oh," she gasped, glimpsing the shadowy form of a mountain lion, creeping out of the pine to the edge of the rock ledge, its yellow eyes intent on the horses and the people in front of it. Anna had no time to wonder about the cat's unusual actions. Ginger came up, whinnying, her front feet rearing high in the air. Coming down, she tried to turn and lost her footing in the soft dirt and rock. Anna yelled as Ginger started sliding sideways, the horse scrambling frantically to stop herself in the small avalanche of shale and dirt.

❁ ❁ ❁ ❁ ❁

Chelsea watched in horror as Ginger fell, rolling to her side, throwing Anna. She bounced like a rag doll onto the rocks that littered the canyon floor.

She let up on the reins, giving Corky his head. For all his chunkiness, he managed to back down the trail, and when it widened enough, he scrambled to turn around. He started back down the path at a fast, sure-footed clip. Tears soaked Chelsea's face; both hands held the saddle horn tightly as the little Appy headed unerringly back to the ranch. The gate was still open as he trotted through, past the barn and down to the horse trailer parked under the cottonwood in front of the house.

"Steve, Steve, Anna's hurt! Steve!" Chelsea screamed while she clutched the horn, sobs choking her.

The screen door slammed against the house as Steve and Mike came running.

"Where, sweetheart? What happened?" Steve's voice soothed.

Chelsea stuttered between sobs, "Her—her horse fell down with her. Horses were scared of something, but—Ginger…couldn't turn around; she rolled down, Anna fell off, she's hurt, I couldn't stop Corky."

"I'll take the four-wheeler, Mike. I should be able to go up that canyon a little way, and they've not been gone long, so she can't be too far in."

Eyes wide, tears streaming, Chelsea listened.

"I'll stay here and unsaddle Corky and take care of Chelsea. Should I call for an ambulance?" Mike asked.

Chelsea felt Steve pry her hands from the horn. "It's okay, Chelsea. It's all right, and I'm going to find Anna. Honey, how bad do you think she's hurt?" She felt him pulling her off, cradling her, brushing the hair from her tear-streaked face.

Corky let out a shrill whinny, and they all looked up to see Ginger limping into the far gate of the pasture. Chelsea saw her brother's eyes open wide, catching his bottom lip between his teeth before he spoke.

"Mike, we need help: call Emily, the ambulance, and my mom. Chelsea, honey, I got to get Anna. You stay here with Mike, okay?"

Chelsea nodded, a sob escaping as Steve lowered her to her feet. She reached for Mike's hand.

"Good girl. Everything will be fine. Help him with Corky, okay? You can do this. Corky needs you." Steve sprinted for the barn.

Mike shouted after him, as Chelsea held on tightly. "Steve, call me when you can; there's reception on this side of the canyon. Keep me updated."

Chelsea watched Steve wave in answer.

❀ ❀ ❀ ❀ ❀

Anna slowly came back to consciousness, the world swirling around. Her left arm throbbed in excruciating pain, pulse pounding in her head. Opening her eyes slowly, she tried to focus on the large rock in front of her until the spinning made her stomach threaten mutiny. Snapping them closed, she hoped it would stop the momentum.

Tentatively moving, testing her limbs, she realized her back was against a large boulder. In agony, she pulled up her legs and pushed off with her right arm, her left arm aching and dangling uselessly. Squirming, she was able to prop herself up against the rock behind her. Even with the world careening, Anna could hear the stream a few feet away, and realized she was at the bottom of the canyon.

Ginger was nowhere around. Something wet and sticky ran down the side of her face, the metallic smell letting her know it

115

was blood. The left arm now burned with an intense fire. She glanced down; the hand and wrist crooked to the left, and in the middle of the forearm, she wondered what that jagged thing was sticking out. Bracing against the rock, she closed her eyes again to stop the dizziness.

A pungent, musky odor floated on the slight breeze. Recognizing it as an animal odor, Anna knew the cougar must be close. Opening her eyes, she stared at the big cat crouched on a boulder across the stream, about thirty feet away. Its tail twitched, and there was hesitation in its baleful, golden eyes. Amazement registered in her scrambled mind that it was this close. *It's not acting normal. Usually, they are like ghosts. The smell of my blood must have drawn it in.*

She kept still despite the pain and light-headedness, staring down the mountain lion until it shifted on the stone beneath it. There would have been no outrunning it, even if she was in the best of shape. Overhead, a crow called, warning of the silent standoff below it. In the tense quiet, even the buzzing flies sounded loud. Suddenly, the mountain lion swung its head to the right, gazing down the canyon, listening. The distant rumble of a motor vibrated in the still, summer air.

The big cat turned, limped off and disappeared. With a big sigh of relief, Anna slipped into the blackness that had been held at bay by fear.

Even through the veil of black, she heard Steve's growl in her ear. "Anna, open your eyes. Look at me." Struggling through the fog, her eyelids heavy, she tried to look at him, wondering why he was upset with her. His face was out of focus.

"What?" she murmured. "Let me rest; it's spinning."

"Listen to me: you have to wake up,--do you hear me?--stay awake--look at me! Where are you hurt? Does your neck feel okay, Anna?" The fear in his voice made it gruff.

116

Why is he hollering at me? This isn't my fault; she thought irritably.

"No, my neck doesn't hurt. My arm burns. My head is throbbing," she mumbled, wondering why he still called her name, anger spiking his tone.

"You got to stay awake, Anna Sanchez--you can't sleep! Do you hear me?" She was too tired to care or respond, welcoming the blackness that drew her in.

❀ ❀ ❀ ❀ ❀

Steve didn't have time to curse. He worked furiously to keep her conscious, using every ounce of his focus, and First-Aid training. He knew, from the blood and bruising he could see--and her half-conscious state--she had sustained a head injury and a possible concussion, if not a fractured skull. Worrying about the compound fracture of her arm, he pulled off his t-shirt, wrapping it, trying to keep dirt from getting into the jutting bone. His fingers probed up the back of her neck, searching for any swelling or abnormality. Since she had been able to get herself into a sitting position, he was going to chance it that she hadn't broken any vertebra. The ambulance couldn't come up the trail; he'd have to take her down with him.

As if handling the most fragile of items, he picked her up, cradling her.

"Anna Sanchez! Answer me!" Her eyelashes fluttered, but she didn't open her eyes.

Carefully, he maneuvered down to the four-wheeler, awkwardly throwing a leg over the seat, gingerly holding her across his lap, steering one-handed and driving slowly back down the canyon.

"Anna, open your eyes. Talk to me." Desperation tinged the sound of his voice. "I can't lose you, girl. I just can't. What is it

117

with you; can't you stay out of trouble? Anna! Wake up, come on, look at me," he shouted over the roar of the engine.

She roused. "Quit yelling at me; my head's spinning...."

Waves of nausea rolled through his belly, his pulse tripping with adrenaline. The four-wheeler seemed to crawl; he wanted to be at the hospital now. His thoughts were jumbled, fear whipping like a Chinook wind. He couldn't lose her, be without her--dang it; he loved her. There was no doubt: he couldn't live without the girl in his arms.

Tears ran down his cheeks, turning cold in the moving air. Brokenly he begged her again, "Anna, sweet, open your eyes. I love you. Stay awake, please."

At the end of the ridge, he slowed, struggling to get his cell phone out.

"Thank God, a signal," he said out loud, dialing clumsily. "Yeah, Mike, she's pretty bad. No, she's got a strong pulse, just fast. Hard to tell what the blood loss is. Did you call everyone? Thank God, I'm almost there."

The idea of eternity seemed shorter to him than the time it had taken before the barn came into view, the ambulance waiting below at the house. Paramedics raced to him, a backboard in hand. They slid her from his lap onto it, busily strapping and securing her.

"Rodney, her name is Anna Sanchez, and she's twenty-four years old. She's in and out of consciousness, compound fracture of the left arm, and I think she's going into shock. Must have hit her head pretty hard in the fall. That's all I know. Emily Higgins is her cousin and works at the hospital. She could give you more info," Steve reported to the busily working medics. He was thankful for the time spent in conversation with Anna over the past weekend.

Rodney, a hefty built medic, nodded. Steve had worked with him in Search and Rescue a few times. "'Good job, Steve, but you're right: she's going into shock. Did she give you any idea of how long she was out?"

"No, she hasn't been fully conscious with me." Steve's answer pushed out around the tightness in his throat. A movement at the window revealed Chelsea peering out, her eyes red from tears. He gave her a thumbs-up and a big, fake smile.

A cloud of dust parted, revealing his mother's beige Chevy Malibu. As the car came to a halt, she jumped out, running to Steve. "Honey, how is she?" Fear filled her blue eyes at the sight of the blood on Steve's chest.

"Don't know, Mom; it looks bad. I want to ride in with her. Chelsea watched it all happen--she's pretty freaked out."

She started towards the house, saying back over her shoulder, "Okay. Well, I called the church prayer chain; you just go take care of Anna."

Steve stepped up as they loaded Anna. "Hey Rodney, is it okay if I ride in with her?"

"Yeah, keep talking to her. See if you can get her to respond."

❀ ❀ ❀ ❀ ❀

At the hospital, Steve worked on his fourth cup of coffee. He'd flipped through every magazine in the waiting room, paced the halls, and thought about taking up smoking before Emily found him.

"Well, you were pretty accurate in your assessment. They had a rough time setting the compound fracture in her arm. She came through surgery just fine, though there were a lot of bone fragments, so they had to put in a few pins to stabilize the break. The swelling has to go down before they can cast it. No skull fracture, but a bad concussion, some fractured ribs, a very small brain bleed from the impact, and blood loss. They're putting her in room two-twenty if you want to go down and wait for her. Thank heavens you were out at the ranch. I appreciate you staying around here for her."

Out of the corner of Steve's eye, he caught sight of a familiar figure. Rob Miller shuffled down the hall, dazed, Mary Beth holding his arm. Her glance slid over Steve, her eyes empty, not registering his presence.

"Rob, you doing okay? Can I get you something?" Emily softly questioned.

"No, it's all right; I'm on my way out. Thanks, Emily," he mumbled brokenly. He put his hand on Steve's shoulder. "Dad passed this morning."

A lance of pain shot through Steve's stomach; the blood drained from his face for the second time that day. "Hey, man, I hadn't heard. What happened?"

Rob choked out the words. "Heart attack, just gone. He got up, was doing chores, and he didn't come in for breakfast. We found him in the barn." Mary Beth pressed her tear-streaked face against his shoulder, sliding an arm around his waist.

"Let's go. We need to get your mom home," she urged.

"Sorry to hear about Anna, but she's going to make it, right?" Rob rubbed his forehead wearily.

"Yeah, she's doing well, made it out of surgery."

"Good, got to go now." He resumed his shuffle, Mary Beth supporting him.

Steve's relief over Anna was pushed aside by a wave of sorrow. His eyes still wide in shock, he turned to Emily. "I talked to Herman just a week ago. He seemed healthy as a horse."

"You never know when your time is up, honey." Still in disbelief, Steve nodded.

❁ ❁ ❁ ❁ ❁

Steve stared out the hospital window overlooking the valley. The town of Lander lay like a quilt of quiet neighborhood squares stitched together by roads and trees. The mountains rose in the background, stretching across the west. Blind to all of it, he was deep in prayer, thanking the Creator for Anna's narrow escape and asking to give solace to Rob and his family.

He loved her. It was a shock each time the thought flashed through his mind, so new and strange. It interrupted anything else he was thinking. It was a pain, joy, and a fear all rolled into one. He wasn't sure of what to do with this new emotion or how to proceed. But one thing he knew without a doubt: today had given him clarity. He knew what he wanted more than anything else in the world.

Reaching out, he pulled a finger along the edge of the window sill. While she healed, he would have a little time for planning. Could she love him like he loved her? There was the distance to contend with also. She loved Ft. Collins. That was evident in how she had talked about her hometown this last weekend. Where he lived wasn't all that important to him, but he was getting ahead of himself.

A noise behind him warned of someone approaching, and he turned from the window. George moved slowly towards him, appearing uncomfortable. He stuck out his hand. "If I remember correctly, you're Jack Johnson's son, Steve, right? I hear from Emily we have you to thank. So what happened?"

Steve shook his head, answering, "I don't rightly know. I suspect the horses were spooked by something. The vet says the mare took a tumble, scrapped her hide up pretty good and sprained a back hock. When my sister first told me how things happened, I was afraid the horse had rolled over Anna. From what I've now gathered, she was thrown."

Evelyn, George's wife, bustled in with coffee. Steve groaned inwardly--he needed solid sustenance.

121

T

"How long have you been working out there, Son?" George reached for a coffee.

"The last couple of weeks."

A welcoming smile spread across Evelyn's full features. "I've heard a lot about you, Steve. Nice to meet you, only wish it wasn't under these circumstances."

Before Steve could comment, George continued, "Emily says you're a hard worker, and you know your way around a ranch. Are you wanting full-time work? Comes with some perks."

"Really? What did you have in mind?"

"Well, I need a few hands to help out. Bunkhouse ain't any fancy fixings, but it'd save you on gas if you live there. We'd work out the pay depending on what all you can do. Fencing will be first on the list if you are interested."

Steve blinked, staring hard at George. He had prayed, asking for direction, for a place to stay and a way to start on his plans. In one quick moment, his prayers had been answered.

He held out his hand. "I'd be honored to work for you." They shook hands, the only contract needed.

A clamor of squeaking wheels outside the door warned them of the approaching patient and her entourage of nurses. A tall, reedy, red-headed nurse backed in, pulling at the foot of a portable gurney. Glancing over her shoulder, she gave a quick bob of her head.

"If you folks want to step out for a moment, we can get her situated."

A clicking, murmuring blood pressure machine followed and another nurse attached it to the form on the bed with a long, black cord. A couple of glistening bags of clear liquid hung on a silver hook, attached to plastic lines that disappeared under the covers. After the gurney was lined up next to the waiting hospital bed, George and Evelyn headed for the door. Steve followed, anxiously looking over at the still shape under the white mound of plain cotton blankets. Dark, purpling bruises stood out stark against Anna's pasty skin, the swelling in her face making a grotesque mockery of her former beauty. He didn't see any of this, the vision of the girl this weekend implanted over the wounded girl of now.

The door to the room closed in a hushed sigh behind them. Steve watched the bustling hospital staff ducking in and out of rooms down the long hallway. Evelyn and George wore worry on their faces in different wrinkle patterns.

"She will be okay, Steve." Evelyn patted his arm softly. Was it already evident that he loved her so much that he was near panic?

The shrill scream of an anxious machine sounded behind the closed door. Suddenly, a red light flashed over the door mantle, warning Steve, Evelyn, and George that they were in the way of the descending crowd of hospital staff.

Robynn Gabel

Chapter 9 – Relationships

"Not more food," Anna groaned as Steve reached the shade tree and the old, weathered bench she sat on. Clean-shaven, well-rested and newly tanned from outdoor labor, he looked like the quintessential modern cowboy.

"Yup, high noon in the West. I'm starved."

Watching him reach into the picnic basket to set up lunch, she sighed, softly saying, "You know, I should thank you again." Gratefulness laced each word.

"Yeah, well, I like being your knight in shining armor instead of just an irritating handyman." His tone was light, but his expression was somber.

"Great. Well, don't get used to it. I liked you as Sherlock better."

They'd not had a chance to talk privately since the accident. First she'd been surrounded by hospital staff, and then by family when she got home. She missed their banter.

The bench squeaked under his added weight as he sat down, her heart fluttering at his nearness. Inspecting the decaying wood under them, he asked, "How long has this been up here?"

"Hmm, I don't know. Been here as long as I can remember. This place has always been kind of my getaway. Quite the view isn't it? Go ahead and eat. I'm still full from breakfast."

It was easy to be comfortable and content with Steve, even in the silences. The picnic lunch finished and packed away, he stretched his long legs out in front of him, put his arm along the back of the bench, and looked down at her. The wind and cottonwood tree conversed in rustling whispers above them. The breeze felt good in the hot sun, but in the shade its caress was cool. She shivered slightly.

"Are you cold? Come here; I won't bite. For Pete's sake, you have goose bumps."

"And just who is Pete, that I should worry about his well-being?" she sassed back.

Taking off his cowboy hat, she noticed he had an indecipherable look in his eyes and an easy smile ended in her favorite crinkles. *It's okay. He's not Miles, just relax. I should have thought to bring up a sweater, so either take his offer or go back to the house.*

Anna battled the old roller coaster ride: wanting to let her guard down and open her heart. *What if he turned out to be another Miles?* There was no way she'd make the mistake of falling in love before discovering his flaws. When she was young, Anna had vowed she wouldn't marry a man like the father who had chosen alcohol over spending his life with her. She wasn't following in Mom's footsteps either, always struggling to survive. And she wasn't going to jump haphazardly into life without a plan, the way so many of her classmates and friends did.

But--at this moment--suddenly feeling like a small child craving to be held, her resolve wavered. Leaning on his shoulder, she allowed him to wrap his arms around her. Resting a cheek against his chest gingerly, she heard the soft thud of his heart, noticing the uptick in rhythm.

Just because you have the same effect on him that he has on you doesn't mean you can play with his heart, she lectured herself. *I'm not falling for a cowboy. It's just a little snuggling; that's all. Friends hug all the time.*

The last few days played through her mind. The first recollection after surgery was Steve's anxious face, leaning in to whisper to her, "Hello there." Scruffy whiskers and dark shadows of worry gave him a haggard look.

Another memory teased, just out of reach. It came back in a rush: the world spinning, the pain, cradled in his arms, his angry voice fearful, crying out "I love you." Did she hear that? Did he really say it? Or was it just part of slipping between the world of dark and light? What would it change if he did say it? She would be heading home in a few weeks, back to the world she was comfortable in, and this interlude would just be a fond memory.

He rested his cheek against her hair; his slender hand moved to rub her arm. Tilting back her head, she looked into his eyes. The color he wore determined their tint. With the light-blue, western cut shirt, his eyes had a haze of blue.

He held his breath, bringing his hand up slowly as if he might frighten her away with any sudden movement. Timidly, he reached out his finger to touch her cheek. She felt the gentle stroke and held still as it slid down to her jawline and continued to the base of her throat. The light contact left a warm path that she felt even as he retreated. He hesitated but seemed drawn to brush her cheek again, only to trace around her lips, this time, his eyes focused on the path his finger drew.

Who would have thought, in the wilds of Wyoming, there could be such a gentleman? Why does he have to smell so darn good? Oh, what am I doing? Closing her eyes, she felt his arm tighten under her shoulders and the side of his warm chest press against her. *Just a few minutes more, even if it does feel good,* her conscience warned.

Feeling strangely weak, warmed with yearning, she opened her eyes, giving in to the urge to raise her good hand to touch his tanned cheek, the smooth skin taut under her fingers. Inside, a little voice asked, *what are you thinking?* That was the problem: Anna was no longer thinking but feeling, giving free rein to all her senses. Sighing sensuously, she smiled at him.

Steve froze, his breath expelling in a quiet huff. He bent his head slowly as if waiting for her to push away and flee. Instead, she leaned into him eagerly, her lips parting to receive his, delighting in their softness.

This is how you got in trouble with Miles, smiling once, being nice. That's all it took. Stop now before it gets out of hand, the little voice trumpeted. Suddenly, she pulled away, embarrassed by her ardor. Desperately searching for something to say, the first thing that came to mind popped out. "What, you don't want to shout at me to stay awake?"

His eyes widened. "You remember?"

"Well, not much, but I did wonder why you were yelling at me. I wasn't sure if my head hurt because you were shouting or if I had landed on it."

"Lady, you sure know how to ruin a romantic moment," he groaned. He reached out to cup her face with his warm hand. "I'm just thankful I didn't lose you."

Her heart thrummed, the burning in her stomach wasn't from too much breakfast. "So that kiss was just to make me feel better, right? So I wouldn't think I look too ugly?" She felt light-headed and silly. Taking his hand away from her face, he stared at her thoughtfully. She knew he could see the ugly, purple welt on the left side of her forehead, and the angry black eye.

"I suppose I look horrible."

"Like you fell down a mountain, but underneath it, you're still beautiful."

Anna shifted under his gentle gaze. "What?"

He shook his head. "Anna, you have no idea how lucky you are, do you?"

"I think luck had nothing to do with it, just good friends and guardian angels. Before you brought lunch up, I was trying to remember how I got to the hospital."

A slight shudder went through him. "It was pretty bad; you were in and out of consciousness during the ride to the hospital. But the worst part was when you came back from surgery and crashed. I thought we'd lost you for sure then."

Gazing pensively out over the little family cemetery that lay in front of them, he said with an uncomfortable edge to his tone, "Well, you don't have to search far for your lineage."

Anna sobered. "Yes, they're all here, including my father. Those three new headstones are my grandfather, grandmother and mom." Her voice cracked on the mention of her mom.

Ominously, he said, "You know you almost ended up a name on one of those headstones, don't you?"

Stiffening, she leaned away from him. "Yes, just another reason country living sucks as I see it. You don't have to worry about wild animal attacks in the city."

"Hmph," he snorted angrily. "No, just stalkers, pollution, drive-bys and crime. Like that won't take a few years off your life."

"I fully understand the gravity of the accident. It wasn't like I went looking for trouble. What is your problem? One minute you're kissing me--the next, lecturing me."

Leaning forward, elbows on knees, he rubbed at his face with both hands, and dropped them, his voice low, expression pained. "Lady, I know you wanted just friendship, but I don't think I can

129

do it. I know you don't want to hear this, but, I want more. I'm not sure if I'm ready for this, or if you are either. But when I held you in my arms, thinking I was going to lose you, all I wanted to do was to protect you, keep you from ever suffering again. Thinking of my life without you made me realize: I want you in it."

Eyes widening, her mind scrambled for the meaning behind his words. *Had she gone too far? Was it already too late? He couldn't be declaring his feelings, could he?* Anna was used to controlling how far relationships went. It was coming too fast to get a hold of it. And though there had been declarations in the past from others, this time, it felt so different.

"Steve," she breathed the word.

"Look, I think I lo…." She put her fingers to his lips, stopping him. Shaking her head, she said firmly, "We need to talk. Not right now, but later. I can't think right now."

He caught her hand, kissing the palm. Tipping her face to his with one slender finger, he leaned in, his lips ever so gently meeting hers. Anna's breath came faster, her bruised ribs protesting with a painful stab. Grabbing at her side, she gasped.

Lifting his head, he loosened his hold quickly. "Did I hurt you?" A frantic worry shone in his eyes.

"Sorry, I'll be okay. Give me a second." The pain slid away, subsiding. Speaking so softly he had to lean in to hear her, she said, "Let's just take this slow. One day at a time, okay?" Lightly, he slid his arm around her shoulders, gently squeezing in response. No words were needed.

The sounds of boyish laughter floated up the slope as Emily's boys chased each other around the ranch house. "So do you miss your nice, quiet house, or are you glad to have the company?" His tone was casual, no trace of the previous frustration.

"Well, it is a little overwhelming, and Emily is definitely in the mothering mode. But it's okay."

"Well, Boss, unless I get paid for making out with you, I think I'd better get back to work. You should be resting anyway. I'll help you get back down."

"Yes, that'd be a good thing--not sure of my balance." She was thankful her voice sounded cool and controlled.

Gently, he slid his arm around her waist, and they slowly made their way down the path to the ranch house. Her uncle's truck pulled up just as they reached the porch.

"How are you doing today?" George called, as he got out of the truck and came up to the deck.

Anna smiled gratefully up at Steve. "Pretty good with all the help around here."

George glanced at the arm Steve held tightly around her waist. "I've some business to discuss with you if you're up to it."

❀ ❀ ❀ ❀ ❀

Steve had a hard time not pulling her closer so he could feel her slim body against his. Instead, he gently guided her towards the house. *Damn, that didn't go as planned. I finally have some time with her, and try to get it out there, and somehow it didn't go anywhere. She doesn't make sense sometimes. Why didn't she want to hear that I love her?*

Emily met them at the doorway, stepping around them and out onto the deck. "Matthew, John, time to come in, boys," she called. "I don't want them far from the house with that cougar roaming around here. Hi, Dad. Come on in, folks."

Bustling to find water glasses, Emily searched among the moving boxes while scolding Anna. "It's about time you came in. You need to be resting."

Steve felt her arm tense, a frown line appearing between her delicate brows. "Emily, you have a 'mother hen' complex. You know that, don't you? I'm a big girl. I know when to come in."

"Don't sass me, Anna Sanchez. After that scare you gave us all, you need some caretaking."

Steve chuckled quietly under his breath.

"Do you have all the legal documents for the ranch property here, Anna?" George interrupted.

"Yes, over there at the desk--bottom drawer--the file labeled 'Ranch Deeds.' Why?"

Matthew and John came through the front door, bringing with them the chatter of children. "Boys, wash up; then I've got some treats here for you to take upstairs. The adults need to talk," Emily directed, pulling out a few bags of fruit snacks.

Steve headed for the big, oak table Emily had brought from her house in town. He winked at Anna, watching as she ducked her head, pink glow moving up into her cheeks as she used her good arm to brace her descent into the chair he pulled out for her. He loved it when she blushed, giving away her embarrassment.

"Dad, couldn't this wait?" Emily asked, giving Anna an assessing look.

George shook his head. "No, we need to contact Mr. Brannen...right away. We have a problem with Rob Miller."

"Why? What's going on?"

Steve noted she seemed to be working hard to focus on George's questions.

"Well, I have a close friend at the courthouse, and he alerted me to a filing made by Rob's lawyer today. You probably already know this, but let me go through it again. Do you know how you get your water?"

"Well, I know it comes off the back ridge--into the reservoir--and don't the Millers maintain the reservoir to have usage of the water?"

"Yes, that's the way it is now. Our great-grandparents originally had a mining claim on this land and dug into that ridge. While they didn't find gold, they did strike it rich in water. They accidentally tapped into an artesian spring that filled the mine. At that point, Wyoming was becoming a rancher's paradise, so they decided to run cows and purchased the surrounding land. They dug out the lip of the mine and started the flow of the stream that we now use to irrigate the hay pastures.

"When Herman Miller bought the adjacent land, he dug wells, but couldn't find a stable water supply. John offered him a deal. In Wyoming, you have to fence out your neighbors' livestock, and putting a fence up that ridge was going to be a challenge. So he told the Millers if they dug a reservoir and maintained it, John wouldn't put up a fence, and Miller's cattle could water there. The stream collects in the reservoir. Then there's a head-gate that can run water to either property for irrigation purposes. They shook on it, a gentleman's agreement. Your grandfather owned the land that both the mine and reservoir sit on; Miller's land borders it."

"Okay, I understand. So what does Rob want?" Anna sounded frustrated.

It seemed black-and-white to Steve who owned the water.

"Well, Wyoming has a strange law, called 'adverse possession,' which essentially means if someone cares for a property for over seven years, they can claim that property for their own. Rob filed for adverse possession of the land and of course, the water rights, claiming the land is not fenced to prove actual ownership and his family have cared for the reservoir for over thirty years."

"What?" Steve, Emily, and Anna simultaneously exclaimed.

George slowly shook his head. "I know. It sounds incredible, doesn't it? The problem is he may have a legal leg to stand on."

"But that would ruin us! How are we going to get water?" The color drained from Anna's face.

"We can drill wells, but it's a hit-or-miss situation. We've got to fight this," George answered, running his hand through his cropped hair.

Steve had come to recognize the signs of Anna's panic attacks. Right now she was rubbing at her temples, bottom lip caught in her teeth, with chest heaving. *Damn Rob! She had been through enough.* Grinding his teeth together in anger, he pictured wiping a cocky grin off of Rob's face with one good swing.

With volcanic vehemence, Anna suddenly smacked the table, startling Steve. She spit out, "Who's his lawyer and how long do we have to answer his claim?"

George's eyes widened in surprise at the flare of temper. Steve cursed quietly under his breath.

"Shush, cussing isn't going to fix this," Emily fumed. "I don't know what has gotten into Rob. It's not like they don't have a nice spread themselves. It's got to be plain greed driving that boy. I can't imagine how Herman would have taken this. Maybe it's a good thing that poor, sweet soul isn't around to see this."

Steve pushed back from the table, tipping his chair back slightly. "He's always wanted to expand the ranch, but Herman kept telling him they had enough. I'd like to wring his neck."

George interrupted. "To answer your question, Anna, he has Mr. Kraken on retainer, and we have fourteen days from being served, to respond. He probably filed since he has settled his father's affairs. I know Herman wouldn't have backed this. I can't believe Rob wouldn't honor his father's agreement. What type of world is it nowadays that a man's word is not his bond?"

Steve felt pride at the sudden fury that shone in Anna's stormy eyes. *She's stunning.* He caught himself, a chuckle almost escaping as he thought, *I'm just glad it's not me she's angry with for a change.*

Vehemence rang in each of her clipped words. "We'll just see about this. I don't need this in my life right now. I don't care what his reasons are. If he wants a fight, he's going to get one."

Steve looked around the table at the different shades of anger reflected in the countenances before him. *Rob has no idea what he's getting into.* A smug smile formed on his thin lips. He noticed there was no wobble as she stood up and strode to the wall phone. Dialing, she waited.

"Yes, this is Anna Sanchez. I need an appointment with Mr. Brannen as soon as possible. Yes, it is a land dispute that involves water rights."

Robynn Gabel

Chapter 10 – Respect

"Damn!" rang against the stillness of the morning. The clatter of silverware in an empty cup followed it.

"What in heaven's name is going on? And pitching a fit isn't going to make it better, girl." Emily shuffled into the kitchen, house slippers slapping against the new tile.

"Damn is in the Bible as well as hell, so don't lecture me. Either you're one brave woman, or you aren't awake yet," growled Anna.

Emily's eyes opened wide. "Okay, so let's start with what is wrong, shall we?"

"What's wrong? Outside of being nowhere remotely close to a decent coffee shop, this ungrateful, decrepit machine picked this morning to give up making the swill it considers coffee. Nothing has gone right since I've got here. I don't know how I'm going to get anything finished up with this new soap opera with Rob. I can't drive, I hurt, I'm cooped up here and can't do anything, plus I'm tired of being on edge, wondering if Miles is going to put in an appearance. So I don't know, you tell me--what is there not to swear about?"

Anna turned to look over the tea bag selection, wondering how many tea bags equaled one cup of coffee, feeling Emily's stare behind her.

The storm clouds outside couldn't compete with the darkness of the storm brewing in the kitchen of the Windswept Ranch. Anna had never been a morning person, and she never understood people who enjoyed starting their days bright and cheery. There didn't seem to be anything that could pull her out of the hole she had sunk into. Coming from a college-based life of scheduled classes and routines to the chaos of the last few weeks had finally taken its toll. Now the only thing routine in her life seemed to be the panic attacks that hit whenever she stressed.

To top it off, she had a funeral to attend. It was only out of deep respect for her grandfather's and Herman's friendship that she had decided to attend the memorial for Herman Miller that morning.

Emily's soft voice cut through the angry fog that enveloped her. "You have so much to be thankful for. I know this has been hard. I have no idea the stress, pain and grief you must be feeling. I just want you to know I care."

The tears clogged her throat, eyes stinging. Anna turned, putting her one good arm around Emily, accepting the hug in return. Stepping back, she rubbed at her temple. "I'm sorry, Emily. I'm just feeling sorry for myself."

"Well, it's just everything catching up with you. I can't believe you've held up this long, girl."

The back porch door squeaked open, and Steve appeared. Looking at the pieces of the dead coffee machine, he turned a bemused smile to Anna.

"Being an appliance repairman this morning?" He gave Emily a quizzical look. Out of the corner of Anna's eye, she saw Emily shaking her head and gesturing to him to zip his lip.

A feral smile curled her lips. "So if you're so good, Mr. Fix-It, why don't you just try putting it back together and resuscitating it? Call me when the coffee is done." Turning, she flounced out of the kitchen, knowing that Steve and Emily probably cringed when she slammed the bedroom door.

A little while later, there was a soft knock. "Yeah," Anna called.

"Hey, I'm heading into town. I'm on call, and they are short a staff member in the E.R., so I have to go in. Steve agreed to take you in for the memorial if you still want to go. Are you doing all right?"

Anna opened the door. "I'm okay. Just go; I understand, and I'm sorry for this morning's rant."

Emily nodded and headed out. Anna could hear Steve tinkering in the kitchen. *Great, didn't want to have to go in with him, but I guess it could be worse. Yeah, it could be Miles.* A tight smile crossed her face. *I need a walk. Maybe that will change my attitude.*

She wandered down to the barn; the wind pushed with an attitude of its own. Ginger nickered to her from the side pasture; General and Midnight pushed against the fence, eager for attention. Grabbing the bucket hanging on the wall inside the barn, she filled it with grain as a treat for the excited horses. There were things about the country she loved, but she'd never admit that to anyone. Gazing up at the ridge, she noticed a puff of dust. Behind the rocky lip of the ridge, an old, rutted road led to the reservoir. *Who'd be driving up there? Or, maybe the wind is just stirring up the dust, and I'm paranoid.*

"Would you like a cup of coffee?"

Anna jumped at the voice, whirling around, instinctively raising her arm. She hadn't heard Steve approach over the racket caused by the wind.

Freezing in place, his hand still extended with the steaming cup, his face registered surprise of his own at her reaction.

Leaning over, grabbing her aching ribs, she gasped for air. Steve approached with caution, touching her shoulder gently. "Anna, are you okay?"

Shaking her head, moving away from his touch, she headed to the barn's tiny bathroom. It sported an antiquated sink and a rust-ringed toilet that no amount of scrubbing could make white. Splashing water on her face, she gripped the sink as the pounding of her heart subsided. Steve stood in the entryway of the barn, reflected back to her in the wavy, dusty mirror. *Damn, he almost gave me a heart attack. How can I keep him at a distance when I'm practically living with him? How the hell did he get that coffee machine working? It's a good thing he's so handy because I really could use that coffee he's holding.*

Reaching for the mug, she gave him a weak smile. "Sorry. You just startled me. You have no idea how much I appreciate this coffee."

His return smile didn't quite erase the serious look in his eyes. "Those panic attacks are getting worse, aren't they?"

Anna turned her back to him, sipping at the coffee. "I'm fine."

"Hear I'm taking you to a memorial service. Do I get to drive the Vette?"

She turned around, arching an eyebrow. "Oh, you wish. I'm afraid the only insurance you're covered under is the corporation. You will have to drive my grandfather's old truck. Sorry."

"You know you don't have to go, especially if you aren't feeling well."

"I'm going. I need to get out. End of story," she snapped.

"Have you always had that wee bit of temper, Anna, my girl?"

Giving him her back, she headed towards the house, not bothering to answer him.

❀ ❀ ❀ ❀ ❀

She was quiet during the ride into town, which didn't seem to bother Steve. He hummed, drumming on the steering wheel, looking anywhere but at her. That suited her just fine.

The church was filled wall-to-wall with people and the crowd spilled out into the front foyer for the memorial service. Steve stood with his family at the back of the church, while Anna sat, given a seat due to her injuries.

Looking over the crowd, she spotted Rob, amazed at his appearance. He had changed from an easy, laid-back rancher to an aged, serious-looking businessman. Gone was his ever-present cowboy hat, his suit impeccable in its cut and newness. A wave of empathy washed over her for his mother, the tiny, frail-looking woman leaning on his arm, dazed in sorrow. Seating her, he started the proceedings, conducting the memorial service with flawless decorum.

Leathered, lined faces, all having seen the worst in weather and years of toil, stood up and praised the man whom death had stolen from them. By the end of the eulogy, there wasn't one eye in the crowded church that had not shed a tear for the loss of Herman Miller.

As the receiving line crawled after the service, Anna wrestled with just leaving or giving her condolences. Again, out of respect for a man who had done so much for her family in their time of need, she stayed, supported by Steve's warm, muscled arm.

He dropped his head down, his lips grazing her hair, before whispering in her ear, "You're doing great. You look beautiful."

Feeling suddenly grateful for his presence and remorse for her foul mood earlier, she smiled up at him, hoping he could see the truce in her eyes. She knew her face resembled a brightly colored Halloween mask, but he stood straight and proud, guiding her through the crowd. Leaning into him, she felt his strong body against hers.

As they got close, Mary Beth, standing next to Rob, looked over at them, a perfect, sad smile on her face. Anna felt relief, and then almost smiled when it dawned on her Emily had guessed correctly. It seemed Mary Beth had been after Rob after all, and now she had him.

Rob's eyes narrowed ever so slightly as Steve and Anna came forward. She held her hand out to Rob's teary-eyed mother.

"I'm so sorry--I just don't know what to say--so sorry."

Hugging Anna, she murmured in her ear, "Oh, honey, thank you. You're such a dear to come out after what you've been through. You just take care of yourself."

Mary Beth looked at her, nodding regally as if receiving a humble subject. Rob stiffly shook her hand, mumbling, "Thank you." Anna looked him in the eye, knowing he saw her brief, courteous acknowledgment of his loss. Then she moved on, the cease-fire between them now over.

Suddenly, as she headed downstairs for the reception meal, she looked up and saw the plain, wooden cross on the wall behind the pulpit. Peace stole over her. It seemed Steve felt it as well, his arm going around her waist, hugging her gently to him.

A line formed at the serving kitchen counter, laden with inviting dishes. She listened to people chattering around them. Steve shadowed her, making sure he was between her and any jar or bumps.

"Let me get you to a seat, and then I'll bring back two plates for us, how does that sound?"

Anna realized she still tired easily. "Thank you. That would be great."

"Hey, Steve, I'd heard you and Mary Beth broke up. It sure was strange seeing her with Rob," said a skinny, pimple-ridden teenager standing next to him.

Steve turned. "Hey, Pat, let me introduce you to Anna Sanchez."

It seemed he was making it plain to all that he had no further ties to Mary Beth. She felt a little smug knowing this handsome man wanted her with him.

He tensed as he guided her past his family to a separate table. Anna caught his mother's brooding glance in their direction, and couldn't contain her curiosity. "Where's Chelsea and why don't you want to sit with your parents?"

"They left her with a babysitter. I'd like a little one-on-one time with you. When did the doctor say you could drive again?"

Anna didn't miss his attempt at changing the subject. "In two weeks if I'm off the pain meds and don't have any short-term memory problems, like--who are you again?"

Steve lifted an eyebrow, looking askance at her. "Who needs mirror therapy now? Don't even joke about it, Miss Sanchez."

His mood now somber, he helped her into her seat and headed to the food line. Chatting with her table mates, she waited until he reappeared with two plates piled high with home cooked goodies.

Between mouthfuls, she persisted, "I'm not blind. What's going on between you and your parents?"

He leaned back in the chair, arms on the table, his fingers picking apart a biscuit. "They're not sure my change in career paths is the best."

She studied him for a moment. "What are you planning on doing?"

"I'm thinking about following my passion; that's all. Mom would like me to get back with Mary Beth and continue college." He raised his head, looking over at his parents, and then back to the crumbling biscuit.

"I think that's awesome. Any particular school?"

"I'm looking into some tech schools that are supposed to be great for mechanics right now. I probably will go with whichever one will take me. I'm leaving that up to the Lord."

"Well, congratulations on your pick of goals." Shifting back into her chair, she lowered her eyes. "Steve, I like you. You've been wonderful to me. Saved my life, our best worker on the ranch and I consider you one of my best friends right now, but I don't want to be in the way of your relationships."

The bread chunks flew to the plate and bounced off the table. "Anna, you're not in the way. You're the best thing in my life right now. It's been coming on for a while between my family and me."

She tensed against his anger. "So now, who has a wee bit of a temper?"

He sent her the blackest scowl, but then, slowly, a smile grew until his eyes crinkled.

"You got me. So, let's get you home, now that you've had your favorite meal of potluck and before Rob busts a seam over there because you're here." His somber mood had shifted into the light-hearted Steve she liked.

As he escorted her out, she watched him give a curt nod to his family, his only acknowledgment.

Steve's long fingers held her arm gently, helping her to the truck. A folded piece of paper waved in the gentle breeze under the windshield wiper, catching her eye. Anna reached out and grabbed it, and then, with Steve's help, got situated in the seat. Printed in large, black-marker strokes on the outside was her name. Opening the folded paper, she gasped, feeling faint.

Steve opened the driver's door, swinging in with ease. "Well, time to get you home, and...." He glanced at her. "What is it?"

Her throat constricted with fear, and there was no stopping the anxiety wave that crashed over her. Mutely, she handed the paper to him, the words leaping off the page in large, harsh, black letters.

'You Are Mine Anna.'

Robynn Gabel

Chapter 11 – 4ᵗʰ of July

The sound of a scratching, yelping puppy brought Anna out of her slumber. Half-awake, she stumbled to the door to let the pup out. In the faint, early morning light, she watched him race down the hill towards the barn, still barking.

Yawning, she stretched and headed to the kitchen, starting the morning coffee. The memory of Matthew begging for the free, yellow, lab-mix puppy bouncing with its brothers and sisters in a box at the grocery store parking lot made her smile. She couldn't refuse Matthew's pleading look and the sloppy kisses from the grateful puppy. He earned the name of Samson after hours of tug-a-war with anyone who would play with him. She thought sleepily, *what was a ranch without a dog?*

Hearing little feet thumping down the squeaking staircase, she turned to see Matthew's wildly spiked hair, his face infused with morning energy. "Auntie, when are we going to the parade?"

"After you get showered and ready. I let Samson out already. You'll want to give him food and water."

147

While the coffee brewed, she rubbed at her temple irritably. *If Grandpa wrote it down, where would he have put it?* The doctor had warned that there might be some short-term memory problems, and she feared that the holes in her recall had allowed her to miss something.

Mr. Brannen, the lawyer, had dashed Anna's hopes of a speedy resolution to Rob's move to take their water source. "I'm afraid, Anna, your uncle, is correct. Unless you have some proof of the original agreement, Mr. Miller may be able to take the land and anything on it. You can ask for mediation at this time, and I highly suggest it, but it means you may not walk away with continued ownership." Anna gritted her teeth. It wasn't the Rob she remembered, but then, people change with time.

While tidying up the paperwork on the old desk, her fingers brushed along the top of the files she had spent the last few days going through. With the new problem of water rights looming over their heads, her uncle's plan to attend a cattle auction in Riverton next week and buy more cattle to expand the herd might be put on hold.

Picking up a manila envelope that held her grandfather's financial information, a flat key fell out with a tag attached to it. She gave it a quick read, noting it belonged to a safety deposit box.

More pounding footsteps announced the arrival of John. "Morning, Auntie! It's my turn to ride with you. You're taking the Vette to the parade, right?"

"Oh, no, not today, John. I'm sorry. I can't drive; I'm not up to it yet. But you can come with Steve and me if you want."

His little shoulders slumped. "Okay. Do you have anything I can do to earn a couple of dollars?"

"Why? What do you need money for?"

"A new bookstore opened downtown, and I want to check it out," he said with boyish enthusiasm.

"Actually, there is. I left the Vette out in that little rainstorm we had, and it got all dusty. It's in the barn if you would be so kind as to 'carefully' wash it." Anna laughed as he dashed upstairs to get dressed.

After breakfast, the two boys headed out as Anna readied for the busy day ahead. According to travel brochures describing the 4th of July Pioneer Days Parade, it was one of the oldest and biggest in the west, having been celebrated for over 100 years, making Lander famous.

For Anna, it was a childhood tradition and this year she was going to get a treat. Steve had done some work for the local theater owner and he'd gotten permission to watch the parade from the window of the empty apartment above the theater.

"Good morning. You're up early," Steve greeted her, coming through the back porch into the kitchen via the laundry room. Anna had seen very little of Steve lately, and it surprised her how much she missed spending time with him. He'd been busy putting a new coat of paint on the bunkhouse, working fences and riding the ridges, trying to find the elusive mountain lion.

She sighed. "I didn't sleep well last night. Grandpa kept meticulous records--he had to have noted a gentlemen's agreement with Herman on their water-sharing deal. I was thinking all night about where it might be. I even went back through Grandma's diaries; she said nothing of it."

Steve poured a cup of coffee, looking over at her. "Well, it'll turn up: I've faith in that. We need to head to town by nine before it gets too busy."

Shuffling in with a bad case of bed-head, Seth headed to the popular coffee pot. The front door exploded open, and John and Matthew lurched into the living room, talking simultaneously.

"Auntie, come quick! All the windows are broken on your car! And something's wrong with Samson: he's under the car and won't come out."

Emily joined Anna in the living room, sleepily rubbing her eyes. "What's going on?"

"Problem at the barn," Anna tossed out, heading out the door.

She could hear Steve and Seth questioning the boys, as they all followed her down the path to the barn. The sliding main door was usually open unless inclement weather made it necessary to close it. No one worried about break-ins this far out in the country. In its cool interior to the right, the vandalized Corvette was parked next to the tractor. She gasped at the destruction. Fear rose, wrapping her tightly. Her heart started its frantic pounding, the sweat beading on her brow. Emily was down on hands and knees, calling softly to the cowering puppy under the car.

Steve let out a quiet oath, as he walked around the car, glass crackling under his feet.

Even in her shocked state of mind--out of habit--Anna quickly made note of the surroundings, checking to see if anything was missing or damaged besides the car. She reached for her cell phone in her back pocket, dialing the Sheriff. She had seen this before and knew who had done it.

Emily got the puppy to come to her, tail between its legs, yelping as she gathered him up. "Someone hurt this little one. I'm not sure how bad it is."

"Hey, guys, we need to get out of here. Don't touch anything." Anna lowered her voice. "We've got to go. He may still be around here somewhere."

❀ ❀ ❀ ❀ ❀

Steve introduced Anna to the short, stocky owner of the Grand Theatre. His white hair, ruddy cheeks, and beaming smile gave him a Santa Claus look.

"Hi, Anna. Hope you don't mind a little climb."

She was in awe of the huge, steep, two-story, concrete staircase that led up to the emergency exit for the theater balcony and the front door of the apartment. Built in 1928 by a rich California investor, the solid concrete building had been the first air-conditioned structure in town. Being a wise investor, he had designed it like most theaters of that time: with two working storefronts and a cozy apartment above them.

Reaching the top of the sharp incline, they all were a little breathless. Darrell worked the key in the aging lock, finally getting the door open.

"Thanks for letting us do this," Steve said.

"No problem. You did a nice job on that flashing out back. I appreciate you working with me on the cost. I've got to get back downstairs. If you need anything, just come and get me. If you don't mind, lock the door behind you when you leave." He disappeared back into the theater through the emergency exit door.

Anna followed Steve as he led the way to the kitchen. He set two chairs in front of the window, and they sat down, waiting for the parade to start. This morning's incident left a tense silence between them. Anna was hoping to relax and enjoy the bird's-eye view she had of the parade. But she could see him out of the corner of her eye, studying her, his expression guarded.

"When your uncle went over my job responsibilities, one of those was to look out for the property and you. I overheard you telling the deputy you thought it might be Miles. Tell me what's going on, Anna, please."

She rose to wander around the little kitchen, running her hand along the counter, finally turning around and leaning up against its edge. Her brunette hair flipped and waved around her face, framing full lips and high cheekbones. The bruises had started to fade; her arm now encased in a plaster cast to her elbow, it rested in a dark blue sling. Her thin, arched brows were pulled together, hinting at the war raging inside of her.

151

"You're all in danger because of me. Miles Rannet was released from prison for stalking and holding me hostage two years ago." The memory of the sharp edge of a knife pressing against her throat caused her to hesitate. She took a big breath.

"Supposedly, he was cured, ready to go on with a normal life. He broke into my house, stealing my personal information, including my diary. That alone will enrage him if he reads it, and I know he has. There is nothing he doesn't know about me. He uses a hit-and-run tactic, scaring, bullying and threatening in various fashions. This morning was just a warning shot," she stated flatly.

"Hurting small puppies, smashing windows and being a chicken?" Disdain shone in Steve's eyes.

Anna moved back to the chair, sitting down. "I didn't want anyone involved in this. It's my problem."

He leaned forward, his long, lean hands grasping her uninjured one. Intently, he stared into her eyes, saying in a firm tone, "You don't have to do this alone. I'm here for you. Let us help you. We can pull together, like...like water buffalo. We will surround you, and he will have to get through us."

"I won't let any of you get hurt for me," she snapped, pulling her hand away.

He leaned back in the chair, pushing air through his lips in a disgusted 'pheff.' "Anna Sanchez, you've got mule blood running through your veins."

Her lips pulled in a firm line. "Maybe I'm as stubborn as you insinuate, but I can take care of myself."

"In my family, we protect each other. I realize you're an independent sort of gal, but there is safety in numbers. And if I ever get my hands on him, I will personally rip off his head." A tick in the muscle along his jaw reflected the internal strife.

"Hopefully, that will never happen. He isn't just a bully who needs a good thrashing. He has problems. With the local authorities involved, the rest of you will be safe. He's after me. It's my problem." She emphasized each word with finality.

He moved his chair closer, and casually picked up her hand again, his thumb smoothing over her silky skin. She waited for him to say something about her pounding heart; for she was sure he could hear it.

Irritation melted away as she looked into his eyes, seeing the worry there. Gently, she squeezed back; taking in his thick, arching brows, seeing for the first time a scattering of freckles across a straight-bridged nose, and the tousled, ash-blond hair giving him a dodgy air. A loud horn blew, announcing the start of the parade below them.

❁ ❁ ❁ ❁ ❁

Anna accepted Steve's invitation to share his family's 4th of July traditional picnic and fireworks. On the drive out, he drummed his fingers on the steering wheel of his truck, looking out the side window, and back to the road in front of him.

"Are you nervous about me spending time with your family?"

He shot a quick, sideways glance at her. "Well, yes and no. I'm more afraid of what you are going to think of them. My mother can be a little overwhelming sometimes."

"It's okay. I like your family. Your mother is just worried about you."

He stared at the road, a solemn expression settled in. "Remember when you asked if I knew a lawyer? Well, I need you to know some things about me. My life was a mess for a few years, got into some trouble in high school." Pausing for a quick second, he hurried on to say, "But then I realized things had to change. I've worked on it since. This last year I feel I've made real progress."

Anna waited. She knew his secret already. His addiction. The meetings he attended. One evening over tea with Emily, she told her Steve was a recovering alcoholic. Emily had encouraged her to give him a chance, and so far he had done nothing to damage her trust.

"I just wanted you to know there may be some tension between my family and me. We're still working on things."

Before she could ask any questions, he turned into the drive of a sprawling, country home.

Chelsea was waiting for them. She immediately grabbed Anna by the hand, leading her to the pasture to see Corky.

The horse's soft lips nibbled at Anna's hands to see if she had any treats. Chelsea sat on the log fence above him, leaning down to offer another carrot. He crunched it happily.

"I'm glad you came to our picnic and that you're okay. I was really scared when Ginger fell down. I never got to see the mountain lion because Corky ran back to the ranch," Chelsea informed her.

"I know that was a scary day for both of us, but I'm so glad you listened to me, and Corky got you out of there. You saved me. Thank you." Anna smiled up at her.

"I want to show you Snowball. She's my kitty. Come on." Chelsea jumped off the fence, grabbing Anna's uninjured hand, pulling her up the dirt path towards the house.

"She's around here somewhere. She likes to sleep in the lilac bushes alongside the house, so you can sit on the porch while I find her." Chelsea pointed to the porch swing and chairs and then disappeared around the side of the house.

From the spacious porch, the river could be seen winding around the cottonwoods, showing a glint here or there of sunlit water. The sprawling, ranch-style home sat comfortably on fifteen acres dotted with groves of aspen. A horse barn and workshop nestled in among the trees. It was peaceful in the little subdivision that sat at the mouth of the canyon.

Anna could hear Brad's two boys laughing and playing in the plastic pool set up behind the house. A slight breeze caressed her face as she closed her eyes, soaking in its coolness. There were two open windows behind the wicker chair Anna sat in. She could hear voices in the house, recognizing Steve's easily.

He pleaded, "Mom, I'm doing fine out there. The work is easy, the pay is good, and Emily is a good cook."

Irritation was plain in Rosalyn's voice. "Well, I haven't seen you at church since Herman's funeral. Are you still going to your meetings? And I'll have you know that you've lost your chance with Mary Beth."

At the mention of Mary Beth's name, Anna shifted, tilting her head towards the window.

"Mary Beth has moved on; in fact, I suspect she broke it off with me for Rob. I'm okay with that. I feel the best I've felt in a long time. I know what I want to do now. I've applied to several trade schools. I'll probably end up in Colorado somewhere."

"Great, I knew it. How long is this going to last, Steve? Are you just following another impulse again? Have you asked her if she's a Christian? What about being a youth leader? Are you throwing away two years of college? I don't mean to pry, but don't you think you're jumping into this relationship kind of soon? This is your future we're talking about. The choices you make now will affect the rest of your life," Rosalyn retorted.

Well, now I know what Steve was so nervous about and why his mother seemed so cool towards me, Anna thought irritably. *And she wants to know if I'm a Christian--isn't that obvious to her?* She shifted in the seat again.

Steve's voice was fierce in resolve. "Mom, which is it? Are you angrier you lost a possible daughter-in-law or a youth pastor? I understand your concern over my hooking up with a non-Christian;

it's harder on the relationship. There are a lot of things I don't know about her yet, and I don't even know what's going to happen between us. I just know that I've figured out what I want to do with the rest of my life. I thought you'd be happy about that. I'm making decisions, moving on."

Silence. Anna imagined the two of them glaring at one another. *I bet his mother is quite a force of nature when she chooses to be.* Their voices became fainter as they moved off farther into the house.

Her temper started to rise. It wasn't like they had even discussed what would happen when she headed back. They had not progressed beyond a few kisses and the hand holding at the parade today.

She rose restlessly, and headed around the house, following the smell of barbecuing hamburgers in the back yard. Jack and Brad hovered over the smoking grill while Lisa, Brad's wife, cleaned off little Jacob, who strained to get away from her. Tow-headed Kevin was splashing happily in the blue, plastic wading pool. A picnic table covered with the traditional white-and-red-checkered tablecloth sat under a stand of elegant aspen trees that stretched their welcoming arms out to provide shade.

This morning's event had brought back all the old terror. Even now in this Norman Rockwell setting, she felt uneasy, as if she was being watched. She pushed it away, took a deep breath, glanced around, and then squared her shoulders. *I'm going to enjoy this picnic, have fun, and not think of Miles.*

She looked up to see Steve coming off the back porch, a bowl of potato salad in hand. He smiled. "Hey, there you are. I was beginning to worry I'd never get you away from Chelsea."

At that moment, Chelsea came careening around the house, arms full of an unhappy cat, just as Steve stepped down. The collision sent the potato salad into orbit, and Anna instinctively caught the bowl with her one good arm, close to the chest, the contents landing with a wet plop all over her.

156

All three froze as the cat took the moment to escape back into the bushes where she had been hiding. Anna watched Steve's face go through several different contortions while Chelsea's soft "oh" matched the look on Anna's potato salad splattered face.

"What happened here? Oh, Anna, please come inside. Let's get you cleaned up," Rosalyn said quickly, coming out on the heels of Steve.

"Sorry, Mom. It was my fault," Steve offered, Chelsea chimed in to claim it was her fault as well.

"Don't worry, I've more potato salad. Right now we've got to get Anna cleaned up."

Rosalyn held open the screen door. Anna caught the nervousness in Steve's eyes as she carried the empty bowl into the kitchen.

Off the kitchen was a mud room–laundry room combination. After helping Anna wipe down her shirt and get the chunks out of her hair, Rosalyn showed her to the main-floor bathroom.

Rosalyn's eyes were alight with mirth. "I think that you are about the same size as me. Maybe it will be a little large for you, but I have several shirts. Looks like it missed your shorts, but you will have to wash your hair." She moved about pulling out towels, and then disappeared, coming back with several cute shirts.

"Thank you, Rosalyn. Appreciate it," Anna murmured, still feeling it best to keep her distance after what she'd overheard.

Rosalyn's bright-blue eyes scrutinized the slim girl in front of her. "Let me help wash out your hair, Anna. It's got to be hard to do it one-handed."

Anna cringed inwardly; the one thing her infirmities were teaching her was humility. Depending on others for help didn't sit well with her. But there was no denying she couldn't do it one-handed.

"That would be helpful," she said.

Rosalyn went to work, chatting comfortably about how cute Chelsea looked dressed as a cowgirl on the library float. Chelsea's 4-H group had chosen to dress up for different history periods. She was working on drying Anna's hair when she changed the subject.

"With inheriting the ranch, did you ever consider living here?"

"Yes, it did cross my mind, but I have lived in Fort Collins all my life, and love it there. Though I wouldn't rule out ever living here since it seems I have a foot in both worlds. I hope you don't mind that Steve is helping with the ranch."

"We are proud of Steve's initiative to get out on his own and so glad he was there when you needed him. We prayed for your recovery, and God blessed us. I'm so thankful your injuries weren't worse." Rosalyn looked at her with motherly concern.

Anna bit her bottom lip for a second and then plunged in. "You know, I didn't mean to eavesdrop, but I happened to hear your concerns over my beliefs."

Rosalyn's eyes widened for a second and then she patted Anna's hand. "I'm sorry, dear. You must understand there are some things about Steve's past that cause us concern. We're worried about the choices he is making now. It's nothing personal."

Anna nodded. "I know. Emily spoke of his problems with alcohol, but he hasn't brought it up to me. We're not even dating. I think your son is great, but I have worked hard for the plans I have. You're right: he has some things he has yet to work out. It might put your mind at ease to know that I accepted Jesus in high school. I admire your family's closeness. I had no brothers or sisters, or father."

Tears shimmered for a quick second in Rosalyn's eyes. She ducked her head down, looking at her hands in her lap. "I owe you an apology. I'm sorry, Anna. I judged you, and I shouldn't have." She looked up quickly with a brilliant smile that reminded Anna of

Steve. "Let's get some more potato salad out to the boys and get to know one another."

Corn on the cob made a ribbed, ridged mountain. Baked beans glistened in rich, brown sauce. Hamburgers scented the air with a savory, fried bouquet and all the fixings clustered in the middle of the wood table like bright confetti. "All right, everyone, it's time to eat," Rosalyn called out, and they gathered around the table.

Jack bowed his head and grasped a hand on each side of him. "Dear Lord, thank you for this day and the food before us. Thank you for healing Anna and keeping her safe. We ask that you would look out for each one of us at this table. Amen." He looked up. "Let's eat!"

Excited voices went "ooh" and "ah" over the delicious fares, and everyone dug into the mountain of food. Compliments to the cook floated in the air.

"Brad, toss me a hamburger bun, please," Steve called.

"Hey Anna, we need a catcher at our next softball game. You up for that?" Brad started laughing. Lisa hit him in the arm, saying something under her breath.

Steve's eyes danced with wicked amusement. "Well, it sure beats a septic bath, right, Anna?"

Anna shot him a honeyed smile. "I see it's time for your mirror therapy again, Steve."

"Mirror therapy--what's that all about, Steve?" Brad ribbed him.

Steve shrugged. "Ask her."

Uproarious laughter greeted her explanation of the process.

Lisa looked up from squirting catsup on two hamburger buns simultaneously. "After spending an afternoon with these two little dust devils, you can't still be thinking of being a kindergarten teacher!"

"Actually, you amaze me, Lisa. You are quite talented in keeping up with those two. Jacob and Kevin are at such an exciting age and...."

Lisa interrupted, "I would say 'exciting' is an understatement. You have no idea how unpredictable, loud, busy and destructive they can be."

"That's because this is the period of their lives when they will learn the most, so they have to check everything out and learn about it."

Kevin's squeal alerted them too late to be of help. He had taken the mustard bottle while Lisa talked and had given it a mighty squeeze, giving his hair a blast of yellow.

Anna and Rosalyn chatted like longtime friends. She noticed Steve watching from across the table. Anna glanced his way now and then and smiled, enjoying his discomfort.

"Well, we can only follow up that strawberry shortcake with something even better: fireworks!" Jack said, patting his full stomach. The men left the table to start setting up the various odd shapes that promised sparks and showers galore out in the gravel of the circular drive.

While Rosalyn and Lisa cleared the picnic table, Anna sat in the wicker love seat on the porch with Chelsea beside her, watching the two little boys. Jacob curled up on her lap, sleepy after the meal. Kevin laboriously raised a stout leg to get onto the step, clutching something in a chubby little fist. After negotiating each step in a wobbling war, he finally attained the top step, running to Anna. Opening his little pink fist she saw the squashed remains of a grasshopper.

"Oh, Kevin, how did you catch such a big bug, you little cutie?" Anna smiled.

He babbled nonsensically, pleased by her compliment.

"You're quite the child-magnet," Rosalyn observed, as she joined Anna. "I think you've chosen the right profession."

Anna nodded. "I think so. Children have always fascinated me."

The evening had become a cool dusk. Brad held up a packet of sparklers, luring the children from the porch. They bounced up and down eagerly with the adults in tow to help them. As each sparkler lit up, the stars in the little eyes rivaled the sparklers' shower. Anna watched from the porch and Snowball, the reluctant cat, happily replaced the child on her lap.

Steve joined them, sitting on a white, wooden swing. "I see that I have competition for your attention, lady. I'm afraid I dare not disturb that ferocious feline for fear of bringing on more flying potato salad!"

"Funny, Steve." She shook her head.

As Anna lifted the cat off her lap, Snowball grunted, stalking away as if to give them both a view of her furry pantaloons and stiff tail. Anna moved over to the swing, sidling up to Steve's warm side.

"Well, I must admit that potato salad didn't quite go with the color of your hair." Steve chuckled.

Anna leaned her head against his shoulder, tracing her finger up his arm. "If you didn't have such big feet, I wouldn't have to catch a bowl of potato salad one-handed."

"Yeah, I was pretty impressed with that catch--didn't even break the bowl! You must have played softball sometime."

"In my younger days, I did."

"I can't believe how well you and my family, especially my mom, hit it off this afternoon." His gaze was tender.

"She is quite outgoing and sweet--reminds me of someone else I know," Anna said, intertwining her fingers with his, her heart tripping again. She turned her face into his chest, taking in the crisp, clean laundry smell of him, and felt his arm go around her.

"Yeah, Mom is just a momma bear protecting her young, but we love her." Steve pulled her closer, nuzzling at her ear, sending shivers down her neck. His warm lips traced along her cheek, finally capturing the treasure of her lips. When he broke away, he looked down at her, sighing contently, his long fingers gently massaging her arm above the bulky cast.

The sparklers ran out, and the small herd of kids now scrambled back onto the deck to pick out spots to view the upcoming show.

Jack, Rosalyn, and Lisa joined them on the porch, scooting the wicker chairs into place to have a view of the display.

"I see you two stole the best seat in the house," Rosalyn remarked, eyeing them with a serene smile.

"Mom, would you and Dad like your seat? We can move," Steve answered sheepishly.

She shook her head, "No, just teasing you, Son. We are perfectly fine here."

He whispered in Anna's ear, "It's probably a good thing we have chaperones."

Chapter 12 – Rights

The eastern sky glowed gold while the moon, full and heavy, sat on the western mountaintops, waiting to catch sight of the sun's face before fleeing. Steve walked down the little path from the bunkhouse, taking a deep breath of the clean morning air. He opened the door to the ranch house's screened-in back porch. Samson jumped up and down in puppy enthusiasm, his tail smacking into Steve's legs.

He went in the back door that opened into the laundry room and kitchen. Samson followed, his nails clicking on the tile, nosing around for leftover crumbs. Nodding to Emily, he filled a thermos full of coffee. She smiled back, knowing about his secret mission in the barn.

"Is Anna up yet?"

"No, she's been sleeping in since the accident. It will give you more time this morning before you start the chores."

"Who's sleeping in?" Anna appeared in the doorway, hair tangled from sleep, stretching her casted arm up over her head. Samson bounced up against her in greeting.

"Good morning. I've meant to ask you: did you ever go out and check on Momma and her calf?"

Steve watched as she smiled fondly down at the puppy, rubbing his ears. "Yes, Mike and I rode out last week; they hooked up with the others, and the calf's doing fine."

"Are you planning on running the fence today?"

"Yeah, I am."

"Do you mind if I go along? Well, if you'll be back before one. I have the mediation this afternoon."

"Won't be out too long. Yeah, I can have you back before then."

"Good. Then I will pack a lunch for us after I've showered. I can be ready in an hour. Is that okay?"

"Sure--if you don't think riding the four-wheeler will be too much. Mike will be here today working on the pump so it should be okay." He turned and poured a cup of coffee.

They'd all agreed that someone would be at the ranch at all times to make sure Emily, Anna, and the boys would never be alone on the property.

"Well, I'll be down as soon as I'm done."

Steve turned back to her, holding out the filled cup. "Let's start the day right, okay?"

Emily chuckled.

"Thanks," Anna replied sarcastically.

Quite pleased with himself, he headed out to the barn, the puppy bounding along. A crow called overhead, and he quickly scanned the ridges, pasture, and rocky hillside, looking for any lurking figure. Miles was on everyone's mind since the window-smashing incident.

Ginger nickered as he came into sight. She was healing just as fast as Anna seemed to be. He entered the barn, catching the end of

164

a green tarp, pulling it off a wooden form. Samson grabbed an edge of the plastic with his teeth, growling as Steve tried pulling it away. Fresh pine scented the air, and the cream-colored poles looked stout. With sanding, shaping, cutting and pounding, a free-standing, wooden swing had grown under his skillful hands.

Woodworking was a hobby he loved, giving him time to focus on something else when thoughts of Anna kept him awake at night. Her expressive, blue eyes and little mannerisms like flipping her hair nonchalantly fascinated him. Her quick wit in conversations had him running those exchanges over and over in his mind.

Wonder why she wants to go along today. She must be getting bored. Just another chance to get through that 'friendship' wall she keeps throwing up. I guess I need a lesson in patience. I can't wait to tell her about the tech schools I've found.

He'd filled out two online applications for school funding, and several applications for trade schools. There was one located in Laramie, Wyoming, and covered all aspects of mechanics, including automotive engineering. Located in Loveland, Colorado, the tech school he wanted most didn't start its next round of courses until October.

It would allow him time to help bring in the cows for the fall roundup, and tie up loose ends at the ranch. Loveland was less than a half hour away from Ft. Collins. He'd done research on apartments and set up a budget. It would work if he could get a part-time job to help with living expenses. Now, he was working on fitting Anna into this picture.

An hour later, he covered the pieces of the swing with the tarp again and poured gas into the four-wheeler. Throwing fencing tools in the small box on the back of it, he swung his leg over the heavily duct-taped seat. The aging machine grumbled to life.

Driving through the barn door, he caught sight of Anna and Matthew coming down the path. A twinge in the pit of his belly reminded him of the yearnings she stirred when she was near. He shut down the growling four-wheeler.

The lavender top she wore set off the turquoise in her blue eyes. *Why is it when she is around all I want to do is look at her?* His friends all envied him when he had dated the beautiful Mary Beth, but he had been oblivious to her beauty. Anna, on the other hand, drew him in with every move she made.

Matthew handed a lunch basket to Steve, running off to the barn with Samson barking at his heels. With the lunch secured, Anna slid behind Steve, situating her cast up against his back, her slender arm around his waist. Glancing over his shoulder, he noticed her smooth, olive-toned skin.

"So what made you decide to come along today?"

Her expression seemed carefully composed. "I just wanted to get away from the house and spend a little time with you. Since you're on such a tight work schedule, thought this might be the only way. We could also check out the ridge to see if there is any sign of the mountain lion."

He had not seen this side of her: cool and aloof. Her mercurial moods kept him scrambling to figure her out, but he loved the challenge.

"Well, you haven't had a chance to see my great driving skills on this speed machine. It can do turns like no other around here."

The tiniest hint of a smile played across her face. "Okay, Sherlock, though your confidence in the speed of this thing is just a little overrated, don't you think? Just don't tip us over."

He pushed down the crown of his straw cowboy hat. "Hold on, lady. I'll do my best to go slow."

❀ ❀ ❀ ❀ ❀

Anna rested her cheek against his broad back, feeling muscles move as he steered the four-wheeler over the rough terrain. The jarring caused her arm to ache, but they had to talk. She had to slow this relationship down, put it in its proper place.

George admired Steve, saying he was a great asset to the ranch, and even she had to admit he was a hard worker. *I want to leave on good terms. After the Miles situation is cleared up, maybe, just maybe.*

Steve followed the barbed fence line, checking the posts and wire for any slack. The bright sun overhead warmed them. Coming to a stop, he jumped off. Grabbing thick, leather gloves and an odd-looking pair of pliers from the box on the front of the four-wheeler, he went to work.

Straddling the four-wheeler she watched as he deftly wound the wire around the post, the muscles flexing in his forearms, pulling against the resisting wire. The white, cotton, western-cut shirt fit him snugly, his jeans clinging to long, muscled legs. Sweat started beading down the side of his square jaw. His features were pleasantly balanced.

She found herself thinking about running her hands down his chest, his soft kisses, that look of love in his eyes. Sometimes she worried she didn't know how to love. It was an emotion that seemed to be nothing but responsibility.

His voice broke the peaceful silence. "So what are you thinking about there, lady?"

Throwing a leg over the four-wheeler seat and leaning against it, crossing her good arm over the cast, she gave him a long perusal. This was a conversation she was familiar with, having done it many times.

"So what are we doing? You know I'm heading out pretty soon. What do you expect out of this relationship?"

He paused, grabbed his hat by the crown, and lifted it, using his forearm to wipe his brow, hair curly from the dampness. "That's your decision. You know how I feel." His gaze was direct, his eyes searching hers.

"You know how I feel, Steve."

He gave the wire one more twist. "Not really. You haven't said much at all, Anna. You seem to want to be with me; at least, you don't glare at me like you do Rob. You asked that we take this slow, but outside of that, I don't know anything about how you really feel," he said, waiting.

She dug at a little clump of grass with the toe of her shoe. This was the part of the discussion she preferred to avoid: feelings. Looking up at the ridge, considering her answer, movement through the scrub pine caught her attention.

"Steve," she quietly breathed the words, "behind you."

He turned, catching sight of the tawny cat as it weaved in and out of the pine, seemingly unaware of their presence. Slowly, he moved to the four-wheeler, pulling the rifle out of the leather scabbard lashed to the side of the vehicle. Her hand flew out to rest on his muscled arm. Caution and restraint in her squeeze, her gaze staying on the sleek cat, pity in her eyes.

"It's wounded; look at its back leg," she whispered.

Even from a distance, it was evident the mountain lion was struggling with a limp. Anna's eyes widened as two smaller versions moved alongside the big cat.

Steve whispered, "She's got cubs. No wonder she's been so careless. You never see them; they could be living in your backyard, and you won't even know they're around. I was wondering why she would show herself the day of your accident. She was looking for easy prey."

Anna shuddered. "Let's get out of here, leave her be. If you take her out, the cubs could starve. As it is, they may not make it. She isn't bothering us."

The big cat finally noticed them, freezing in place, her little ones doing the same. Then she slunk off, melting into the shadows, her tawny cubs following quickly.

Steve quickly walked to the four-wheeler and gathered up tools. She slid back on the seat, making room for him. They continued down the fence, leaving the ridge, and found a rocky area where the fence was in dire need of repair, and she could set up for lunch. Throwing a little plastic tablecloth over a small, flat rock, she put out cold chicken, potato chips, and fruit on plastic plates.

She sat sideways on the four-wheeler seat instead of straddling it, balancing a plate on her lap, and Steve sat down with his back against a large rock. As she picked at her lunch, she watched him tear into his voraciously.

"My gosh, we need to feed you more!"

"Fencing is hard work," he said after a long draw at a water bottle.

She moistened her lips nervously. "I've made a job commitment in Fort Collins, and I want to get back to my life there. I'm not sure how this is going to work out between us, so let's just keep taking it slow, okay?"

He stared at her for a moment, his expression unreadable. "Okay."

"It's only a six-hour drive at the max; it's not like you can't come down and visit me. And there's texting, phone calls…it's not like we can't connect with each other."

"It goes both ways, lady. No reason you can't come back here and visit too. But what if I told you I might be going to school in your area?" He waited, watching her with a stare as intent as a mountain lion.

"That's great. We can get together. But for now, still friends, right?" She smiled calmly; she had gotten it out there--no commitment, and no promises.

Nudging back his cowboy hat, he gave her a level stare. "What are you afraid of? I'm not Miles. I agreed to take it slow. Why can't we date? You can't kiss me like you do and declare friendship. I know you want more too."

Steve stood up, brushed off his jeans and came to stand in front of her. He placed his hands on the seat on either side of her, leaning in, staring into her eyes, and she could see to the core of his soul. *I don't want this right now! Why won't you listen?* Her mind shouted, but her heart overrode everything, beating erratically at his closeness. His breath brushed her cheek. He gently nibbled, applying pressure to part her lips with his.

No longer holding back, she responded with a gentle pressure of her own, molding her lips to his while raising an arm to slide around his neck, pulling him towards her. He moved in, wrapping his arms around her waist gathering her close, one hand going up her back into her hair, no hesitation, answering her passion.

She slipped her arm down, pushing him away. Seeing the laughter dancing in his eyes, she asked sharply, "What?"

Steve smiled flirtatiously. "So is this dessert? Can I have more?"

"No, I brought pie if you'd let me off here," she growled.

He stepped back, sweeping his hat off, bowing as he said, "Your wish is my command."

What is it with him that I can't stay on track? It was going just fine until he kissed me. Dang, he can kiss! Maybe I'm going about this all wrong. Maybe I should just agree to date and take it as it comes.

After dessert, she watched Steve wrestle with a few more fence posts while she packed up lunch. Anger rose over her resolve that wavered with each kiss. Mind argued with heart, and it seemed her heart was winning.

Anna threw her leg over the seat again, straddling the four-wheeler. "How much longer do you plan on checking the fence line?"

Steve threw his tools into the box. "I was just thinking I'd better get you back early before Emily tracks me down to scold me for letting you overdo it."

"Hmpf," she huffed in reply. "I'm doing fine though I'll admit I'd forgotten how rough the four-wheeler rides are."

He leaned into her, sliding his arm around her waist again, inclining his head towards her. Orneriness slipped into his smile. "So, you never answered me. Do I need to kiss you again to help you make up your mind?"

Unruffled, she gazed back. "I readily admit you are good at kissing, but there's more to a relationship than just making-out, Mr. Johnson. I'm not making any promises, but I wouldn't mind spending time with you."

With a wolfish grin, he said, "Sounds good to me."

❈ ❈ ❈ ❈ ❈

Anna one-handedly dumped the old coffee, rinsing the pot. Checking her hair in the antique mirror on the way out, she headed for the maroon-colored Tahoe parked under the cottonwood. Finally getting a release from the doctor, she had taken to driving the SUV she had inherited while her Corvette was in the shop. The bulky Chevy handled well but seemed very long. *I can just see me trying to park this in Ft Collins. That would be scary!*

Anna and George decided there was enough time before the meeting to take possession of her grandfather's bank accounts, converting them to the corporation's.

Driving into Lander, her mind wandered back over the morning's events. Anna recalled Steve's teasing comments from their picnic. She could no longer deny she enjoyed his company but worried about how Miles complicated her life. She didn't need a love-sick boyfriend to compound it.

Pulling into the bank parking lot, she maneuvered into a spot. Gathering up purse and envelope with all her grandfather's paperwork, she went into the bank.

The bank teller behind the marble counter answered her request. "Yes, Sally over there will help you with it."

Smartly dressed, with raven-colored hair and beautiful doe eyes, Sally smiled pleasantly at Anna, indicating she should take a seat at the desk.

"So you're John's granddaughter. I've heard so much about you. Let's see. You're here to take possession of his accounts, am I correct? Mr. Brannen sent over the transfer paperwork for the corporation. You will have to designate which accounts are for what and who you want signing on these accounts."

George came through the bank door, catching sight of her, and joined them. An hour later, Windswept Ranch had all its banking needs in order.

"Well, honey, we're official, and just in time for the mediation meeting. Do you want to come over for dinner afterward? Evelyn would love having someone compliment the meatloaf she's made tons of." George rolled his eyes.

"Yes, that sounds good. I just have to check on the safety deposit box. If you have nothing else to do, would you mind going with me?"

A few minutes later, in the coolness of a room with only a plain table and two chairs, Anna laid down the long, brown metal box. The flat key fit easily and she pulled up the tin top of the box. Family heirlooms lay before her. Wedding rings designated their owners with little tabs written in her grandfather's neat script. An antique, gold pocket watch with worn, ornate scroll adorning its case lay on top of aging papers. Several more pieces of jewelry lay next to an envelope filled with yellowed bits and pieces of paper. She split it on the table between her and George.

"You go through this pile, and I'll do this one. We have an hour, so if we don't get through it, we can come back." Anna dug in, quickly looking over marriage licenses and deeds until she found the original mine claim. A newer, handwritten notepad page caught her eye.

To Whom It May Concern, Loaned to Herman Miller $1,000.00 for burial expenses of Louise Mae Miller. It was dated 20 years previous, both men's signatures neatly scribed along the bottom next to a notary's seal. Next to that in John's neat handwriting, a year later, he had written 'Forgiven.' Anna noted it didn't say paid, but forgiven.

"Uncle George, why did Grandpa forgive this loan to Herman?"

He shook his head. "You know my brother was never one for outward sentiment, but his heart was full of love. The Millers went through a real rough patch for a couple of years. Herman lost his mom; his herd got scours, and he lost a lot of calves. Then his daughter was killed in a horseback riding accident. Your grandfather said he never loaned anything he needed to be repaid-- you know like the Bible says. He knew Herman couldn't pay it back, so he forgave it, the only way he knew how to show he cared.

Tears threatened; it was hard for her to swallow. She wished she had known him as a child the way she knew him now.

"I didn't know the Millers had another child," Anna said huskily.

"Yes, Louise was her name, and she was beautiful both inside and out. She was only nine years old when she died. It took Herman a long time to come back from it. Rob had a lot of responsibility at an early age." His voice trailed off as he intently perused the paper in his hands. "Hmm, this isn't going to go over well," he said quietly.

❂ ❂ ❂ ❂ ❂

Mr. Brannen's conference room seemed crowded now, the cherry wood table a little less massive, with all the chairs filled. Rob was looking sharp, in a black suit, tie and another ornate rodeo belt buckle announcing his winning ways. His lawyer had a hawkish face, with beady, darting, bird-eyes to match.

Mr. Brannen introduced all the parties present. "Anna Sanchez, this is Mr. Kraken, lawyer for Mr. Miller. I believe you all know George Hanson, CEO of the Windswept Ranch. Mr. Dollen is our mediator for this matter at hand, the property located at...."

Anna watched Rob as the property was legally described, wondering how far she should play her hand. He wouldn't meet her eyes, a firm, stubborn look on his face. She took a deep breath in, sending a prayer heavenward, hoping she would walk out with a good attitude.

Immediately, Mr. Dollen's nasal voice scratched at her nerves. "Let me start by saying I hope we can look at both sides of this matter. Since Mr. Miller has had primary care of the property that contains the reservoir, the source of the reservoir and water rights, but has no proof of that ownership, I would like to know if your corporation can produce any proof of prior or current ownership."

"Yes we can," Anna retorted. She wasn't sure if the surprise on Mr. Dollen's face came from her authoritative tone, or that she had proof. He looked slightly comical with owlish eyes that peered out through thick glasses.

George moved his hand over hers, squeezing, casting a kind look at her. She nodded, taking a deep breath; pushing the dilapidated deed to the mine across the table to Mr. Kracken. He picked it up, perusing it like a bird of prey. He cleared his throat; his piercing look stabbing at them.

"Yes, this is in order. But it is over a hundred years old, and only applies to the mining claim filed. Though the deed you provided in reply to the original filing for adverse possession was in order as well, it does not show that you have cared for the land. Nor have you fenced it, leaving it open."

Anna scowled. "Funny, we pay taxes on that land."

George shook his head at her. Mr. Dollen, the mediator, continued as if she hadn't spoken.

"Now we just have to put some proposals out here and start the discussion. Remember each side is going to have to give something; this is about compromise. I ask," he paused, looking at Anna, "that we do this in a spirit of cooperation with civil language."

Anna flushed with anger, feeling the warmth spreading across her face. George's hand tightened on hers, his features stony. Mr. Brannen calmly interjected, "I'm sure, Mr. Dollen, we're all adults here and know how to conduct ourselves."

"Let me start with my original offer, which was fair and equitable." Rob looked at Anna disdainfully. "I can give you market value for your herd, and current land value, and will be willing to give you ten percent above market value for all equipment and outbuildings."

Anna stared at him in fury. A sarcastic smile carved itself into Rob's face. Mr. Dollen felt the tension and jumped in to diffuse it. "This sounds like a fair offer, but the matter at hand is the dispute over the ownership of the spring and the land it sits on.

"Enough!" Anna snapped. Mr. Dollen's hands fluttered. Mr. Kracken's eyes bored into her. Mr. Brannen leaned back, lacing his hands across his stomach, a huge smile hiking up his mustache. George clasped his hands as if in prayer, and Rob glared at her.

She pulled out a yellowed notebook page. "I will wait if you need proof of your father's handwriting, Rob, but I believe this will put to rest any dispute you think you have with me. And if that isn't good enough proof for you, I have several other documents with your father's signature here that will prove there was nothing but a spirit of friendship and neighborly support among them."

Glancing quickly at the yellowed note, to make sure it was the right one, her grandfather's signature still crisp next to Herman's scrawl, notary seal ink still sharp, agreeing to share the water. She slid the folded paper across the table to Rob. He hesitated and then picked it up, sharing it with Mr. Kracken's beady gaze. Rob's face slowly turning red, he pulled at his collar and laid it down. "What else would you have with my father's signature?" A defiant edge tinged his voice.

Anna looked at her uncle, suddenly unsure of the impact of her next move. George inclined his head towards Rob with a sad look. She slid the next note over.

Rob was silent, his shoulders sagging as he read the aged note. He looked up. "I'm sorry to have wasted your time, gentlemen. Obviously, I didn't research this enough. I drop my claims to the land and water." Regret edged his voice.

Mr. Brannen cleared his throat again. "Would you folks like some time alone? If you need anything else, we'll be right outside." He held the door open as the other two gathered papers and briefcases and left.

She stared at the deflated Rob, suddenly seeing the young, gangly boy of the past. "I'm so sorry, Rob. I didn't want it to come to this."

He sighed, sitting up straighter, looking at her, a tired smile emerging. "It's okay. I knew I was pushing it. I can't expand our ranch if I can't get more water sources. I thought you being a city girl and all--I didn't think you'd have any use for it. I thought you were just being, well, you know."

Laughing, Anna went around the table, offering her hand. "Mr. Miller, let's let bygones be bygones. I'd like to honor our family's previous agreements." Sheepishly, he extended his hand to shake on it.

"Let's get that drawn up in a legal agreement, shall we? So our kids don't end up fighting over this same thing. It seems my family is in your debt." He picked up the second paper.

"Absolutely not, Rob. It was forgiven. A handshake is good enough. I just needed to remind you there was deep trust and love between our families; I didn't want to lose that. Sorry, I played that card."

A deep laugh rumbled up from his chest. "Remind me, George Hanson, should I ever forget, to never play poker with your niece!"

Robynn Gabel

Chapter 13 – Destruction

Emily carefully rearranged the bacon, tomato, lettuce and toast into a neat stack. Anna watched in bemusement. "Really, Emily, it all goes to the same place."

"It's easier if it's organized on the way down," she answered tartly.

The loud clatter of a falling tray made them both jump, looking at the red-faced culprit. Anna glanced around the hospital cafeteria filled with various colorful smocks, uniforms, and blue operating caps.

"I bet you like part-time better than full-time."

Emily nodded in agreement. Wiping at her mouth with a napkin after a bite of the neatly made sandwich, she said, "It's much easier on the feet, plus I enjoy the extra time with the boys and they love it out there. John has wanted to join 4-H for years. It's too late this year, but he's going to raise a steer next year."

"You've no idea what a help you and Seth have been to me," Anna said, staring down at her tray.

"That's what we're on this earth for, honey. To help one another. By the way, sure wish I'd been at the lawyer's office. Dad said you nailed old Rob's hide to the wall."

Anna blushed in embarrassment. "I was just blessed to find Grandpa's note. I wouldn't say I was rude, but I wasn't going to be bullied. If Miles has given me anything, that's more backbone. Rob just lost sight of what really matters."

"So what did the doctor say about your arm?"

"Three weeks tops and the cast will come off. Then there will be a few weeks of therapy. It's doing quite well. Thanks for the invite to lunch, even if it's hospital food."

"What? Don't you like cafeteria cuisine? Where do you think I got all my lovely curves from?" She chuckled.

Anna looked at her, feeling for her outspoken cousin. "I'm not complaining: the food's not bad; I enjoy visiting with you, but it's not like we don't live in the same house together. So was there something you wanted to talk about?"

Emily cocked her head to the side, "Now that you brought it up have you and Steve decided on what to do about living in two different states?

"Uh, doing the same thing we were doing before?"

"You know what I mean. You can't have missed the fact that he is totally in love with you."

"Emily, Emily, Emily, you know I'm not ready for something like that. He and I have talked. We agree we enjoy each other's company, and that's all for now. I wish he was more open, or would trust me enough to talk about his drinking. He tells me when he has to go to a meeting, but he never says what the meeting is about. How long has he been sober?"

"I think about a year. I know you said that you'd never marry an alcoholic, but I think he has a lot going for him. I think Steve is turning his life around. Besides, girl, when you fall in love, it happens when you least expect it and sometimes with someone you never expected. If you ever want someone to marry you, you're going to need to lighten up."

Anna shifted in her seat, turning away from Emily. "You know what the statistics are for divorce, right? It's tough enough when there isn't a problem, but an addiction makes it doubly hard."

"And what would you do if he had, like, diabetes? There isn't a perfect man out there. I wanted a man with lots of hair, but it doesn't mean I love Seth any less."

Anna raised an eyebrow. "You're silly, sometimes." She stirred the cold soup before her.

"I spent a few years in Al-Anon, you know that. I'm not judging him. I give everyone a chance. And it's not just the fear of him being alcoholic. It just seems everything in my life is so complicated right now. Miles isn't the type of baggage a girl drags into a relationship with another guy."

"You don't learn anything unless you attempt it, Anna Sanchez. You know that. Quit using Miles as an excuse. You need to get over your trust issues. If Steve is the guy, go for it. Besides, practice makes perfect, though I would say you two have the kissing thing down pat."

A shy smile supported her lightly blushing cheeks. "Hmm, that's none of your business, Emily Higgins."

Emily snorted. "Look whose twitterpated now!"

"You're too nosy! Thanks for lunch. I've got to pick up groceries now. Find some other poor soul to torture."

❀ ❀ ❀ ❀ ❀

Anna opened the cupboard, slipping the last box of cereal into place. Picking up the empty plastic grocery bag, she looked around the neat kitchen with a sigh of completion. Grocery shopping was not her favorite thing to do. Going into the newly remodeled laundry room, she checked on the drying clothes. Her eye caught the strange print, her eyes tracing the sinuous lines of the Panthers. *Just like Steve and I, circling one another, and trying to figure each other out.* Now she understood her grandmother's fascination with this picture. A little smile graced her lips.

The back screen door opened, and Steve looked surprised to see her. Anna noticed he was clean-shaven, hair damp from the shower, and dressed in fresh, clean clothes.

"My, my, don't you look spiffy."

Steve put on her favorite smile, eyes crinkling and impish in nature. "Yup, all done for the day. I thought I'd come in and see if you'd like to take a walk."

"You're just in time--all my chores are done for now. Where do you want to go?"

"It's a surprise," he said, a broad smile showing off his porcelain-white teeth.

Reaching out his hand, she slipped her delicate one into his, feeling the roughness of it, heart surging. Going out the back porch, they strolled up the path towards the cottonwood tree and family cemetery. She began to make out the squat form of a creamy-white pine structure sitting where the dilapidated old bench had been. A few feet closer, she recognized a swing. Slats in a fan pattern formed the back of the bench, glistening with a clear sealant. The poled wood had been fitted together to accentuate and take advantage of its natural curves and bumps. Besides being utilitarian in nature, it was a piece of artwork.

Anna felt tears welling; never had she seen such a beautiful, handcrafted gift. She ran her hand over the satin finish, sliding onto the slick seat, setting its quiet glide into motion. Stopping, she jumped off and flew into his arms, tears flowing.

"I've--I've never, never been given such--such a beautiful gift," she choked out, burying her face into his chest. His arms came up around her, tenderly holding her. He rested his cheek against the top of her head.

She leaned back. "When did you have time to do this? It's gorgeous, and it's in my favorite spot. How'd you...?"

He traced the path of a tear, wiping it away. "Well, I had someone in on the plot. That's why Emily invited you to the hospital for lunch today. The rest was easy to figure out. You're up here reading or staring off into space all the time. I was afraid you were going to hurt yourself lying on that old bench. I learned wood crafting from my spons--, my friend. Had a big old barn at hand for a workshop and I like putting things together. I had some free time here and there, like at night," he said, embarrassment pinking his cheeks.

"I love it." She stared up at him, knowing the look in her eyes told him all he needed to know.

He bent his head, gently seeking her lips; she rose up on her tiptoes to accept hungrily. The wind kicked up, pushing at them. He ended the kiss tenderly, letting her go. She sat down again, patting the opening beside her.

"Let's see if it can hold both of us."

An eyebrow hiked up. "Doubting my workmanship?"

She giggled. "Come over here, Sherlock. Let's check it out." Rubbing at her arms, she shot a look towards the mountains, eyeing the clouds gathering there. "Think we're going to have a storm tonight, looking pretty grim over there."

"Maybe. Sometimes a front will come over, and we just get a good wind out of it. During the summer months, we get some great heat lightning."

Anna jumped up off the swing, grabbing Steve's hand. "Never mind. Come on down for dinner. It's my turn to cook tonight. If you're lucky, I'll be able to make spaghetti."

Incredulously, he looked at her. "I thought you couldn't cook."

"Silly boy, I never said I couldn't cook. I said I didn't like to cook."

❁ ❁ ❁ ❁ ❁

The raw strength of the wind raked at the trees. Dark layers of gray clouds came to their lightest band on top of the mountain

183

peaks where the sun had set for the night. The tempest tore at Anna's hair, flinging it blindingly into her eyes, at the same time pushing against her, making every step a challenge.

"Thank you, Steve, for walking down with me."

His arm steadied her; he leaned his head in to hear her. "Anytime. Pretty good winds tonight; we should've locked up sooner."

Turning on the light inside the barn, she said, "You know, I've gotten used to the quiet out here in the country. But that wind has such a power it's frightening. In the city, buildings block it, and if I need help, all I have to do is dial 911. Out here, you're on your own."

Good-naturedly, he laughed. "You have tough, pioneer roots: you can handle it. If not, you can always open an Italian restaurant in the city; you have spaghetti down pat."

"Yeah, you think so?" She smiled, pouring oats into the feeding bin for a nickering Ginger. "I'm going to close her in tonight; it's looking rough out there."

"Let me do that. You've only got one good arm--don't want you breaking the other one." Impertinently, she arched an eyebrow. He chuckled as he slipped outside, tugging against the wind to pull the Dutch door inward. He closed off the stall to the outside run, slipping the simple bolt locks to secure them. Inside the barn, Steve checked the back door, making sure the chain was tight. The smell of summer past was caught in neatly stacked grass bales, pungent in the still air of the barn.

Anna noticed him eye the old tractor with contempt as he passed it.

"Old Bessie's been acting up again?"

Steve snorted. "If that's what you want to call it. It throws a temper tantrum when I work that back pasture."

She patted its faded, green side. "Well, we can look at the budget and see if a new one is affordable. Grandpa sure had a knack for keeping things going." Steve groaned his assent.

A pile of pine shavings at the base of a sawhorse caught her eye. "So this is the scene of the crime. I can't believe you did this right under my nose and I never even noticed."

She melted up against him, staring up into his intense gaze. He smoothed windblown strands of hair from her cheek. She felt fingers slide into her silken hair, his other hand going around her waist, pressing her closer while his lips teased ever so slightly. The response came unbidden, as she slipped her good arm around his neck, and pulled him closer. Hungrily, he answered her ardor.

Her skin had an intense awareness of its own as she felt the hand in the curve of her waist slowly move over her hip and come to rest warmly on her backside. Suddenly he pulled back; his breathing ragged. He gripped her arms lightly, looking down at her with wide eyes full of passion.

"Lady, you are exquisite. We need to slow down before, well...." She watched as he glanced around the barn, focusing on the old, slat ladder going up the side of the wall into the hayloft beside her. "Before we have to make use of the hay up there."

Calming her breathing, she said, "Yes, I agree." Raising her hands to his chest, she stepped away as he released her. "I'm sorry." She brushed the hair from her flaming cheeks.

"What are you apologizing for?" Confusion showed on his face, and he had to lean in to hear her soft answer.

"This isn't like me. I don't normally lead guys on like that. I'm sorry."

"Lady, you kiss like no other, but it's not going to be like that. We agreed to go slow, and I'm going to prove to you I'm a man of my word."

The barn creaked and rasped with the wind gusts, along with rustles, bangs, and clanks, here and there, making a conversation of its own in the usually quiet interior.

"Let's head back; I need to get to bed early tonight. Got some repair work on the bunkhouse porch, and a meeting at noon," he said in a voice still gruff with passion.

Avoiding his gaze, she answered, "Sounds good."

In the beam of the flashlight she held, he locked the outside of the barn, struggling in the ripping wind. A shiver ran down her back; she couldn't shake the foreboding that haunted her.

❀ ❀ ❀ ❀ ❀

Samson scratched in the dark, barking furiously as an orange glow lit up the front windows in the bunkhouse. Coughing, stumbling through the haze Steve went to the window, pausing to pull aside the curtains, freezing in surprise. "Damn!" he shouted, scampering to grab his jeans. Hopping on one foot, he frantically dressed as the flames licked under the front door. Grabbing a kitchen chair he ran, coughing harder now, into the back bedroom and smashed it into the window. Scooping up the wiggling pup, he climbed out through the shattered frame. Running to the ranch house, he let out another curse as the night lit up from sparks that flew, like disembodied spirits above the blaze consuming the barn in the valley.

Steve pounded on the front door until Seth opened it to peer out, squinty-eyed from sleep, eyes widening as he saw the raging inferno. He threw the door open wide, running to the bedroom, pulling off his bathrobe as he ran, and hollering, "Fire! The barn's on fire!"

Anna stumbled out, her oversized night t-shirt clinging, her good arm cradling the injured one. "Is it Miles? What's going on?"

In agitation, Samson ran around them all, barking. She grabbed the puppy, holding him to her.

Seth had run back out to the living room, pulling on his pants, pelting Steve with questions. "How long has it been burning? Seen anyone? Have you called it in?"

Anna gasped. "What's burning?"

"Bunkhouse was the first I think. Could have started the barn fire, I don't know how long, just saw it, called 911, they're on their way. I haven't seen anyone. Anna, stay here. Seth, I've got to get down there," Steve barked out.

Running down the path, Seth close on his heels, Steve peered into the dark. Looking through the shadows the flames cast, he tried to see if the culprit was among them.

"We need to get the hoses, get the backup pump going!" Steve shouted as he raced on to the corrals, dialing furiously on his cell phone. "Hey, Mike, we need you here, buddy; bunkhouse and barn are on fire, could use your help. Okay, see you!"

He saw Ginger in the outside fenced stall run. She was wild-eyed, snorting and running up and down the narrow enclosure. He yanked open the gate to the stall run, noticing the Dutch doors to the barn were open. *How the heck did that happen? I know I locked that door from the inside.* Steve flailed his arms at her, trying to get her to go towards the end of the run and the open gate that led to the open field. General and Midnight whinnied as if calling to her. She ducked away from him, galloping wildly into the dark, far from the flaming barn.

Anna came running down the path, a sweatshirt donned quickly over the t-shirt sleeper.

The fiery inferno devoured the dry timber of the huge barn, fanned into a frenzy by the wind.

"No! No!" she screamed painfully.

Steve caught her around the waist, murmuring in her ear, "It's okay. Come back here with me. The fire department is on the way. There's nothing we can do."

She turned panicked eyes to him, and shouted, "Ginger!"

"She's out, she's okay," He reassured her again.

The heat pounded them in rolling waves as the wind whipped, feeding the fire's hunger. He pulled her gently up the path as Seth drug a hose down, coming up short. Above the howling of the wind and the roar of the fire, Seth shouted, "This is as far as it can go; all the other hoses were in the barn."

Steve grimaced. "Any hoses at the auxiliary pump house at the pasture gate?"

"Yes," Anna panted out, her hands clutching her chest. Emily joined them. Up at the ranch house, the boys pressed their faces against the large picture window as they watched the fire.

"Stay here with Emily; I've got to get those hoses." He relinquished his hold to Emily's enveloping arm, running towards the pump house.

With the extra length of hose, Seth futilely sprayed while Steve worked with a hose from the auxiliary pump.

The scream of sirens and flashing red lights split the night, announcing the rural fire department's arrival. The fire chief approached, stepping up close to Steve to be heard.

"Was there any livestock in there?"

"No, they're all out to pasture," Steve answered.

"It looks like the fire's fully engaged. Half the crew is trying to save the bunkhouse. You were lucky to get out of there Steve, and we may not be able to save any of the barn; these winds are stoking it. Let's hope it doesn't spread out to the pasture or up those ridges."

Mike ran down the path, the flaming-orange hell reflecting in his dark eyes, throwing the despair on his face into sharp silhouette. The fire crew started setting up, with Steve's help, hooking into the water sources.

Steve, Mike, and the fire chief, came to where Anna and Emily watched helplessly at the pump house, near the holding corrals. Waves of fierce heat washed over them, warming against the push of the cold wind.

The fire chief spoke quickly, "Folks if you don't mind going back up to the house. It's far enough up the hillside that you are safe in case there is anything volatile left in the barn. We will keep an eye out in case the wind shifts and puts it in the path of ash or cinders. There's nothing you can do here." Steve could see Anna stiffen, knowing she was ready to refuse. He stepped up to her, lightly grabbing her arms. He spoke with firm authority against the din, "Go with Emily, there's nothing you can help with, lady."

Anna shivered; he looked her over, worried, seeing the anxiety was winning. The fire created shadows that accentuated the fear he saw in her. Bending his head down to speak softly into her ear, he said, "Anna, I can't do my job and take care of you too. Please go to the house." She finally nodded, giving in.

A sudden, sharp crack caught their attention as the first huge support beam of the aging barn collapsed, sending a surge of flames tearing at the black of night in defiance.

❀ ❀ ❀ ❀ ❀

Fighting the anxiety attack, Anna leaned heavily on Emily while getting back up to the house. Her heart was racing, breathing becoming a challenge as her legs weakened.

As they left, Anna could hear the fire chief shouting directions to Steve and Mike, "We'll need a perimeter set up, possibly some trenches dug. I'm calling in backup. There are pretty good updrafts from these winds, and there's a lot of vegetation on that ridge behind the barn. Need your help to keep it from spreading--do some sweeps of the area; you know it better than we do."

Back at the house, flashing red lights reflected on the walls of the living room as Matthew and John watched from the window, excitedly pointing to the fire trucks. Anna slowly moved around the kitchen, starting coffee, trying to calm the panic that came in waves through her.

"It's a good thing you videotaped everything in there for insurance," Emily said.

Anna worked to catch enough breath to answer. "We should be able to get something back at least for the building, and equipment. But we lost so much, Emily, things that can't be replaced. Steve put up half the hay from the bottom pasture in there; we needed that feed. Thank heavens we all had our vehicles up here and the Vette's in the shop. It could have been the house, with all of us in it, instead of the bunkhouse. Steve could have been killed." Icy rage tinged her voice as she moved to the window. "You know who did this!"

"You don't know it was Miles. It could have been a lightning strike. The barn could have caught fire from a downdraft."

More flashing lights pulled in, piercing the night. 'Sheriff' could be seen in print down the striped side of the car. Anna opened the front door to the uniformed deputy.

"Evening, ma'am. Got some questions if you don't mind."

Anna nodded. "Wish I could say it's nice to see you again, Sheriff."

She led him to the kitchen table. Emily shooed the boys upstairs so they could watch their heroes as they worked.

"I'll take coffee down to the men while you talk to the Sheriff," Emily announced as she gathered up cups, thermos and sugar to put into a picnic basket.

Anna wrapped her hands around the warm coffee cup, working on calming her racing heart, patiently answering his questions.

"Ma'am, I know you think Miles Rannet is behind this. But until we do a full investigation and figure out exactly what started this fire, we can't be jumping to conclusions. I'll make a pass around the property. You made mention of an old mining road behind this ridge. I'll check it out. I suspect he is long gone if it was him. I hope that will make you feel better."

"Anything you can do is appreciated," Anna said softly.

He made a few more notes and left. She watched from the front windows as he made a run down the little dirt road in front of the house, towards the main road, sweeping the hillsides and ridge with the spotlight on his car.

Locking the bathroom door behind her, the dark circles under her eyes and mussed hair didn't even register as she stared blankly at the mirror. Gripping the side of the sink, she struggled to take in a breath. Finally relenting, she reached for the medication behind the mirrored cabinet door.

What is wrong with him? What did I do to deserve this? All I tried to do was be nice. So many people are now at risk. Steve! He almost died tonight. What do I do?

After a few minutes, a knock at the door interrupted her spiral into the hole of panic.

"Auntie, I need to use the bathroom," John called out.

She quickly wiped the tears from reddened eyes, splashing cold water on the splotches that mottled her face. Breathing was coming easier now, the medication doing its job, and she gratefully sucked in air. Opening the door, she reached out to tousle John's hair, heading back to the kitchen to brew more coffee.

Through the night, the firemen tirelessly battled against the wind that gave breath to the dragon that raged, keeping it contained so it wouldn't spread to the wooded ridges and grasslands beyond.

The morning light revealed the blackened, smoking carcass of the barn. Weary firefighters sifted through the remains, making sure nothing was left of the fire-breathing monster of the night before.

Uncle George and Aunt Evelyn arrived as dawn was breaking, to help assess the damage and give moral support. They gathered around the kitchen table, looking at Anna, Emily, and Seth, who all gazed back, tired and disheveled.

"Your insurance policies are all intact. As soon as it's a decent hour, I'll call Stan. He will know how to start the claim. You lost the truck and tractor?" George queried.

She nodded, her face drawn. The front door opened. Steve and Mike, covered in soot and looking exhausted, walked in.

"Looks like the fire's out. We ran the ridge and outlying areas, and pretty much just kept an eye out to make sure it didn't spread."

"Thank heavens Samson woke you up, Steve. I guess you got some overtime coming, young man," George said.

"No, sir, I'd have helped anyone in this situation. You know, I've been thinking. How does he get away?--how can he be watching us?--there aren't many places to hide out here." They all listened intently.

"So what's your theory, Steve?" George's lined face showed his concern.

"I think he's been in the barn all along. When I got there, the Dutch doors were open. Those doors--we locked them from the inside. We didn't have to worry about him getting in; he was there all along. We never checked the upstairs storage tonight. The wind made so much noise we wouldn't know if he was around. The fire chief says the first fire started at the bunkhouse, and it looks like arson. There's a chance the wind could have sent cinders that may have ignited the barn, but he doesn't think so. He believes that was arson too."

"It makes sense," George said, lost in thought.

Anna's skin crawled when she realized just how close he might have been all along. "But why did he single you out? Why start the fire at the bunkhouse? Is there anything left?"

"We can go down and check it out if you want. The crew is just cleaning up." Steve led the way.

In the stark light of day, the blackened skeleton of an old tractor, a charred truck, various convoluted pieces of metal, and a large amount of twisted timbers in burnt agony was all there was left of the barn.

On the hillside to the north sat the bunkhouse. Blackened windows stared blankly; half of the roof was burnt away, and the charcoal outline of the new porch Steve had built could be seen.

Exhausted tears ran down Anna's face unchecked. They huddled together in silence, staring at the destruction.

Robynn Gabel

Chapter 14 – The Proposal

The estate auction came at an opportune time. There was a long list of equipment, including several tractors, household goods, and cattle.

Steve had agreed to go and learn the ropes, but he was disappointed that Anna wasn't able to go with them. He found himself wanting more time alone with her, but he was working towards making that a thing of the past. George interrupted his thoughts.

"So when we get there, let's check out the tractors first, then look at the cattle," George directed.

"Sounds good to me. What is it with you Hansons that you have to drive antique trucks?" A huge grin stretched across Steve's face.

"We just take care of our vehicles. Call us frugal, I guess. This old Ford has been good to me through the years." George patted the dusty dash.

They pulled into the fairgrounds, George easily finding a place to park. Steve followed him as he headed over to the hulking equipment. George made quick inspections of the well-used tractors, shaking his head. "Nothing here that's going to help us out."

"Hey, is that you, George? Haven't seen you in years! How're you doing?" A grizzled old cowboy with bowed legs hobbled over to George, extending a hand covered in age spots. George introduced Steve, and then waved him towards the cattle as he stayed behind to chat with his friend.

Steve wandered down the alleyway, looking at the bulls in the paneled pens; his eyes noting weight, size, muscling, and body build but his mind was far away. Stress had been building, like a steam engine, pushing against his mind.

Just that morning, he had spoken with his AA sponsor about his plans. Jim was a tough old Vietnam vet, who had given not only six years of his life but also his leg in the war. He'd struggled with drug and alcohol addiction for many years, only getting clean for the last eight. Steve looked up to the hardened vet who pulled no punches.

He fished the little black box from his jean's pocket, staring down at the tiny rainbows caught in the facets of the diamond. It was burrowed in the black velvet, gleaming in promise. He could hear Jim's voice, cautioning him against doing anything impulsively. Steve was good at impulse, having blown some of his careful budget to get this sparkling beauty. It carried his hopes for the future in its crystal heart.

Remembering her dusky-blue, shining eyes when he had presented the swing to her, he'd gone over and over what response he might get to this gift of his heart. Would she accept his proposal for marriage? Was it too soon, too fast? His mind ran over his plans again. If she said yes, they would have all of next year to arrange the wedding while he went to school. She was to go back to Ft Collins this week, but he hoped if she accepted his proposal she would stay longer so they could plan their lives together. He couldn't - wouldn't - imagine that she would say no. What girl didn't want to get married? Have the wedding of her dreams? He pocketed the little box once again, sighing.

"Over here, Steve," George called, bringing Steve back to the moment.

"Here's a good lot. Can you see why?" The group of thin heifers milled around, coats dull and with a few ribs showing, coats.

"I don't know. They look a little on the underfed side."

George sported a sly grin. "Yes, which is why the bidding won't go high, but they aren't sick, no injuries, and even though thin, with a little feed they'll be a good investment and sound addition to the herd, especially if any of them was bred this past spring.

Steve tipped back his hat, perusing other pens.

"Look around and see if you can find any others you think might be a good deal, and I'll check them out for you." George was enjoying being back in his element. Steve knew he was learning from the best.

Walking along the pens, eyeing each group of cows up for auction, he asked, "How'd you know Evelyn was the one?"

George squinted for a second, saying carefully, "Well, Son, I just knew it in my gut. I wanted to spend time with her; no other gal was worth looking at. We got along terrific; I wanted to punch any guy that even looked at her. Why? Have you been thinking about Anna?"

Steve stopped by another pen, black heifers staring back at him, a scraped hide here or there, a little more weight, but looking sound. He looked down at the card, reading the notes on the lot. "How about these?"

George took a moment to study them. "Yeah, they'd do, depending on the bid price. But you didn't answer my question."

Steve ducked his head. "Yeah, I'm thinking about her a lot."

"You've got good taste, Son, but she's been through a lot. Think you got your work cut out for you, but if she's the one, hang in there. You've got my blessing." George clapped him on the back. "You'd make a good partner in this group. I'd be honored to have you, and you'd be a good 'investment' for her." His gravelly laugh startled the penned cows. "Now, bidding starts after lunch. We can come back for the cattle. I didn't see any equipment worth bidding on so let's go tractor shopping."

✿ ✿ ✿ ✿ ✿

Anna woke immediately when the shot rang out. When she had first got to the ranch, she wondered if she would ever get used to the silence of the country, missing the hum of the city. Not that the old house didn't squeak, crack and groan, especially at night when it was the hardest to fall asleep. So letting the radio softly lull her to sleep became a habit. But lately, since Miles had returned, dead silence was the only thing she could fall asleep to, giving her peace that all was well.

Quickly throwing on her robe, finding her slippers, she ran to the front porch. Seth was already there, dressed in his suit for work, his gaze skimming the hills in front of them.

Her voice trembled when she asked, "Where'd it come from?"

"I don't know. I let Samson out about a half-hour ago. I haven't heard him barking, but it was close--I think up on the ridge."

Seth stepped off the porch to peer up around the backside of the house. Steve joined them, hair tousled, looking half asleep, huffing from the jog from the trailer that had replaced the bunkhouse.

"Seth, where'd that shot come from?"

"I don't know. Are we sure it was a shot?"

Steve eyed the ridge behind the house. "Yes, sounded like a small caliber, but it was a gunshot."

Anna left the porch, whistling, calling for Samson, wandering around the cars parked under the cottonwood tree. Steve shadowed her, glancing now and then at the back ridge, as she walked down the path to where the barn had stood, calling for the puppy.

For the last week, a flurry of activity had cleared out the rubble left behind in the barn's burnt shell. A steady stream of insurance adjusters, fire inspectors, dump trucks and contractors had kept Anna busy.

Steve had been just as busy. With several new hired hands and help from Mike when he was free from the hardware store, they already had a frame rising from the ashes. Sitting beside the frame, several fresh lumber piles were stacked neatly. Trusses sat next to a crane on loan that would lift them into place. Rob had gathered a group of volunteers together from the church, and tomorrow, Anna and her family would host a good, old-fashioned barn-raising.

Anna chewed her bottom lip. "I don't see him anywhere. Usually, he comes running when any of us call for him."

"I'll look for him; you just go and get some breakfast in you. I'd rather you not be out here, lady. You're a target this way."

She looked around quickly one more time. "I do have a lot to do today, but we need to know where that shot came from. I'm not feeling good about this." Anna felt her heart thumping loudly.

Seth was waiting for them on the porch.

"I'll keep an eye out, Seth. Mike is supposed to be here in about a half hour so go ahead and go into work. I can handle it." Anna could see Steve's eyes were dark with tension.

"Thanks, but I don't need to be there just yet. I'll stay until Mike shows up. We can't take any chances, especially if that piece of excrement has a gun. I'm going to call the Sheriff."

Anna walked slowly up the path to the little cemetery, taking a break from the day's labors. The morning had been hectic with the Sheriff helping in the search of the hills and surrounding property. They had found fresh tire tracks on the back ridge above the farmhouse on the old mining road, finally giving some indication of a possible Miles connection. Up to this point, if it was him, he had been as stealthy as a mountain lion. They had found bullet casings and cigarette butts at the edge of the road, where a car had parked. From the mining road, someone could walk to the edge where rocks and a jumble of shrub hid the observer, yet gave a bird's-eye view of everything going on in the valley below.

When hearing their findings, Anna made an appointment with a security company. They would be installing motion sensor lights--and alarms--for the house and the new barn when it was finished.

After the Sheriff had left, they had a visit from the brand inspector for the new cattle that greedily grazed in the pasture. He went to work checking the bill of sale from the auction against the brands of the cows in the field. Filling out paperwork afterward had finished off the morning.

George and Steve had not only brought home another forty-five head of cattle but also a shiny, new tractor that sat under the cottonwood, waiting for the new barn to house it.

Almost to the rise, she felt a gentle wind. It gently caressed the leaves of the cottonwood, as if asking for forgiveness for the tempest of several nights past. Reaching the swing, she noticed an inert bundle of fur at the base of the tree. She froze, staring, hoping to see some sign of life, knowing deep inside there wasn't any. Looking up at the ridge, knowing she was alone but still fearful, scalding tears dripped down her face. She bit her lower lip, tumultuous emotions lashing through her.

Down at the house, Steve pounded away, fixing more boards on the back porch. Anna didn't want to disturb him; she wanted to do this herself. With slow, weary steps, she followed the path back down to the side of the house where a shovel leaned up against it. A few minutes later she struggled angrily, one-handedly, to dig a hole in the little cemetery, cradling her cast against her side. *Why does everything I love have to die, to leave me? I miss them all; why did they have to go?*

With each shove of the shovel and each awkward struggle to get the dirt to the side, the anger grew, the pain tearing at her chest. Slowly, sobs grew until, like a drowning person breaking through the water's surface, she fell to her knees, holding onto the shovel, finally taking that first full gasp of air. Release washed over her as the flood of tears poured. All the emotion she had carefully hidden and buried now surfaced in the wave of anguished moans.

With a shaking hand, she laid the faithful puppy to rest, along with her long night of grief and sorrow. On her knees, smoothing the last of the dirt with her hand, she had no tears left; her heart no longer raced. She sat back on her heels, filling her lungs with air, feeling light-headed.

I'll have Steve make him a little headstone later. How am I going to tell Matthew that Miles shot our little Samson? I can't take this anymore! Enough! Something snapped inside of her; in an instant of total clarity, her resolve cemented into place. White-hot anger gave her focus. She knew what she had to do. First Steve almost being burned to death and now Samson's death, it was a dire warning. No security system would ever be enough. There was no one who could protect them all. Leaving--that was the answer. To lead Miles away from the only family she had left, before the two boys became his next target or he succeeded in killing Steve. Fighting him in a public area, on a turf they both knew well--Ft. Collins--was the only way to make this game fair.

Snapping the phone open, she noted there was a good signal, and speed-dialed Chris. Anna obeyed the canned voice's direction to leave a message. *"Hi, Chris, call me when you get a chance. We need to talk. He's gone too far; we need to start planning, have a game plan in place before I get home. Thank you."*

She laid the shovel up against the tree, and sat down on the swing, leaning back, grateful for the gentle motion. It was decided: she would leave right after the barn-raising tomorrow instead of waiting for the end of the week. All the pertinent things had been accomplished. Everything else could be handled via phone. Emily, George, and Seth had a good handle on the ranch; with Steve and Mike helping, it should go smoothly. Miles would follow if he were even still around. After he was caught again, she would be able to go back to a normal life. Finally have the family she craved.

There was packing to do, but right now, she just wanted to close her dry, scratchy eyes and rest. She felt the smooth slats under her, thinking of Steve, his eyes, his laugh, and his shy kisses. Exhausted, she lay down, sleep stealing over her, bringing peace.

"Anna." She opened her weary eyes, looking at him. "Anna, you okay?" he asked quietly.

Steve stood before her, his hair slicked back, a black tie against a white shirt, tucked into slim, black jeans. His stiff arms awkwardly held something behind his back. She opened her eyes wider, surprise bringing a smile to her lips.

"Well, hell-o, good-looking. What's the occasion?"

Steve shrugged nonchalantly. "Just trying to impress you, hoping you'll give me a raise." From behind his back, he pulled out a bouquet of red, velvety roses.

Her light laughter floated away on the gentle breeze. "Oh, how beautiful." She sat up, scooting over, beckoning him in. He sat down, and she gently took the roses from his outstretched hand. Holding them up, inhaling deeply, she smiled gratefully. "I really needed these. How thoughtful. I will definitely put a good word in with the CEO for that raise."

For a few seconds, they just rocked back and forth. She felt him looking down at her, and a thrill of excitement went through her.

"You know, I have to say, seriously, you clean up quite nicely." She stared up into his eyes, trying to read the emotion there.

"I must say, lady, you look beautiful when you're sleeping."

"Oh! How long were you there?"

"Not long, just came up. Noticed you were doing some digging. Why didn't you get me?"

Anna stared out at the little mound of fresh dirt, her throat closing. "I found Samson. Miles shot him."

Steve jumped up, swearing. Pacing back and forth in front of the swing, his gaze swept the ridge, looking for any sign. "Why the hell didn't you come get me?"

"He's not around; the Sheriff was sure of that. There wasn't anything you could do for Samson. Besides, I needed to handle it. Just leave it at that, okay? I've had a long day. Just sit here and hold me, please."

Hesitating, looking around one more time, he gave in, sliding close to her. She leaned against him, reaching over to slip her hand into his. He interlaced his fingers with hers, sighing deeply.

"Let's talk about something else, shall we?"

She looked up, smiling.

"I want to go to Colorado to the tech school. You know that, right?"

"Hmm, you have my number. Call me; we can get together. I know I'll be busy working, but I wouldn't mind going out with you, like a proper date. You know-- dinner at a real restaurant."

"What?--you don't like potlucks? I thought I'd check out the local church and see if we could crash one of their carry-in dinners." The smile didn't quite replace the worry in his eyes.

She pushed away from him playfully. "Being funny again, I see."

His thumb slid over her hand absently. "Do you think we're good together, Anna?"

Rubbing at the side of her right temple, wondering where this was going, she answered, "All I know, is that I feel safe with you. I know you have a good heart, that you probably have problems-- don't we all. I think we have a lot in common. You know Corvettes almost better than I do." She smiled again. "We have fun. It's just a lot has gone on in the last two months. You have been a tremendous help; you're a wonderful friend. I don't know: does that make us good together?"

Letting go of her hand, he put his arm around her shoulders, and she let him pull her to him. Reaching up, he brought the back of his curled fingers down her cheek. She felt it create a path of touch that lingered. His fingers continued their slide down her neck, uncurling under her chin, tipping her head to meet his ardent lips. She lost herself in the response, craving human contact after the emotional purge of the afternoon. She searched the depth of the kiss, feeling his smooth, perfect teeth, her breath coming faster.

A moan from deep in his throat answered her passion, and he gathered her into his arms. His fervent lips traced a warm path across her cheek, to her ear and down her neck, causing delicious shivers to run through her body. Her palm slid over his chest, moving over muscles hardened by ranch work. She broke free, staring into wells of love in his hazel eyes.

"Oh, Steve," she said, breathing the words as she shifted away, scooting to the end of the bench. She craved more of his caresses, but the little voice warned she'd gone too far once again.

Steve stood up, his back to her, hands in pockets. Staring out towards the ranch house, he asked, "Have you ever, well, had any other boyfriends?"

She shifted on the seat; she'd never had this conversation, having kept her dates to only one or two times before distancing herself. But Steve was different, so different. She took a big breath.

"Yes, I've dated before, I'm not a nun."

He glanced back at her, a rakish grin appearing. "Well, I never thought of you like that. Just wondering what you expected from a gentleman."

"Depending on how much of a gentleman you are," she said and then paused, looking mischievous, "I would think several dates, some good kissing, which I think we have down pat, and a real dinner, would be a realistic expectation and...."

His laugh interrupted her. He turned, leaning his shoulder against the outside support pole of the swing, crossing his arms, eyes narrowing speculatively.

"But what I think you're getting at is what do I think of premarital sex?"

Steve's eyes lit up, a wolfish grin taking over. "Well, Watson, I see you have deducted correctly."

"Well, my dear Sherlock, when I was in high school and college, I didn't date much, didn't have time to. I've always had the belief that sex was something I wanted to share with the one person I was going to be spending the rest of my life with. Does that answer your question?"

Shoving his hands into his pockets, darkness crept into his eyes. "Could you trust someone who has been with others?"

Anna studied his face, seeing the pain there. Gently, she asked, "Let me guess: Mary Beth?"

He straightened, pulled his hands out of his pockets, raking one through his hair and looked out over the little cemetery.

"I did some things in my teen years I regret. Yeah, Mary Beth and I were intimate, and...well...there may have been a couple of others."

"I'm not going to judge you. It is up to each person what they choose to do. I guess I'd just have to know: is it something that's important to you now? Because being faithful in a relationship and marriage is very important to me." Looking into his soul, she found nothing hidden there.

"You may have heard rumors about me. But I've walked clean this last year, Anna. There is more you need to know. I want you to know everything about me." He twisted a twig off a low hanging branch.

"I would like to get to know you. I want us to trust each other, be able to tell each other anything, to communicate well. Just take your time. I'm in no hurry."

"I just don't know where to begin. I'm not always a good person."

"None of us are completely good."

"Maybe I'm no good for you."

"Let me be the judge of that," she said, tenderly gazing into his tortured eyes.

"I…I have a monster inside of me, but I've worked to control it. I'm trying now. There have been bad times in the past, but things are going well now." Tossing the twig away, he rubbed a hand over his face. "And now you've come into my life, and all I can think of is you. I want to spend the rest of my life with you."

Anna shifted on the seat, squeezing the bouquet closer, and smelled the sudden fragrance of the jostled flowers.

He shuffled nervously, staring up at the top of the ridge. He glanced back, his gaze intense, searching hers.

"We both agreed we needed time, and I still want to do that. I just felt now was the time to do this, before you went back to Colorado. I thought maybe we'd like to give this relationship more commitment. I have to ask you something. I don't quite know where to start, even though I've gone over it a hundred times in my head."

She noticed his hand in his jean's pocket, nervously fingering something. Then he pulled it out, keeping it hidden in his hand. Taking a big breath, he knelt at her feet, his head bowed. He looked up at her, his eyes hopeful. Her breath caught at the back of her throat, and she held it. *No, no, please don't. Not yet!* He reached for her hand, kissed her palm and placed the ring case there.

"Anna Marie Sanchez, will you consider spending the rest of your life beside me as my wife?"

Her eyes widened in disbelief, a wilted smile not quite making it.

"Steve."

She could see the sweat beading on his forehead, his eyes panicked, his breath catching.

"Look at the ring, please, Anna." She slowly opened the box. Falling tears glimmered in brilliant competition with the dazzling diamond resting in velvet. Again, all she could muster was, "Oh, Steve."

He waited, his eyes beseeching her.

For a moment, everything froze. A wave of new emotions crashed inside of her. *What to say? Is he the one? We could do this; we could work at this. Maybe later. How do I tell him to wait, to be patient? I could say yes. I want to say yes....*

Samson's crumpled body flashed through her mind. Sitting up straighter, carefully composing her expression, she remembered her resolve to protect them all. Closing the lid carefully, she said firmly, "I can't right now."

Silence hung between them. Steve stiffened. Confusion in his eyes, a blush began to grow as embarrassment took over. She reached for his hand, placing the ring case back into it.

Her voice broke, choking out, "I'm so sorry, Steve. Let's talk about this."

Silently, he stood up and walked away.

Chapter 15 – Falling

Hammers and nail guns thudded, circular saws whined, and the sound of conversations filled the warm summer air. Everyone moved with purpose, accomplishing their jobs. Tables covered with white cloths waving gently in the breeze sat under the big cottonwood in the front yard.

Anna manned the local watering hole from the porch, serving water, coffee, Kool-Aid, and cookies on small card tables. Brad came up, grabbing a water bottle, his smiling blue eyes crinkling in the corners just like his brother, the resemblance ending there.

"I see they found a job for a one-armed catcher," he joked.

Anna smiled in return. "Hopefully no catching today, but it is a good place to greet everyone who has turned out to help. How are the boys doing?"

"They're doing great. Jacob still talks about the pretty teacher. You made quite the impression. Sorry about your barn--seems like if you didn't have bad luck, you'd have no luck at all."

"Never heard that one before," she said, chuckling. "But thank you for coming out to help us."

"Glad to do it. How are you holding up? How's the arm?"

"Pretty good right now. I'm healing well, from what the doctor tells me."

"How's Steve working out here? You know you stole one of my best workers."

"He has been our right-hand man. He knows a little of everything and is quite handy at fixing anything."

"Yeah, he was always taking things apart at the store, but he'd usually get them working again. Well, I hear them hollering for me. Better get back to work."

Emily brought out a mound of sandwiches, pausing to ask, "What's going on with you and Steve? The tension is like cement."

Anna shrugged. "Just a disagreement about the future, nothing more."

"Well, he's got that glare down pat. Good thing you don't melt easily. By the way, I've got Mary Beth working in the kitchen making sandwiches. She's a pretty good hand if I say so myself."

"I think she's good at being an opportunist, but Rob seems to enjoy her company," Anna said, watching the barn crew.

"After the next batch of sandwiches, I'm going to start working on the dinner fixings. You doing okay here?"

"Yeah, I'm doing fine."

Emily nodded, heading for the tables.

With a puzzled look on his face, Rob stepped up, grabbing a water bottle. "Hey Anna, the boss man down there sent me to ask if you still want a side door out the back like in the old barn. Is everything okay between you two?"

Anna gritted her teeth, but smiled pleasantly, answering, "Please tell him it needs to be like the original, so yes, a door out the back. How's it going, Rob?"

"Better than I'd hope. We've got a really good crew. The trusses are in place; now we are working on the walls. It helped that Steve and Mike had most of the framework already done. After today you should have the basics done, leaving just the roof, wiring and some finishing."

"You have no idea how much I appreciate this. I'm so happy we're on speaking terms, let alone having your help."

"Awww, Anna, I'm just doing what I should've done all along. I feel bad I put you through all that. Did you hear? It looks like we may finally have found some good water on the last drill. We've been blessed."

Anna caught sight of Steve walking by. A scowl was all she had received from him before he stared straight ahead again, heading out to a group gathered at one of the pickups parked alongside the dirt road. She couldn't miss the pain in his eyes. *I hate leaving with him so upset.*

Rob swore quietly under his breath. "I hope he's not doing what I think he is. Excuse me." He headed back down to the barn.

Anna felt her heart lurch and a horrible, twisted sensation in her belly. She couldn't miss the glowers Steve had sent her way all day, each one a stab in her heart. *Why doesn't he just yell at me and get it over with? I need to tell him why we have to wait. Can't he see I'm protecting him? We can work this out.*

She tried talking to him that morning when he came in for coffee. Stony silence was all he'd give her, turning his back to her as he headed out to pound away on the barn.

Anna kept busy as the day progressed, noticing she saw less and less of Steve. By afternoon, the smell of barbecuing steaks filled the air. Emily and Anna set up the last round of food as hungry workers sat down at the tables for dinner, under the cottonwood.

"Hey, Anna, want a beer?" Tim waved a can at her. He was one of the new hires who had worked on framing the barn in the last week.

"No, thanks," she called back. Several of the workers had brought in coolers, sharing what they brought. She didn't like the taste of alcohol, but never pushed her tastes on anyone else.

She caught sight of Steve hanging out with a few friends near the drive. Mary Beth approached him, receiving a dark look when she spoke to him. They stepped off together, her hands gesturing as she talked animatedly, a thunderous look crossing Steve's face. He shook his head 'no,' throwing his hands in the air, and strode angrily back to the group as they laughed raucously. Mary Beth hesitated for a moment and turned away, her shoulders slumping, wiping at her eyes.

Rob took her attention away from the scene playing out on the road as he stepped up onto the porch. "You always manage the best cook-outs; it's worth the work just to get the dinner."

Her laughter bubbled up. "I'm not the cook, though. That'd be Emily. She is quite the organizer, isn't she? That green bean casserole you devoured is her specialty."

Over Rob's shoulder, she noticed Steve shooting a thunderous frown their way. Rob moved in closer, putting his arm around her shoulders, giving her a slight hug. She stiffened.

"Well, it was delicious as always. Hey, I noticed that George brought in some new heifers. He must have picked those up at the Anderson auction, right?

Nervously, she took a step back, disengaging Rob's arm. Steve tossed away the can he was holding, anger evident on his face. She answered Rob quickly, "Yes, he got over two-dozen head. A little thin, but with some good grass, they should fill out nicely. You need to check with him; he can tell you what he'll be doing on herd count and feed. Your offer to sell us some of your hay to replace our loss is really going to help. Again, we're in your debt."

Rob gave her his best head-turning smile. "Glad to be able to help."

"Need any help cleaning up?" Mary Beth asked quietly, stepping up beside him, her normally beautiful eyes reddened. Rob slipped his arm around her waist, looking down at her proudly.

"Can always use another hand...literally," Anna chuckled, holding up her arm with the cast.

"I'll let you girls get busy." Rob stepped down, moving away.

"If you'd like to carry the cooler in with the Kool-Aid, I'll pick up the cups. I can do that at least."

Mary Beth glanced at her. "So when does the cast come off?

"Hopefully in a few weeks."

"Hey, Anna!" Steve shouted raucously, stumbling towards the porch, a worried-looking Mike right behind him. He tripped on the first step, swayed into the porch railing and leaned against it. His face filled with disdain, looking like a stranger to her. Anna stepped away from the rank odor of alcohol wafting her way. His lip curled in a sneer, his eyes dilated. "So, hearing all the juicy stories from Mary Beth, are you?"

She said nothing, watching him with narrowed eyes.

Rob had doubled back when he heard Steve's shout. Brad joined him, both watching and listening.

"Just leave, Steve. You've screwed up enough lives," Mary Beth angrily blurted.

Steve snarled back at Mary Beth, "Well, you're just nothing but a...."

"Steve!" Mike hollered.

Defiantly, he turned to Anna again, with an edge of derision to his slurred speech. "I'm not good enough to marry, just to work for you, right? Why don't you just go back to the city and take Rob with you."

Anna could feel the ice in her stare; lips stretched in an angry line.

"Hey, Steve! It's time for you to sleep it off," Rob barked.

Steve turned to stare at him for a moment and then swung at the unsuspecting man, connecting solidly with his jaw with a sound thud. Rob stumbled into the porch, and then with a furious roar sprang back, tackling Steve, both rolling to the ground.

Anna moved forward, but Mary Beth brushed by her, jumping off the porch, yelling, "Enough! Both of you quit!"

Brad waded in, grabbed Steve, and held him back. Mike put his hands against Rob's chest, pushing him away as he swung, trying to get another punch in at Steve. The struggling men glared at each other. Anna stalked down the stairs and strode towards Steve. He looked at her, and suddenly took a step back into Brad, who let go, stepping to the side. Both brothers put distance between themselves and the fury in her eyes.

Anna's voice thundered in the silence. "Steve Johnson, this is ridiculous! I never said I wouldn't marry you. I didn't say no; I said not now!"

A small gasp came from Mary Beth.

"You didn't let me explain. Miles almost killed you! I'm trying to protect all of you from him. I've got to go home to get him away from here. Besides, marrying me won't fix your life. You need to sober up and get your act together. So you have some choices. Until then, Mr. Johnson, you know where I'll be."

"So did you tell Miles the same thing? Is that why he hates you so much?" Steve snarled. The silence deepened further, the wind not daring to stir a leaf above them.

She hesitated, shocked. Then she lunged forward, pulled back her hand, and smacked him, the sound cracking loudly in the quiet. Steve stumbled back, gaping at her in surprise, a red splotch forming on his cheek. Furiously, she stomped into the house, hearing Brad berating Steve behind her.

"You deserved that and more! I should finish kicking your butt right here and right now! When are you going to learn not to mess up a good thing? You need to get out of here...now!"

Anna sat at the kitchen table, rubbing her temple. A few minutes later, she heard Mary Beth come in carrying a drink cooler and watched as she set it on the counter. She leaned up against the counter with a calculated look.

"So how does your knight in shining armor look now?" Sarcasm dripped from her voice. "I just want to warn you; there are things you don't know about him. For instance, has he told you that he's an alcoholic? That he's only been on the wagon for a year, until today?"

Anna looked up at Mary Beth in disbelief. With predator intensity, Mary Beth stepped in closer, saying in a low tone, "He's a hopeless drunk; that's what he is. He's nothing but heartache and irresponsibility. I should know--I picked up the pieces for six years." Scorn hardened her brown eyes into blackened disks.

Anna spread her good hand out on the table, arm stiff, head down, cradling her injured arm close. Looking up, she glared at the dark-haired beauty defiantly. She slowly rose to stand. Mary Beth faltered, stepping back.

Putting a hand on hip, Anna spoke slowly, her words clipped. "First, I want you to know that I found out what you said to Chelsea, and if you ever try scaring a child again, I will personally take you out. That was the lowest thing I've ever heard: you're despicable. And as far as Steve being an alcoholic, Lander is a small town and full of gossip. I knew what I was getting into, but I also know where your loyalty has been the six years you supposedly had his back and was so in love with him. But that's between you and God.

"Something else you need to know about Steve: I think you were part of the problem. You enabled the hell out of him, trying to get him to depend on you, making sure he had anything he wanted. No wonder you didn't know what to do with him when he finally sobered up. Stay away from him."

Mary Beth's eyes narrowed, and her mouth turned into an ugly line. "Well, as if the gossips in town haven't figured out what you were doing out here to get him to propose marriage to you! So are you pregnant? Is that why he had to ask you to marry him?"

Anna squared her shoulders, saying in an ominously level tone, "I think you're the biggest gossip in that bunch. Leave it to you to think that's the only way to get a guy to propose."

Surprise popped Mary Beth's almond-shaped eyes wide, perfect lips opening as she sucked in a breath. She lashed back. "You don't know anything; you think you're so good. I've loved Steve since the 11th grade. I'd do anything for him," she said and paused, big-jeweled tears falling.

"We were prom queen and king. All I ever wanted was to get married, be his wife. It was perfect until he started drinking. He ruined it. Not me! He kept saying if I loved him, I'd go out with him, cover for him, get him beer, let him party, and sleep with him. What did I get in return? So, yeah, judge me if you want, but when Rob told me he loved me a couple of years ago, I told him I couldn't leave Steve."

She paused, grabbing a napkin to dab at the steady stream of tears. "Chelsea caught Rob pushing a kiss on me, and I'll admit it was wonderful having a guy who wanted me, offering a real relationship. I thought if I just hung in there long enough, Steve would change. When he got sober, I thought he'd finally realize he loved me."

Her voice broke; she took another deep breath, continuing, "But he changed all right. He never called, just acted like I was nothing. So I decided breaking it off would wake him up. Instead, it did just the opposite and Rob, well, he needed me when his dad died. Rob has been there for me, to pick up all the pieces; I did the same for him. So don't judge me, you witch." Through the tears, she mustered a challenging scowl.

Anna hesitated, seeing clearly how love and desire had shaped Mary Beth's actions. How disappointment in the one she'd loved had taken its toll, slowly replacing her love in inches with resentment.

Shaking her head, she knew pity was evident in her eyes as she looked up. Speaking quietly, she said, "It sounds like you've been hurt. I understand that. Love is built on respect. It isn't bargained for. It isn't bribed."

She took another step forward; cautiously, Mary Beth stepped back. "So, you can keep chasing Steve, or accept that Rob cares and respects you. Give that relationship a chance. And since you know Steve's faults so well, just let him go. Forgive and let go of the bitterness or it will destroy you. Get on with your life. Now if you will excuse me, I have some cleaning up to do." Anna walked away stiffly, heading outside to face curious stares.

Looking up the hill, she desperately needed somewhere to sit and think, but the swing was the last place she wanted to be. Hugging herself, she headed around the house for the back porch. Anger welled now that the adrenaline wasn't flowing. *How come I'm such a sucker? I fall for all the damaged guys in the world. Or I'm too nice to them and get them stalking me. I knew better! You can't trust an alcoholic. And I was falling for him. I knew I was. I must love him, or it wouldn't hurt this bad now.*

Mike intercepted her. "Hey, are you okay?"

"I'm fine," she said with a sigh.

"Well, he had no right talking to you like that, and when he sobers up, I'm telling him. You don't deserve to be treated like that. It kills me; he's been sober for more than a year now. I can't believe he blew it like this."

"Mike, he's hurting. He'll be hurting worse when he wakes up."

"Well, he's always been known to act on his whims, but everything you said: it was right on. I hope he remembers it. It's no excuse, but he's in love with you. That's all he's talked about for the last month."

She felt the warmth of a blush stealing across her cheeks. "I care for him too," she murmured.

"Are you still leaving soon?"

"Yes. In fact, I'm heading out tomorrow."

"I hope he's not running you off."

"No, I decided to leave sooner because Miles tried killing Steve and shot Samson. He's escalating, and I have a good friend in Fort Collins who can help me out with this."

"Well, he's passed out right now; we'll keep an eye on him. If I don't see you before you leave, drive safe and take care of yourself."

Anna nodded. "Thanks, Mike. You take care of yourself too." He headed towards the rebuilt bunkhouse.

Emily came around the side of the house. "Are you okay?"

Anna could see she was not going to be able to slip off, so she turned and headed towards the front. "I'm doing okay. Everyone heading out?"

"Yeah, they are just finishing up. Mary Beth is down at the barn, sobbing in Rob's arms. It seems you've been busy today tying up loose ends before you leave."

Consternation furrowed Anna's brow as she worried her bottom lip for a moment with her teeth. "There has to be a full moon, I swear. Everyone has an attitude, including me."

"Well, I don't know about a full moon, but girl, you sure know how to shut a guy up!"

"Oh, Emily, that was so rotten. How could he say that? He knows I have done nothing to deserve Miles's attention. That was such a low blow." Anna rubbed at her temple again.

"Well, honey, he deserved what he got. As drunk as he was, I doubt he even felt it. I couldn't help but overhear you and Mary Beth in the kitchen too. Maybe I don't have a good Christian attitude. I can't help but think she's had that coming for a while."

"I hate to say this, but it felt good to finally say it to her face because I've certainly been thinking it. You've no idea how close I came to punching her."

Emily giggled so hard she snorted like a piglet. "Oh," she choked while trying to speak, "you're on a roll, girl! That would've been something."

"No, it wouldn't have. She's hurting just like the rest of us. Besides, we've already given the town gossips way too much fodder as it is."

"Hey, we're usually the subject of all the gossip in Lander. And you can not only catch, but swing a mean punch. Remind me not to piss you off!" a deep, male voice boomed behind her.

She turned, seeing Brad's broad smile sporting the same perfect, white teeth as his brother. Again, she felt the warmth of a blush creep up into her face.

"Oh, I'm so sorry. I don't know what got into me."

"No need to apologize to me. I know exactly how you feel; you just got to him before I did. I wanted you to know I'm sorry for my asinine brother's actions. You're the best thing that's ever happened to that half-wit."

Anna managed a sickly smile. "I just feel responsible. I know I shouldn't, but I do."

"My brother has been spoiled for a long time. He has always pitched a fit when he doesn't get what he wants. And Mary Beth just gave him whatever he wanted so he'd stay with her. I feel for her; she does love him in her way, but it's not good for him. A girl with backbone and grit is really what that kid needs--someone just like you!"

Staring at the ground in embarrassment, Anna shook her head in uncertainty.

Brad continued, "Well, I'm going to finish putting things away. I heard you're heading out--don't blame you after today. You take care of yourself, and call me when you get down to Fort Collins, so I know you're safe. I wish it could have worked out for you two." He gave her a quick hug.

She reached up with her good arm to hug him back. "Thank you. Tell him I said goodbye and I hope he makes it through this."

Brad nodded and sauntered off.

She walked down the path towards the newly resurrected barn. The smell of fresh wood hung heavy in the heat. Inside the spacious, new building, she was in awe of how much they had accomplished. Overhead, solid trusses held up the weight of the vaulted ceiling. Cream-colored boards, set together tight and neat, made up the walls. The workshop, bathroom and tack room sat empty, waiting to be filled. It was set up exactly like the old barn. She watched through the open barn doors as Seth thanked volunteers and saw them off.

Leaving the barn, she walked back up to the house, thanking departing friends along the way. Rob's black SUV pulled up next to the cottonwood tree, and George opened the back doors to put a toolbox into it. Rob jumped out to help, and they chatted for a few minutes. Anna stole a quick look, noting Mary Beth sat stiffly in the front seat, staring straight ahead. Dark sunglasses hid any sign of distress.

Rob came up to her, his eye puffy, his jaw swollen, but she saw only friendliness in his demeanor.

She reached up to tenderly touch the side of his face. "Thank you again. Unfortunately, it looks like it's going to bruise pretty good. Sorry for the ruckus here today."

His smile was lopsided. "I'm just glad it's all out in the open, and I'm going home with the girl I love. Thank you for talking some sense into her." He winked at her.

Anna stared in bewilderment. Rob shook her hand. "Just take care, and stay safe." With lightness to his step, he headed to the vehicle, grinning as if he had just won the lottery.

✿ ✿ ✿ ✿ ✿

Seth swung the last suitcase into the back of the Vette's hatchback, carefully closing it. Anna stood on the porch, looking towards the new barn.

"Auntie, I'm going to miss you," John said, wrapping his arms around her waist. Anna lowered her head to kiss his fragrant hair.

"If you behave, you may have my room until I come back. How's that?"

John quickly wiped away a tear, his eyes lighting up. "That'd be awesome. When are you coming back?"

"I don't know. Soon, I hope." She turned to Emily, grabbing her for a long hug. "Oh, how I'm going to miss you." Anna stepped back, giving her a piece of notepaper, along with a manila envelope. "The packet arrived yesterday in the mail. Be sure he gets these, would you?"

Emily nodded, trying to hold back the tears that brightened her eyes. "You call--you hear me?--the minute you get in, so I know you're safe."

Anna slid into the low-slung car, and it started with a roar. She looked up at the bunkhouse, hoping again he might step outside, but the door stayed shut. She waved at the forlorn- looking group on the porch as she drove down the dirt road.

Pulling out onto the highway, she set the cruise control on the purring Corvette, letting the powerful car glide along, taking her with it. There'd be no racing today, no joy in the speed of the engine; she felt drained. Marveling at all that had happened in the last two months, she thought, *it wasn't that long ago I thought my only problem was what to do with the ranch. That seems simple now.*

She kept glancing in the rearview mirror to see if she was being followed. Nothing looked out of the ordinary. Chris had helped her put up a safety net the last time; they could do it again.

All her thoughts seemed to wander back to Steve. Anna hadn't seen him since he had been hauled to the bunkhouse. He'd not been up for morning coffee, so she left, wishing she could have at least said goodbye. Already, she missed his presence, his easy humor, and charm. The thought of his kisses still warmed her. With so much still up in the air, her heart ached at leaving him. She was angry that he had gotten drunk rather than talk. And then there was his comment about Miles. How could he say he loved her, and then say what he said, drunk or not?

It took many Al-Anon meetings for her to forgive her father. She had vowed never to get involve with any addiction, or anyone who had one. She knew the hard work, the ups and downs, and the chances of recovery. Relationships were hard to handle, let alone having a problem to start with. Anna knew she had a tender heart and tried to protect it with only solid relationships and dreams of a healthy marriage. She needed to walk away. Steve might never be able to kick the addiction. It was obvious he used alcohol to

222

medicate his feelings. He hadn't even begun to deal with it. How could she ever trust him? Why did it hurt so much to even think of breaking it off with him?

Outside the car window, Anna watched tumbleweeds roll and bounce as the wind tore across the prairie, pushing them. She felt like one of them, a windswept heart tumbling painfully through life.

Tears pooled and then ghosted down her cheeks as she finally accepted the reason behind the hurt. *I fell in love, damn it. I can't believe I love a drunk. The one thing I swore I would never do.*

Robynn Gabel

Chapter 16 – Resurrection

Built in the 1800s the bunkhouse had been the original home on the property. Small and utilitarian, it had been built sturdy and had endured a difficult century. Re-roofed, and remodeled since the fire, it stood again stoically weathering anything time threw at it.

Steve had it all to himself, and in the silence of its thick walls, his love-tattered mind slept off his binge. Slowly waking, he struggled to come up out of the abyss of shadowy memories.

It was the worst part of the hangover. Not being able to recollect anything but bits and pieces that made no sense. Sometimes, people would tell him things that had happened, and like shards of a broken mirror, he would piece it together, but the facts would always be skewered along the lines of the jagged glass. Sometimes, he simply didn't want to recall anything, especially if the memory was too painful.

He'd let the monster out again; now he would have to deal with the destructive aftermath it created. Foggily, he remembered swinging at Rob, and disappointment in Brad's eyes.

The one thing that did stand out clearly in the shattered mirror pieces was Anna's face. Had he seen hate, loathing, or revulsion in her blue eyes? At the time of his drunken haze, he couldn't decipher it. What had he said? What had he done? Rolling over in bed, he pulled the pillow over his head, trying to push away the memories and slip back into sleep. It didn't matter because right now he loved no one, most of all himself.

A strong knock shook the new door. Steve sat up quickly, the world spinning for a second. Bleary-eyed, he looked around the small bedroom, feeling disoriented. More pounding on the door drove him to stumble through the small kitchen into the main room, where he opened it. Squinting against the bright sunshine, he recognized the portly man standing there.

His long, gray hair was pulled back at the nape of his neck into a ponytail. Strong, rugged features showed years of alcohol and drug use in scars and sallow-colored flesh. An old, camouflage shirt minus the sleeves showed tattooed arms muscled by the passion of working out.

"Come on in," he said through parched lips.

Jim stepped in with an awkward gait. Steve motioned to the right where a small, wood dining table sat in the corner with three rickety chairs set around it. He hitched his prosthetic leg into a position to sit, filling one of the chairs with his stout frame. A veteran of Vietnam, Jim was as tough on the inside as he was on the outside.

Steve opened the door of an antique refrigerator, pulled out a chilled bottle of water and took a long swig of it before turning his bloodshot eyes to the patiently waiting Jim.

"Thanks for coming out. Would you like some water?" he mumbled.

Jim shook his head. Steve could see his dark brown eyes scrutinizing him.

"What?" Steve gave him a belligerent stare in return.

226

"You know why you make such a good alcoholic, old buddy? You're passive-aggressive and have poor impulse control."

Steve pulled up another dining room chair, nicked and worn with age. He snorted. "Got all the therapy talk down pat don't you, Jim, old buddy? But, okay, I'll admit proposing on the fly was a bit impulsive, and there wasn't much thought in getting drunk except I was pretty pissed off and I felt like crap. You're probably right. Lay it on. I deserve it all." He sucked at the water bottle like a parched camel.

"You know better than that--I'm not here to lecture. You aren't a kid. Nothing I can say will make a difference. I'm here because you called. What do you need?" Jim settled a large packet on the table next to him.

"Well, you already know I went on a binge yesterday, fell off the wagon. I blew it." He looked up with defiance in his bloodshot eyes. "So what's new? I'm a damn alcoholic: isn't that what we do?"

Jim's thick lips went into a straight line. "Well, yeah, we do that on occasion, but it's not what we want or are proud of. So what do you want?"

The empty water bottle took flight across the room. Steve stood, shoving the chair aside, pacing the small living room of the bunkhouse. "I wanted her to see that I loved her, was willing to change for her. I wanted her to marry me." He stared out the little square-paned window lined with bright red curtains. "I wanted a normal life, to start over. I wanted to have a beer occasionally, and it's not a big deal. I wanted to be normal. That's what I wanted. It's still what I want."

"Okay, so let me get this straight: you got drunk because she rejected you because it didn't work out the way you wanted, and because you can't be normal? You are pissed off, and you're just going to be a drunk now because that's the only thing you know?" There was a sharp edge to his tone. He smoothed back a lock of graying hair. "So I ask again: what do you want, Steve?"

227

Steve stared at Jim as if he had two heads. "I quit drinking because the court said I had to. I was an embarrassment to my family, and they told me I had to quit too."

Jim shrugged. "So you were a good boy and did it for them, right? What about yourself? If you want to drink, then drink. If you want to be sober, then be sober. But don't do it for everyone else and then be mad about it when it don't go your way."

Steve glared at him. "Just tell me what to do and I'll do it."

"That's not how it works, and you know it. You get sober not for your parents, not for your employer, not for your friends, not for your girlfriend."

"This sucks," Steve growled, pacing the room.

Jim watched him, his face devoid of emotion. "So again, I ask: what do you want?"

"I did what I was supposed to, I quit--remember? A whole year of sobriety. That was supposed to make everything better. You tell me what I'm supposed to do now."

"Nope, I can't. You're missing the big picture here. I'm glad you fell off the wagon. You haven't been staying sober for yourself but for everyone else. You were doomed to fail."

Steve's shoulders dropped in defeat. "I just want to be like everyone else. I don't want to be called an addict. I thought if I worked hard at it, everyone would think differently of me-- things would get better. No, I don't want to drink anymore; it's not the answer either. I just want to have a career, a wife, even kids, if God is willing."

Jim's face softened, his voice low and strong. "Now there's the truth of it. When you want to quit because it's something you really want, then you are on the right path. I have a friend who's diabetic. He said that when he was told he could no longer eat anything he wanted, all he could think about was what he couldn't have, and he was mad. He said he went overboard and ate anything he wanted...until he had an insulin episode, almost went into a coma. He felt sorry for himself. He had to change; he no longer could do what he wanted or what others could do. That's just like us. Yeah, we just want to do what we want, be like everyone else. Instead, we have to work at it, reason and deny ourselves what we want most. We all want the easy way out."

Steve froze, staring at him, emotions changing like a color wheel across his face. Jim waited patiently. Flopping back down in the chair, Steve crossed his arms over his chest and stretched his legs out in front of him.

"All right, I drank because I wanted to. Because it tasted good and because for a while I didn't feel like I was going to blow up and smash something. I was angry and felt like crap. I was going to show her that I could do anything I wanted and truthfully, I would do it again."

"Sounds pretty much like all of us. I remember doing the same thing when I got turned down for a job promotion in eighty-eight. Only it took me three months to straighten out and come to my senses. How long is it going to take you?"

Wearily, Steve rubbed at the stubble on his face. "That's why I called. Do you mind taking me into the meeting at noon today? Brad took my truck yesterday."

Jim nodded, a beaming smile stretching his scarred countenance. He waved the packet and note. "I hope this info makes your day a little brighter. Emily gave this to me when I got here. We chatted for a while. She told me what Anna said yesterday; I think that girl is a keeper."

"If she'll ever speak to me again." He got up, crossing the space to grab the packet. Sitting back down, he tore into it to read the welcome letter telling him he had been accepted into the tech school. He opened the small notepaper and recognized the neat scrawl.

Hey Steve,

Hope you are doing better. I want to apologize for not saying goodbye. We still have a lot to talk about. Call or text me, if you make it down here, or stop in and say hi, okay? I have listed my address below.

Anna

Guilt and embarrassment rolled over him. After what he had done, how could she want to talk? Hadn't she made it clear that she didn't want him or marriage? He knew all too well she had never said that she loved him. He didn't know if he could 'just be friends.' But despite his relationship problem right now, he knew one thing for certain: he wanted the schooling.

"I got in. I start in October." He looked up, a tired smile breaking across his cracked lips.

"Never doubted you, buddy. I knew you could do it. Let's get you cleaned up and back on the road to recovery, shall we?"

❀ ❀ ❀ ❀ ❀

Anna steered the agile Vette around the pickup truck, pushing on the gas, shooting the rumbling sports car onto the exit ramp. A green sign flashed by, announcing the approach of Ft. Collins.

"Anna Marie Sanchez, you're going to get a ticket if you keep driving like that," Carolyn announced.

Anna grinned. "Do you need anything from your apartment, since we're down at this end of town?"

"No, I'm fine. They've already started replacing the windows. What I can't figure out is why he had to break every stinking one. What's up with this guy?"

230

Anna stared at the car in front of her. "He can't get to me, so he has to take it out on everyone I know. Are you sure he didn't take anything? You didn't have anything written down anywhere?"

"Nope, nothing missing, just a huge mess. Thanks again for letting me stay with you. And for the record, I think quitting your job was wrong. I understand you thought it was putting the kids at risk, and subbing keeps him guessing as to where you're at, but it's still not right."

"Just part of the game," Anna said with a shrug of her shoulders.

"Did I tell you? I got another apartment just one block from my work."

"He didn't scare you into moving, did he?" Anna glanced at her friend.

"Absolutely not; he just gave me a 'window' of opportunity." She chuckled. "You'll also be happy to know that the security is tight at this complex. Speaking of moving, have you ever thought about living in Wyoming now that you own a ranch and all?"

Anna shook her head. "It's not that simple. But I must admit: I miss the slower paced life there. You never know."

"Aww, I don't want to lose my shopping partner."

"There's more to living, than malls and the newest fashion."

"Oh, you definitely spent too much time in Wyoming. How could you say such a thing?" With a jaunty flip of the steering wheel, tires squealing, Anna turned the corner onto the main artery of town.

"Geez, Anna, can't you drive normally?" Carolyn groused until she looked over to see the young man on the sidewalk grinning, giving them a thumbs-up for the maneuver. "Hey, pull over. I want his phone number."

Anna laughed. "Not today. Besides, I thought you were seeing Joe."

"Are you still having Friday date nights with Chris?" Carolyn countered.

"If you could go on those dates in my place, I'd trade you in a heartbeat, silly girl!"

"Does he still think your date night will draw Miles out?"

"We're hoping he'll take advantage of the only constant in my schedule."

A frown creased Carolyn's brow. "It sucks. You're just being bait."

"I'm a target either way, Carolyn. This way, at least, I've got some control over my life."

"Well, when this is over, I hope you don't mind if I ask him out."

"Be my guest." Anna shook her head at the memory of Chris's empty goodnight kiss. It was then that Anna knew, without any doubt, she still loved Steve. And that wasn't the first clue. When waiting on the phone, or distracted, she found herself doodling his name on everything. Feeling silly, as if it was a first-grade crush but frustrated because he hadn't called her.

"Still haven't heard from Steve?"

Anna glanced at her perceptive friend. "Well, does a text count? He texted he got accepted into the tech school in Loveland and thanked me for the suggestion. That's been it." Her voice held a note of pained irritation.

"Well, give him time."

Flippantly, she threw back, "And how much time do you suggest, Miss Freud?"

Carolyn giggled. "You two will work it out."

Anna accelerated slightly to get through the yellow light, glancing in her rearview mirror and seeing a little white Toyota behind her.

"Carolyn, I know I sound paranoid, but that little white car has been with us since the mall. Have you noticed?"

Carolyn glanced in the side mirror. "I haven't been paying attention, but if you're worried, I can call Chris."

Biting her lower lip, Anna thought for a moment. "No. Let's see if I can lose whoever it is. If not, then we will call. Hold on."

Picking up speed, she turned right again, heading back to the interstate. They were quiet now, both watching the mirrors. The white car slowed, falling back, but still seemed to shadow their moves. She made another quick right onto a two-lane through street, ducking around the late-afternoon Saturday traffic. Several blocks later, there was no sign of the Toyota.

"I'm going to head home, but to be on the safe side, I'll drive around the neighborhood, just to see if we run into anything suspicious."

Carolyn looked out the back window. "I think we're just paranoid. I don't think they were following you. How about we call for pizza delivery tonight?"

"Sounds good to me," Anna said, as she drove into the driveway to the little garage.

As the garage door closed, Anna retrieved shopping bags out of the back of the Corvette, missing the white Toyota that quietly passed by on the street out front.

❀ ❀ ❀ ❀ ❀

Steve glanced around at the familiar faces gathered for the Johnsons' Sunday dinner.

"Here's to a new start on life, and straight A's in the future!" Steve raised a glass, and laughter mingled with the clink of glassware as they all toasted.

Two months had sped by as Steve had helped Seth and Emily get the ranch prepared for winter. With the cows off summer range, and winter feed put up, Steve was now free to move on to school in Colorado.

Cutting into the huge steak on his plate, Brad said, "Hey, leave it to you to find a school that gives grades on taking things apart. You should get straight A's; you're pretty good at that."

A few snickers erupted around the table. Steve smiled. "I'd better be getting good grades, or I'll have to take up another job to pay for tuition. Those grants have some pretty stiff guidelines. So, now to why I asked for all of you to be here tonight. I've been working on Step Nine in AA, and I needed to resolve some things before I leave."

He looked into the curious faces, meeting the dark brown eyes of Mary Beth. "First let me start with you." She looked down at her plate, holding Rob's hand tightly.

"I appreciate all that you did for me. Especially all the times you pulled me out of gutters and kept my brother here from beating me to death."

Brad faked a scowl at him and then started chuckling. "As if you didn't deserve a good thumping."

"Contrary to your beliefs, bro, beating the crap out of somebody doesn't deter poor behavior," Steve intoned in mock seriousness. Laughter greeted their brotherly banter.

Steve shook his head at his brother, continuing. "Anyway, I'm sorry Mary Beth. I wish I could take back all those years you wasted trying to make me into something. I'm sorry I used you and treated you so poorly. I'm happy that Rob's in your life. He's a good man; you deserve him, and he loves you like the loon he is!"

"Hey now," Rob growled playfully. Mary Beth looked at Rob with a soft smile.

"Sorry, I'll miss the wedding, guys. I won't be able to come back at Thanksgiving, but I wanted you to know I am truly sorry for the pain I've put you through. You'll always be part of our family, Mary Beth. Thank you."

The family around the big dining room table clapped and expressed their agreement with Steve's statement.

When the noise had died down, Mary Beth said quietly, "You're welcome and thank you. Apology accepted."

"And Rob, I haven't forgotten about my last drunk and taking a swing at you. Sorry, man. No excuse for that one."

Rob shook his head. "Hey, I understand. I've had a few incidents myself. Forgiven and forgotten." Steve extended his hand, and Rob gave it a quick, firm shake.

"Mom and Dad, you've heard it before, but I'm saying it again with a clean and sober heart: thank you. It's a puny word next to all you've put up with and done, but it has all my heart in it. I will be paying you back every dime. I'm so sorry for all the embarrassment I caused you, all the sleepless nights, and all the heartache. Just, thank you, for hanging in there with me."

Tears glinted in tiny rivers down his mother's face, and Jack held out his hand. "Son, we're just proud of you." Steve grabbed the hand his father extended with both of his hands, and with one strong shake, forgiveness was given and accepted.

He continued, "Brad and Lisa, for all those nights you had to go and pick me up, clean me up and put me up, thank you, and especially to you, bro, for not killing me when you had every right to!"

His brother laughed again, and then, sobering, said, "Forgiven, if you can just stay straight, bro."

"One day at a time. I'm going to do my best."

Steve turned to Chelsea, sitting next to him; her face scrunched in pain. "And Chelsea: for all the times I was late or rude or not there at all when you asked me to be, I'm so sorry, pipsqueak."

Chelsea threw her arms around Steve, pushing her face into his chest, a quick sob escaping. "I don't want you to leave; I want you to stay here."

Steve wrapped his arms around the crying girl, his head resting on her silken tresses, tears shimmering in his hazel eyes.

❁ ❁ ❁ ❁ ❁

The sun announced its rising with an orange-sherbet glow across the eastern horizon. The air had the nip of a freeze in it, leaving its handiwork across the windshield of his pickup. Steve threw the last suitcase into the packed truck and started scraping at the lacy frost.

His father stepped out onto the porch. "Son, before you leave, I need to talk with you."

"Sure, Dad, just a minute."

A few moments later, he was warming his hands on a cup of coffee in a kitchen filled with golden sunshine.

"Your mom had to take Chelsea in early today, so she said to tell you goodbye, and she packed this little snack for you." His father handed him a small picnic basket.

Steve laughed. "Yeah, a snack all right."

"I've never been prouder of you. Wished it wasn't so far away; if you get into any trouble, well...." He hesitated. "I trust that you aren't, but we're not going to be around."

"Precisely, Dad, which is why I chose this path. I need to be out, away and on my own."

His father nodded. "I agree. It's a wise decision. You've put a lot of thought into this. You plan on seeing Anna while you're down there?"

"I've got to apologize to her, and I don't know where it will go from there. I've prayed a lot about this. You know, she's never

236

told me she loves me, but I know she cares. I know she's the one. I love her, Dad. But I'm going to wait on the Lord to open or close the door this time. So far, this move is looking like the right direction. How'd you know Mom was the one?"

Jack looked at him for a quiet second. "We were best friends, Son. We took it gradually, took our time, and kept praying. And as you said, all the doors opened. We were two halves that made a whole. That's all I can tell you."

Steve stared out the window. "Well, it's unlike anything I've ever felt before. I cared about Mary Beth, but I didn't feel this. I miss Anna, can't stop thinking about her even now. We get along so well, can talk about anything, and have so much in common. I've never known anyone like her. I don't want anything or anyone to hurt her. I've never felt this protective, except for my sister and mom."

Jack looked into the dark pit of his coffee. "Well, it sounds pretty serious. I think the world of Anna, and if she's the one for you, I'm behind you. Leave it up to the Lord. You're in our prayers. We'll support any decision you make. You know that, right?"

"Yeah, thanks, Dad." Steve stepped up to give him a bear hug, turning away quickly, hiding the threat of tears in his eyes but also missing the tears welling in his father's eyes.

237

Robynn Gabel

Chapter 17 – Reconnect

The clatter of silverware meeting plates, and soft music--mixed with various voices--created a cacophonous sound. Like everything else in the city, it made Steve feel hemmed in, crowded.

Pleasantly, he asked, "May I take your order?" The elderly couple popped their heads up over the menu, reminding him of a pair of alert Meerkats. They both wanted to know about the special, and then they ordered.

He moved quickly around the crowded, black-lacquered tables to the kitchen, picking up empty dishes along the way. The service door swung busily with a steady stream of waiters and waitresses. The popular downtown restaurant in Ft. Collins served Italian cuisine, including a spaghetti Steve didn't think he'd ever get enough of. Its walls were paneled and painted olive green, mustard and burgundy, giving it a rich atmosphere. Putting the order in, he returned to the table with bread and drinks. He enjoyed his new work routine. His outgoing personality helped him earn plenty of tips.

"So you doing anything after work?" a dark headed, bearded Sam queried between their runs to the kitchen.

"Yeah, I've got a date with an engine manual. You?"

"You work too hard! Why don't you hang with us after the shift? There's a new club around the corner that opened like a month ago that's supposed to be pretty good."

"Thanks, but I've really got to study Sorry."

Sam shrugged. "Well, there's next week."

Steve's order was called up. He headed out the door with a heavy-laden tray. Looking over the crowd, he suddenly recognized a familiar face and his heart skipped faster. He smoothly delivered the plates to the couple. "Is there anything else I can get you?"

The Meerkat man peered over his large glasses. "More bread if you don't mind." Steve nodded, turning with the tray, glancing over his shoulder toward the table near the door. There was no mistaking Anna; her features were burned into his memory. Had it been only three months since he'd seen her? It didn't seem that long at this moment.

Escaping back into the kitchen, he leaned against the wall, his heart now in full race mode. He grabbed at Sam's arm as he went by.

"Hey, Sam, you waiting on table two?"

"Yeah, they come in every Friday, like clockwork. Why?"

Steve shook his head. "Just wondering."

"Well, good luck getting her attention off Mr. Model Man." Sam grabbed another order and pushed through the door.

Picking up a basket of bread, Steve took a deep breath and headed back out. Surreptitiously, he stole glances her way every chance he had. She sat with her back to the dining room, the tiny, silver light above the table setting off her creamy skin. Ruby highlights glinted in her hair as she gazed out the large window to the busy street. Her date looked like someone out of a commercial

240

for an expensive perfume, his eyes darting around the restaurant, seemingly more interested in the crowd than Anna.

"May I take your order?" he asked two young ladies. The blond gazed up from under heavy mascaraed lashes with a flirtatious smile while he tried to stay focused, keeping out of Anna's line of sight.

Her redheaded companion asked in a nasal tone, "What's the special?"

Steve rattled off the choices of the evening, adding, "But my personal favorite is the spaghetti. The marinara sauce is out of this world."

"I'll try it. And did you know you look like my first husband?" the blond asked, chortling.

Steve stared for a second. "Ma'am?"

She giggled. "I'm not married yet. Are you?"

He laughed nervously. "No, just a starving student trying to make a wage. I'll be right back with your drinks." As he turned towards the kitchen, he glanced again towards Anna.

A myriad of emotions flooded him each time he saw her. First, relief that she looked well: her arm free of the cast, her laughter as musical as he remembered. Then, worry: what if she saw him? What would he say? Then, jealousy: that one surprised him. He wanted to be the one across from her, because no matter how good-looking that guy was, he wasn't good enough for her. As she turned to glance around the restaurant, he ducked quickly into the kitchen, losing track of what he needed to do.

"Man, you're preoccupied tonight. You almost took me out there, buddy," Sam remarked, smoothly moving his loaded tray away from the swinging door.

"Sorry," Steve mumbled.

Venturing forth again, he brought out an order, picking up dishes and reading her body language from across the room. She appeared relaxed, but her legs were crossed, she angled away from her date, and her hands were on her lap under the table. She was being polite, not totally engaged with the man across from her. Steve remembered how she used to lean into him to listen, her arms on the table. When she'd talk, her hands fiddled with things, or she would gesture with them in excitement.

He came back into the dining room after leaving an order with the cook, noticing Anna was gone and immediately felt the void her absence left. It had been a long forty-five minutes. Now, memories percolated at the back of his mind as he went on with his shift. He'd put off seeing or contacting her because he feared being rejected again. He needed to apologize, to ask for forgiveness for hurting her during his relapse. But would she let him back into her life?

"Steve, are you sure you don't want to go out with us? You've been out of it all night; I doubt you're going to get much studying done in that frame of mind. Take a break, buddy. I think you need one," Sam wheedled.

"Thanks, some other time maybe. I just need to go to bed early for a change."

"Okay, but you're missing out. See you tomorrow night."

The crisp night air was fresh with the scent of mountain pine, erasing the smells of restaurant cuisine. He took a deep breath, trying to clear his mind. He knew taking a job in Ft. Collins might put him in a position to see Anna, but it had not been his intent. He'd based the decision on pay and job availability. He hadn't received any responses from job applications in Loveland. When the restaurant job came up, his friend from AA put in a good word for him and helped him to cinch it.

By the truck dome light, he checked the street address on the very creased and worn note from Anna. He located her house one night, when he had nothing to do, finding it was only a twenty-minute drive into Ft. Collins from Loveland.

The traffic was light, and the beat to his favorite music lightened his mood. He didn't know what he was going to do when he got there, but he felt drawn to drive by her house again. He'd struggled with how to reconnect, but tonight a door had opened. It was a sure sign he should try.

Pulling up to the curb, he cut the headlights and engine. A wan, yellowish glow squeezed around the drawn curtain, a dim light illuminating the porch. An older, silver compact car squatted in the driveway. He wasn't sure if it was her car, but he couldn't imagine the Superman of good looks owning anything that drab. There was no sign of her Vette, but he suspected it was hiding in the single-car garage. With his heart racing again, he sat trying to get up the nerve. He crossed his arms on the large steering wheel, resting his head against them. It was late. Maybe tomorrow. Maybe he should just text her, maybe….

A flashing red light, which reflected off his window and side-view mirror, brought him out of his thoughts. He looked up, seeing in the glare of headlights behind him, the figure of a cop rising out of the cruiser parked behind his car.

"Great," he groaned. What had he done? No parking zone? He glanced around, noting other cars parked on the street. His tags were current in Wyoming, and he knew he had time yet to apply in Colorado for a new license and plates. What was the problem?

There was a tap on the window; he rolled it down, receiving the glare of a flashlight shining into his eyes.

"License and registration, please, sir," a gruff voice commanded.

"Uh, yeah, just a second. Is there a problem?" Steve reached for his wallet, searching for his license, his mind panicking when he couldn't find it. Where had he last used it? Oh great, this morning at the bank. Did I put it back into my wallet?

"Hmmm, I don't have my license, sir. I think…."

The cop abruptly cut him off. "Out of the truck, now please."

Worry began to build. "Officer, I'm sorry, what is this about?"

"Just get out of the vehicle, now." He quietly called a series of numbers into a little black microphone clipped to his lapel. Steve slid out of the truck. The cop reached out, grabbing his arm.

"Up against the truck with your hands on the hood, sir. Legs apart please."

Steve gave up questioning, instead following the directions, fear setting in.

A neighbor woman, wrapped in a thick house robe, stepped out onto the porch, watching as another police cruiser pulled over in front of Steve's truck, more flashing lights illuminating the scene vividly. Voices crackled over receivers in both cruisers.

Steve looked towards Anna's home, seeing the curtain move to the side slightly, a dog barking loudly. Great. She can't miss me now.

"Sir, I need to know why you were parked out here on the curb," the gruff voice commanded again.

He hesitated. "I was trying to decide whether to visit a friend."

"Do you realize what time it is, sir?" The second officer was now going through the truck. Finding the registration, he returned to his cruiser.

"Have you had anything to drink in the way of alcoholic beverages tonight?" the voice behind him continued.

Steve's temper flared; he whirled to face the bulky cop. "No! What in the hell is the problem...?"

The officer moved rapidly, roughly seizing Steve's arm, twisting it up behind his back, and shoving him up against the truck. Steve heard a click and then felt the cold metal of a handcuff ensnare a wrist while his other wrist was grabbed and pulled around to be trapped by its match.

"What the hell have I done?" Steve snarled.

A black sedan pulled up, a single flashing light on the driver's side. Anna's date of the evening emerged gracefully, staring intently towards Steve. He spoke into his phone, "No, it's not him. It's someone from Wyoming."

Several more neighbors had gathered now, watching quietly.

The first officer had pushed him face down on the hood of his truck. Steve could feel cold metal under his cheek as he stared towards the house. The door flew open; Anna ran down the steps, and a lean yellow dog followed at her heels. She stopped to look at the scene, her eyes widening. He watched as recognition of the truck dawned in her eyes; then she looked at him. She took off again, running around the truck, pushing at the officer.

"No, no. He's not Miles. This is Steve Johnson."

The cop released him, stepping back. Steve straightened up off the truck, turning, leaning into it. Anna threw her arms around his neck; tears wet on her cheeks. The dog jumped up, putting its paws on his leg.

"Steve!"

✿✿✿✿✿

"Well, I can see I shouldn't have been worried about Anna coming back here. That was quite an arrest!" Steve chuckled while fondling the silken ears of the golden dog against his leg.

He wondered if the detective ever smiled as Chris's intense gaze swung towards him. "The call came in from a very active neighborhood watch group here. They are a big help to our department with this situation. Thank you for handling this so well, Steve. I appreciate your understanding of the circumstances."

"Teach you to lurk in the night, won't it, Sherlock?" Anna's eyes shone bright, despite the late hour. "Why didn't you just come to the door?" The dog left Steve's gentle administrations to brush up against Anna, her golden, feathered tail softly thumping against her leg. She leaned down to capture the gentle face between her hands, looking into adoring eyes.

Steve shrugged uncomfortably. "I wasn't sure if you would want to see me after my… rudeness at the barn raising."

Anna looked up, leaning forward, her blue eyes soft with forgiveness. "Didn't my note tell you anything?"

Chris watched their interaction silently, his face devoid of emotion. "Anna, if Steve is going to be an active part of your life, he'll have to follow the protocol we have set up. You will have to let me know where you two will be at. You can add him to the schedule of check-in calls as well."

Anna cocked her head to the side, a mischievous glint in her eye. "Well, it depends on whether Sherlock here can get up enough nerve to call or text me. If I remember right, we did agree on a real dinner date."

Between the two of them, Steve felt as if he was under interrogation. He straightened up in his chair, squaring his shoulders, directing his attention to the brunette minx in front of him. "I'm willing to be part of anything that will take this Miles character out of your life. I would love to take you to dinner, Anna Sanchez, anytime you are willing. Just pick the place."

"Well, they are having free hot dogs down at the Chevy dealership tomorrow if you want to go?" She giggled.

Steve had missed their sparring, feeling a little rusty. "No, Anna. A real dinner, remember? No potlucks either."

"Well, after all of this excitement, I need a quick minute; I'll be right back, gentlemen." She headed off down the hall to the bathroom. The dog followed her with a click of toenails on the wooden floor and a waving tail.

Chris's smooth voice broke the silence, "So how long have you known her?"

"I met her five months ago when she needed work done at the ranch." Steve watched Chris's expressionless face, catching a flicker of emotion.

"I could tell by her greeting outside, she is quite fond of you, and Delilah seems to trust you as well." Suddenly, in a panther-like move, he leaned across the table with a fierce glare, speaking in a low, threatening tone. "This girl deserves a break. Know this: if you hurt her in any way, you'll have me to deal with. Understood?"

Steve stared steadily back, understanding fully the jealousy in Chris's expression a moment before. "I'd never hurt her, and will stay only as long as she wants me to. You have my word on that."

Anna stepped out of the bathroom, joining them, her smile radiating delight. "I'm so glad the two of you got to meet, even if it was under such circumstances."

"Well, I'll be on my way. I think we've covered all the bases here. Welcome aboard, Steve. We can always use more support in this problem. You know what is needed now, and you'll be a great asset to us. Remember: the key to this is communication. Anna, see you next Friday at our usual time." Chris looked pointedly at Steve and then ducked out into the night, Anna resetting the alarm after him.

She turned to him. "I can't believe you're here! How long have you been in Colorado? Where are you staying? Really, why haven't you called before now?"

Steve laughed, holding up his hands. "One question at a time, lady! Let's see…I've been here a couple of weeks, started school right away. Jim set me up with some friends of his and I'm staying with them until I can get an apartment." He grew serious. "I told you: I didn't know if you wanted to see me. I haven't called because I needed to talk to you in person."

He sat across from her at the small, cozy wooden dining table, feeling complete, content and not wanting this moment to end. The dog plopped at his feet with a sigh.

Anna looked under the table at the dog. "I can't believe she acts like she has known you all her life."

"Where did you get her?"

"It's a long story, but she's a rescue dog, and she picked me to be her owner."

"She's beautiful. What's her name?

"Delilah."

Tenderly, Steve smiled, getting the connection right away.

"You're looking so good, Steve. I mean, healthy, happy." She blushed, looking away.

"I've been busy, but missing you."

She looked down, tracing a little design on the tabletop. Steve took a big breath, diving in.

"Anna, you already know this, and I wish I had trusted you, telling you first thing, but I'm an alcoholic. The meetings I go to are Alcoholic Anonymous meetings. That lawyer I referred you to was the one that helped me when I got my second DUI. After I had learned your father was killed by a drunk driver, I was afraid you'd have nothing to do with me. I was sober for over a year until the day of the barn raising. I was hurt, angry because you rejected my offer of marriage. That was absolutely no excuse for me to go off on a drunk. I see now it wasn't the right time, I didn't want to lose you, hoped you would stay if I proposed. Can you forgive me? I can't make any promises, but I want to change, be a different person. I would like you to be in my life again."

He held his breath, his heart hammering, waiting for her answer. She'd propped herself up on her elbows, face in her hands, watching him closely as he talked. She leaned back, her hands flat on the table now, taking a deep breath, letting it out in an audible, "phff."

"Well, since we are finally being totally honest with each other, I owe you an apology too. Remember I said my father was killed in a drunk-driving accident? I didn't tell you he was the one drunk and driving. He killed not only himself, but also two others, a young couple. He left behind two orphans that day, besides leaving me. My mother told me when I was ten. I remember being hurt, and angry that he didn't love Mom or me enough to be sober for us. I went to Al-Anon for many years, and I still catch a meeting now and then. I knew about your drinking problem, but I always give someone a chance to show me who they are. I don't believe in labeling people. We can rise above any handicap. I wanted to give you a chance, and for you to trust me enough to share it with me."

Steve looked long and hard at her, trying to figure out if he was frustrated with her, or happy to be in her presence again. "Okay-- a new day, new start. How's that?"

"Agreed!"

"I've got a meeting tomorrow, so I need to get going. I'll call you, and we can get together if you're free." Steve stood to leave, hoping that it was yearning he saw in her crystalline blue eyes.

She hesitated. "You don't have to leave, and it's late. The sofa makes into a sleeper."

He arched an eyebrow. "Stay here? What will the neighbors think?"

"Not much. This isn't like Lander. Besides, Carolyn is staying in the spare bedroom and will be home in half an hour."

Delilah stood, wagging her tail, looking up at him with soft, brown eyes that seemed to be begging him to stay.

"Okay." He flipped open his cell phone, making a quick call to his host in Loveland.

She grabbed sheets, blankets and a pillow from a hall closet, and headed to the plump sofa. He grabbed the cushions, stacking them neatly beside the couch. Within minutes, they had put together the bed.

"Would you like a cup of tea or something to drink, or do you just want to go to bed?" Anna asked shyly. She seemed as uncertain as he was feeling. With her so close, after all that time, sleep was the last thing on his mind.

"Tea sounds great." He followed her to the kitchen, leaning against the counter, watching her move with the grace he remembered. The silence between them tangible, quick looks sent back and forth. He wracked his brain for something to say, not knowing where to start. She went past him, heading for the table, and he could stand it no longer. He reached out, gently catching her arm.

He looked down into her upturned face, his finger hesitantly touching her cheek. She slipped her arms around his waist, resting her face against his chest, a gentle sigh leaving her.

Wrapping his arms around her, he pressed his cheek against her hair. The delicate fragrance that belonged only to her filled his heightened senses. As a man in the desert, dying of thirst, he greedily drank in the feel and smell of her. He felt whole again, a sense of well-being settling throughout him.

She looked up at him, her eyes the color of a calm mountain lake, desire unmistakable in their depths. He reached his finger to bring up her chin, leaning down to test her soft lips with his. He fully sampled her eager response, feeling every sense coming alive with the electric yearning to hold her forever.

She responded, moving in against him. He gave a little gasp and gathered her closer. One hand slid down to the small of her back, his other sliding up into her satiny hair, and lacing his fingers in it; he pulled her lips in closer. A tiny moan slipped from deep in her throat.

He suddenly stiffened, his hand dropping to her shoulders, ever so gently pushing her away to stare into her eyes, his voice sounding husky to him. "We have to stop before I take what is not mine to take."

She stepped away, taking a deep breath herself. "You can't take what I willingly offer." He'd never seen this look before, her eyes enigmatic. He hesitated, feeling shaken.

"I love you, Anna Sanchez. I'm willing to wait until you're ready. I won't be making that mistake again. This is your call."

The alarm system clicked, unlocked, and the front door opened. Steve sighed.

"Anna, whose truck…oh!" Carolyn's face was comic with surprise.

"Carolyn, you're home early. I'd like you to meet Steve Johnson."

"The one and only Steve Johnson, the one I've heard so much about? The one I've been wishing would call my stubborn friend?"

"Carolyn!" Anna grimaced.

Steve held out his hand. "Yes, I'm the cad."

Carolyn shook his hand, a giggle escaping.

"You are a lot more handsome than she described."

Anna rolled her eyes, a huff of exasperation escaping.

"He'll be spending the night on the couch if you don't mind, Carolyn."

"No, I don't, not at all. Welcome, Mr. Johnson. Make yourself at home."

Steve caught the sly wink she sent Anna as she flounced into her room, calling a good night.

"Like I've said before, lady, it's a good thing we keep getting interrupted," Steve said, his smile ending in little crinkles at the corner of his eyes.

Robynn Gabel

Chapter 18 - Fate

Miles Rannet was the perfect example of what fate was: just a string of very small coincidences occurring in an improbable chain reaction. Like the day Ben Sanchez left his friend's house drunk, to climb in behind the wheel of the car that would become a weapon of death. The two little orphans left behind didn't know that they would be forever linked--with the now fatherless child--through one coincidence after another.

"Take one more bite, sis. You gotta," he whined.

She closed her eyes tight in pain, her lips in a firm line, a blue-veined hand waving him away. He stared helplessly at the clear tubing delivering the chemo, a toxic combination of chemicals that seemed to be doing more damage than good.

He pushed away the tray containing the untouched lunch and sat by her recliner in misery. The invisible hand of cancer was slowly squeezing the life from her. She was all he had left, the only one who'd ever loved him

When their parents were killed, they'd been taken in by an aging grandmother and passed on after her death to an uncle who couldn't have cared less about what happened to them. Theresa, three years older than Miles, had lovingly filled the role of mom.

She'd been diagnosed with breast cancer only a year ago. The outlook was grim as it had metastasized but she started chemotherapy with the hope of beating it. He snuck in to see her during treatments because he knew she was being watched. They would meet in unlikely places like movie theatres or shopping malls.

Theresa stirred, coughing, her eyes wearily opening to peer at him dully. "Water," she rasped.

He hurried to bring the straw up to her peeling lips. After a few swallows, she took a breath. "You know I love you, but I'm tired, really tired."

Jerking his head back and forth, he refused to accept her words.

"Have you taken your medication today? Remember, you promised."

He shook his head yes, but didn't look her in the eye.

"Okay, then you need to go and tell the police you made a mistake. Please, for me." She struggled to breathe, the words taking all her strength to put forth.

Licking his bulbous, pink lips, he set them in a stubborn line. He watched as she squinted, her pale blue eyes working to focus on his features, pity shining in them.

Taking another shuddering breath, she labored to speak. "Please, promise me you'll turn yourself in. Forget that girl. She isn't worth it."

❀ ❀ ❀ ❀ ❀

Anna watched Delilah run down the path, tail waving behind like a feathered flag. Steve hunched his shoulders under the leather coat, the brisk wind causing a chill. The autumn leaves had fallen long ago, leaving only a few stragglers left to complain drily in the breeze. Delilah ducked off the path, picking up a scent in a bush that was just a bunch of burgundy sticks.

Walking hand in hand along the path, Anna leaned into Steve's side. "I'm taking the Vette in this Saturday to Pete; he's going to do the final fall tune-up on it. I should have done it sooner, but things have been a little hectic. It's probably my last chance to drive it this year."

"Then you're back to your little Ford. Such a traitor you are, driving a Ford," he teased, looking down at her.

"Have you been down and seen the new Z06 at the Chevy dealer?"

He sighed. "No, I don't dare until I get the student loans paid off."

"Dinner still on for Monday night? What should I wear?" Her cheeks smarted in the brisk wind.

"Do you really have to wear anything?" Steve moved out of her way as she went to swing at him playfully. "It's nothing fancy. You're beautiful in anything."

"I still don't know why you can't let me in on the secret."

"It's just something a few friends are helping with, so just enjoy, Watson."

Her blue eyes studied him, trying to get a hint, but Steve looked away towards the exploring Lab.

"So how did your first test go?"

"Outside of missing the question about the airbag, I did well. I can't believe I missed that one. So many of the systems are interconnected nowadays. I never thought I'd have to know anything about airbags!"

"In my Vette, all it takes is about fifteen miles an hour to pop an airbag on impact, and in my Ford, it's about ten."

She noticed Steve staring at her. "What?"

He shook his head. "Now why would you ever need to know such a thing?"

"Because I've thought about what I'd do if Miles ever grabbed me in the car. I'd ram it into something, and when the airbags deployed, I would escape. Why?"

Anna watched Steve's lips clamp into a tight line, his jaw squaring. "It irritates me you'd have to think of things like that. I'd still like to get my hands on him."

"I hope you don't. I wouldn't want you to go to jail for the rest of your life: he's not worth it."

He looked at her with what she thought of as his 'thinking' look. His brows slightly drawn, his lips pursed, and his eyes serious.

"Would you ever think of living somewhere else?"

"I don't know. I'd like someplace that has at least one good snowstorm before Halloween."

"So Colorado gets the same Halloween snowstorm Wyoming gets every year?" Steve's eyes twinkled with humor.

"Oh, yes. I remember one year being a princess and having so many layers on I didn't need anything to poof out the skirt!"

"But you didn't answer my question. Would you live anywhere else?"

"You're thinking of Wyoming aren't you. I don't know. I grew up here. Know my way around." She stared off towards the mountains that rose on the skyline.

"Do you think this is the best place to raise kids?"

"Now you're hitting below the belt." She smiled. "Okay, yes, I have thought about other places to live."

"Well, it's just something to think about." His expression was enigmatic.

"Delilah," she called. The Lab returned low to the ground, legs flashing, to bounce up onto Anna at the last minute. They had walked the entire path in the little nature reserve ending back at the parking lot. "Well, I'm off to meet Carolyn to go grocery shopping. I will call you when I get there."

Anna felt his warm hands cradle her face as he lowered his head to lightly kiss her, a tingle spreading through her limbs as she returned the favor.

"Just drive carefully, okay?" Steve murmured.

❀ ❀ ❀ ❀ ❀

Sitting in the parked car under the shade tree, Miles mindlessly devoured hamburgers as his bulging eyes skimmed page after page of the diary feverishly. "Even hate is just another side of love. It is the burnt crust left after losing or being rejected from love. It is the lack of love, yet the knowledge of love. Hate in its purest form is just the underside of love. And hate can be melted by the gentlest of love."

He chewed on his pink lip. *What the hell did that mean? Why does she have to talk in riddles, write worthless poems? Couldn't she just say that she loves me?*

Miles felt stabbed over and over by what he'd read in her diary. Though she didn't profess love for anyone else, he frantically searched for written proof of the love he was convinced she felt for him. He sought for only one thing in his beleaguered existence: love.

"Denial is an emotion that in its own right can be blinder than love." He struggled to accept what Anna had written earlier, that she despised him. Miles fought against the hatred that was trying to replace his all-consuming love for her.

He folded all his trash methodically, setting it next to his neat stack of notebooks on the seat. Starting the car, he shot out into traffic, a horn blaring at him for cutting it so close. Miles sneered into the mirror. Driving by the apartment Carolyn had recently vacated, he smiled. She'd been an easy target. When he broke the first window, it felt so good he decided to break them all but only after he had the information he searched for.

In a quick, messy search, he'd discovered she scribbled all her important appointments on the calendar hanging on the fridge. Under the column 'Saturday,' he found what he was looking for.

Two o'clock-Mall-Movies-Anna.

❀ ❀ ❀ ❀ ❀

In the lull between September and Thanksgiving, the large party room in the restaurant was usually empty, waiting for a reception or the holiday season to fill it. Tonight, in its spacious center, a single table sat, with gleaming silverware, wine glasses, and posh plates. Several garlands of tiny white lights hung around the room. Columns and trellises left over from a recent wedding gave a romantic backdrop. It was to this table Sam escorted Anna and Steve for dinner.

Anna caught on right away that Sam was in on the plot. She recognized him from Friday night dates with Chris in this very same restaurant.

"Oh Steve, this is so special. Thank you!"

Steve flashed her favorite eye-crinkling smile, as he nodded to Sam.

"Miss Anna Sanchez, may I present your first real date with Mr. Steve Johnson," Sam said in his best professional tone, ending with a flourish of his hand and a bow.

She inclined her head regally, but couldn't keep a straight face, breaking into a giggle. "How'd you pull this off?"

Steve leaned in conspiratorially. "I had some good inside help, plus we are always dead on Mondays. I can recommend several things if you'd like."

Sam shook his head. "Hey, that's my job. You're the customer, remember?"

Anna watched as Steve worked to stiffen his features into a formal look. "Yes, I would like to hear the specials for the night."

Turning to Anna, Sam asked, "I want to know how he convinced you to have a date with him over that other guy you come in with all the time. You can't think he's that handsome!"

"You're just jealous you didn't have the nerve to ask her, Sam. Don't insult the lady's tastes, just take our order."

The ordering process went quickly. Anna enjoyed the light banter between Steve and his co-worker. The door swung closed with a quiet swish.

"I brought some sparkling apple cider just for this occasion, and it was in my price range as a starving student." He opened the bottle with flare, pouring the light amber liquid into wineglasses. She noticed his thin, artistic hands, the nails neatly trimmed, at odds with his vocation of mechanics. There were so many little mannerisms, so many things about him she could watch for hours.

The flickering candlelight reflected in his eyes. She loved the hazel color that would change to fit the hues around him. Right now they looked gray and were watching her intently. *So I wonder if he's going to ask again because this time the answer is yes.*

She had finally admitted it to herself the night he had slept on her couch. Anna wanted to spend the rest of her life with Steve. She hadn't gotten much sleep thinking of him, so excited he had come back into her life.

"I was wondering: are you uncomfortable talking about your father?"

She hesitated for a second. "No, why?"

He looked down, his lithe fingers picking apart a dinner roll. "I was just curious about your family. You don't ever talk about them."

"I didn't grow up with much family around. I guess it was mostly my mom and me against the world. I learned to take care of myself pretty early on. It wasn't that Mom didn't take good care of me; I just had to be independent with her being a single mom and sole supporter." Anna was curious as to what he was searching for.

"What about your father's parents?"

"Well, my grandfather met my grandmother when he was stationed at the Marine base in Yuma, Arizona. She came across the border on a work visa, worked in a little restaurant in San Luis. She got pregnant, and they got married, but after the baby was born, she ran back to her family in Mexico. So Grandpa Don sent my father, Ben, up to live with his parents in Riverton, Wyoming. Grandpa Don joined my father later after he worked through the problems he had with drugs and alcohol. My mother and father met at a football game between Riverton and Lander. Talk about your small-town rivalries! Anyway, she became pregnant with me. They ran away together to Fort Collins where my father had some friends. And here I am today."

She wondered at the emotions moving across Steve's face as she recited her scant family history. The salad arrived; he continued his questions.

"Didn't you miss having brothers or sisters? Why didn't your mother ever re-marry?

"She said it was because the right one never showed up again. Mom was artistic and a dreamer. She flitted to one thing after another, though we always managed to get by on her teaching salary. And of course, I wished I'd had brothers and sisters. I envied my classmates. I envy you having Brad and Chelsea. That's probably why I like children."

"Hmpf, I'll give Brad to you. He can be your brother."

"Steve! You know you love him."

"Yeah, it's a love-hate relationship for sure." He arched an eyebrow, tilting his head to the side, again watching her. When he gazed at her that way, with such intimacy reflected in his eyes, she felt as if she was the center of his world. The heat of a blush rose, she looked away.

"Well, I think you are fortunate to have such a wonderful family. I love Chelsea. Can I ask you a personal question?" She took a bite of her lasagna, waiting for his response.

He laid down his fork, reaching for his glass. "Well since this is our first date, and we're supposed to get to know each other, I say, sure, go for it."

"When did you start drinking?"

Steve grimaced. "I knew you'd ask, just didn't think it would be tonight. But fair is fair-- probably when I was fourteen. That's the first time I got drunk. How about you?"

Her eyes widened in surprise. "Me? I've never gotten drunk. I don't like the taste or smell of beer. I haven't found a wine I like either. But that's just me."

He shot her a quizzical look. "Well, I guess I'm safe with you then." They both started laughing. His hand reached across the table to grasp hers. *How can just his touch make me feel so weak?*

Sobering, his eyes dark, he continued, "I've given my drinking a lot of thought these last few months. First it was just to be cool, to fit in; then it became something to do. Then I just wanted to drink to drink. Then I started getting into trouble. My family began coming down on me, which I deserved. I drank to escape the problems. But it started affecting everything in my life. I thought it would make me feel better. It was a vicious circle. I couldn't make it through a week without having to drink. If I had one, I had to have more. After my D.U.Is, I was court ordered into treatment,

261

and there I learned some coping tools. I started trying to dig myself out."

"I think you've done well. It can't be easy to do," she murmured.

He let go of her hand as Sam interrupted, "Can I get you anything else this evening?"

"No, thank you. That was delicious! Can I get the recipe?" Anna gave him a teasing smile.

"Well, the only way you can get the recipe is to work here, and then you can never quit," Sam answered with a charming smile in return.

"Come on, Sam, you had your chance the last few weeks and didn't have the courage to ask. No fair flirting now," Steve said, challenge in his eyes.

"You didn't tell me you had a head start! Hey, Anna, if he ever gives you a hard time, let me know: I always have extra dishes for him to wash!"

"Yeah, right." Steve handed him payment for the dinner in the black credit card holder.

Anna slipped her arm into the coat Steve offered. "What a gentleman you are, Sherlock."

"Ah, my favorite nickname. It makes me feel so smart, except when it comes to you." Steve slipped his arm around her waist, holding her close as they walked to the truck.

"Well, at least we haven't had to do mirror therapy lately, so I think you're figuring it out."

He leaned his head into her, laughing as he opened the door, helping her in.

Anna noted he skillfully negotiated the busy, nighttime traffic. "You've mastered city driving pretty well for a country boy."

"Thank you. I've spent some time learning all the shortcuts too. It's just a grid of sorts. But it tests my patience."

"Well, I noticed I had to speed up and get back into the swing of things when I got back here." She grinned.

Anna's cell phone came alive musically. She answered as Steve pulled up in front of the house. Jumping out of the truck, he opened her door, waiting.

"Hi, Carolyn. Yes, we just got here. Oh, no! When did that happen? I'm sorry, Carolyn. No, I understand. We can go some other time. Well, take care of yourself and travel safely. I'll keep you and your grandmother in my prayers." Anna folded her cell phone closed. She slid out of the truck, Steve slipping his arm over her shoulder as they walked to the house.

"What was that about?" Steve asked.

"Carolyn's grandmother fell and broke a hip. She is going down to Colorado Springs this weekend to be with her. Darn! We were going to go to the show on Saturday. I wanted to see that movie too. So it looks like I'll have to wait; hopefully, it's here for a while yet."

"Well, I can cut the AA meeting a little short. If you just want to meet me at the parking garage, I can go with you."

The porch light shone down on them in the cold winter twilight. "Oh, that would be great! Sure it's not going to cut into the meeting? What if it runs long?" She leaned into his chest, bringing up both hands and clasping them together to keep warm.

He smiled down at her, encircling her with his arms, hugging her closer. "I'll be okay. They have a meeting on Wednesday night also."

"That would be great! I'll pay since you are a starving student and all. See you there; I'll call when I leave. And thank you; tonight was wonderful."

Delilah scratched and whined on the other side of the door, hearing their voices.

"You'd better get in there before she tears the place apart. So just a quick kiss tonight, lady. No tempting me beyond what I can handle," he said, a wicked gleam in his eyes.

❀ ❀ ❀ ❀ ❀

Miles vigorously scrubbed the red, compact car's tacky carpet. Once beige, it was now becoming a sickly gray as the dirt and grime bubbled up in the carpet cleaner. Miles had on two pairs of rubber gloves, protecting his pudgy hands. A face mask protected him from the fumes of the chemicals he feared. He worked for a swarthy, used-car dealer, cleaning and transporting cars and being night security. In return, he got paid a little cash under the table and use of a small shack out back, which suited both him and his shady employer.

Done with the car, he stripped off gloves and mask and headed to the shack. A 1950s calendar hung askew on graying walls, a tidily made cot snugged into a corner. Even with the age of the building, it had a compulsively organized look to it, nothing out of place in the tiny kitchen in the corner opposite the cot. One chair and end table occupied the corner opposite the door. Changing out of his mechanic's overalls, he pulled a suitcase out from under the cot, picking out a change of clothes. Taking a key out of his pocket, he smoothed a stubby finger over it.

Fitting it into a lock in the door next to the kitchen, he opened it into a tiny bedroom off the main room. On the left wall was a collage of pictures, Anna the subject in all of them. A twin-size bed with a flowered coverlet and bright, plump pillows sat against the right wall. There were no windows; the dim bulb hanging from the sagging ceiling cast the ghost of a wan light in the room. Next to the bed, a nightstand with a vase of bright, fake flowers was the only decoration. A portable commode sat in the corner opposite to the bed and a colorful throw rug filled in the tiny floor space. From the leg of the sturdy bed, a chain lay curled in a perfect coil, a metal cuff at the end of it, waiting for its captive. Running his hand over the pictures on the wall, he smiled, licking his lips. Glancing one more time around the room, he locked the door behind him carefully.

Tonight he had the use of the compact car; it needed to be on the lot by morning. Finishing, he closed up the maintenance shop, checked the doors to the little office, locked the chain to the lot and he was free for the night.

On the clean seat lay a thick notebook. It was full of notes, dates and observations. He'd figured out which neighbors called in on the neighborhood watch; he recognized all the undercover cars, knew the hours when it was the best to spy and had access to many different cars, making Miles almost invisible.

Opening the trunk of the compact, he threw in a black sports bag filled with gadgets he'd bought to eavesdrop with; he sometimes caught snatches of phone conversations. He fancied himself a connoisseur of disguises and had used them to do things such as walk stolen dogs up and down the street. Several times, he'd even hired himself out to sweet Mrs. Dover to trim her bushes and mow her lawn. Miles spent more time in this neighborhood than in the dingy shack at the used-car dealership.

Zipping out into traffic, he began his methodical search. Though Anna tried hard to vary her schedule, she still had her favorite spots. Miles had managed to put a tracking bug on her Vette while in Wyoming, as well as her silver Ford when he broke into her house last summer. All he had to do was tune into the GPS signal. But when she wasn't driving her car, it became detective work. He'd check out her preferred places where he'd look for her friend's cars.

Driving down the main drag, Miles swiped his hand over his greasy, thinning, brown hair impatiently. Steve was back in her life. That was evident by the white pickup with the Wyoming plates he saw parked in the front of her favorite restaurant. Jealousy clawed at him as memories of their kissing in the barn came back to him. He chortled to himself: *That one had cost her a barn and a dog.*

Luck was with him tonight. He found a good parking spot. Hatred contorted his face as he watched them leave the restaurant; Anna leaned into Steve's shoulder, smiling up at him as he hugged her closer.

"Oh, gag me," he said out loud as Steve opened the door of the pickup with flair. Pulling out, he passed them, turning down a side street. Miles doubled back to become a phantom behind the truck as it pulled away from the curb.

It was almost as bad as watching the detective go to dinner with her; only that one didn't seem interested in her. Miles was well aware that the only constant in Anna's schedule was the contrived dinner dates. *He thinks he's so smart, Mr. Detective Good Looking. He isn't fooling me again. I'm not going back to a psych ward either.*

For all of Miles's physical shortcomings, nature had balanced it with a cunning, intelligent mind. Having been the brunt of many cruel jokes and socially inept, he had watched from the sidelines, learning human nature better than most psychologists. It created a Machiavellian craftiness. He used it well in the stalking game.

Tailing a vehicle--ducking through the traffic, seemingly an accidental shadow--was another of his honed talents. He innately sensed which way they would go. Very rarely did Miles lose his prey.

Driving slowly past Anna's house, Miles watched as Steve helped her out of the truck, putting his arm around her. A hot pain lanced through Miles' gut. She was his! How dare that filthy creature touch her! Hatred twisted itself into a mocking smile on Miles' face.

If all went according to plan, Anna would finally be all his by Saturday.

Chapter 19 - Endings

It was a rare night for Chris Stein if he got more than five hours of sleep. Besides processing the discouraging events he witnessed, his mind constantly worked at trying to put pieces of puzzles together.

This morning, a big piece had just fallen into place, and he was worried. He'd gotten a call on one of his active cases. Here in this sparse apartment, he felt pity for the life that had ended too soon.

Theresa Rannet still lay in the old brown recliner, her eyes staring at the ceiling, jaw slack. She was nothing but a frail remnant of a human being, consumed by cancer, which, in its greed, had killed itself too.

Turning, the coroner looked at him over glasses perched so precariously on the bridge of his nose that Chris expected them to fall off at any moment.

"So natural causes, right?"

The coroner bobbed his head. "Yeah, I'd say about five o'clock this morning. From all indications, I'm pretty sure her heart gave out. She was taking a pretty stringent chemo regimen, from what I was able to get on her medical files. I'll know for sure after the autopsy. I don't see any indication of foul play; all her medications have been accounted for. No suicide note. There was nothing out of kilter really, except someone had covered her up with a blanket and tucked it in around her. So someone was either here with her, or found her before we did."

Chris nodded, his fingers flying, soft clicks sounding as he took notes on his phone. "So who called it in?"

"The neighbor who normally takes her to treatments. When she didn't answer the door, she used the key Miss Rannet gave her for emergencies."

"Mind if I look around?"

"Nope, you know the drill."

There were no indications that Miles had ever stayed in the house, but he knew Miles had a hideout somewhere. Chris looked for notes, phone numbers, or bills that might suggest how she got money to him or where he was hiding.

On a wooden bookcase, an enlarged, fuzzy picture showed a happy couple and two small children in a heavy, gilt frame. Beside it, a young Miles stared blankly in a graduation picture, Theresa smiling in another. Scattered in the array were pictures of a vibrant Theresa compared to the withdrawn, moody-looking Miles.

The deviant mind fascinated him, but what bothered Chris most about Miles were his eyes. Emotionless, empty, they never showed any depth or spark of personality. *Dead fish eyes,* Chris thought with a chill.

It didn't help that nature had also dealt Miles a raw deal in looks. Bulging eyes, round over-sized head, ears akimbo, pudgy lips, a blob of a body, ungainly, and unmatched.

On a bulletin board in the kitchen, a business card caught Chris's eye. Why would Theresa need a used-car salesman? Her almost-new Camry sat in the driveway. On a corner desk, he shuffled through bank statements and letters; finally, a handwritten note caught his attention.

"To Whom It May Concern, I bequeath all my earthly possessions to my brother, Miles John Rannet."

Running his eyes down the list of items that included a 38 revolver, a chill ran down his back. Thinking back over the psychiatric report from the prison, Miles's diagnosis was Anti-Social with a Delusional Disorder, the psychosocial perspective being exacerbated by childhood abuse. The affective symptoms were violent, physical outbursts, with anger and disdain towards authoritative figures.

Treated with medications and extensive counseling, he had seemed to turn a corner until released. If Miles was off the meds, which was typical for this diagnosis, then he would be dealing with mood swings. If he knew his sister was dead, it could be the event to push him from patient, methodical planning to a psychotic break and impulsive actions. And now, without a doubt, Chris knew Miles had a gun.

Chris's phone buzzed with Anna's ring tone. He answered, "Hello? Hello, Anna? Are you there?"

❁ ❁ ❁ ❁ ❁

"Now that was a chick flick," Steve grumbled.

"What were you expecting with a title like that? Car chases and guns blazing?" Anna tossed her hair back over her shoulder, glancing up through her lashes at him flirtatiously.

Their voices echoed in the parking garage along with growling motors and tires squealing up steep ramps. They moved to the end where the Vette and truck sat side by side against the wall. This level was a little less crowded, being near the top of the garage.

"I must admit the book was far better than the movie, but I think that's because you can get into the characters' heads, instead of an actor trying to portray that on...." Anna suddenly pulled Steve to a stop beside her, taking in a sharp breath.

Miles stepped out from beside Steve's truck, his eyes narrowed, an evil sneer plastered on his pasty, blotched face.

"Anna, my sweet, how are you?" his voice grated out.

Her heart took off, ears pounding with the sound of it. Anna's lungs burned, struggling to grab suddenly air.

Steve stepped out in front of her and went into a slight crouch as if getting ready to tackle the flabby man in front of him. Watching a twisted smile go across Miles's face, she shivered slightly. Anna knew that smile.

"Watch him. He's up to something," she murmured to Steve. He gave a minuscule nod, keeping his eyes on Miles.

Anna's attention had riveted on Miles, who stared in contempt at the man between him and his prey. Then, he looked at her. "I thought you would be with Carolyn today. Why did you hook up with this piece of crap? He wasn't part of the plan, my sweet."

"You need to deal with me, Miles." Steve's tone brooked no argument.

"So, think you're a tough guy, do you? That you can protect her from me?"

He gestured towards Steve's pickup. A superior attitude leaked out through his sardonic smile.

"What is it with rednecks and the rifles hanging in the back window of your beat-up trucks? Lot a good they're doing locked up in there right now, huh? You're just a stupid, shit-kicking cowboy."

She couldn't see the look on Steve's face, but the quiet threat in his voice told her of the fury rolling through him. "I will--and can--protect her, especially from someone like you."

270

"You know she doesn't love you. She's using you. She leads you on then tears out your heart…just for amusement."

Steve shifted ever so slightly. "It seems, Miles, you're the one with a problem. Let her go; get on with your life. If she's as you say, then count yourself lucky to have figured it out. Find someone who can love you."

Miles's dead-fish eyes took on a malevolent gleam. "She loves me! And she's mine. If everyone would just stay out of it, we'd be able to work this out. Today it's my turn to be with her. You're in the way." Suddenly, his hand came out of his coat pocket; the ear-splitting shot of a gun going off twice reverberated loudly throughout the garage.

Concrete splintered behind her, the shards pelting her shoulder. Anna's breath cut short as she held it. Steve wavered and slowly toppled to a heap at her feet. Emotions closed off, her mind kicked into self-preservation. *Don't scream, don't look down; just get him away from Steve, before he shoots again.* Stepping over Steve, she reached for Miles.

"It's okay. Let's get out of here before the police arrive."

The voice in her head shouted directions. *Think! Get him to your car, get control of this situation. Talk to him. You know what he wants.*

"If we take off now, we can get away. Let me help you. Let's take my car; it's faster and parked right here."

She touched his arm gingerly, repulsed at the contact. Miles licked his lips, staring at Steve. The hand holding the gun trembled. Pulling him gently towards the Vette, she continued to listen to the voice directing her. *Don't look back; you'll fall apart if you look.* While holding Miles's arm, her other hand reached into her coat pocket, pressing the dial key for Chris on her cell phone. *Please, please, pick up*, her panicked mind pleaded.

"I'll drive you wherever you want to go, just you and me," she murmured to him. Miles's eyes were glassy now. Shuffling his

271

feet, he looked back at Steve. He swiveled his head to Anna suddenly, glaring at her in suspicion.

"Get back!" He yanked his arm out of her grasp, turning the gun on her.

Anna gazed back at him in surreal calm. "Of course, Miles. What do you want to do?"

For a moment, Miles chewed on his bottom lip. His bulging eyes darted around the parking garage. Fear, anger and panic crossed his pasty features in different stages, finally dropping into a mask of calm. He pointed with the gun towards the car.

"Okay. Get in and drive where I tell you. Remember I have a gun and I'll shoot if I have to." Anna nodded, moving slowly to the driver's door. She knew he hadn't noticed, during his tirade, Chris's muffled voice in her pocket, saying, "Hello? Hello?" Her only hope now was that he could hear the conflict going on. Or maybe he could trace the call--or track her by GPS—as long as he just stayed on the line.

The car rumbled to life, ready as always for her command. Glancing in the rearview mirror, her pounding heart surged again: Steve wasn't anywhere behind her. Backing out, she quickly glanced to the left, seeing the blood on the concrete but no Steve.

Miles fumbled with the seat belt while waving his gun. "Take a right out of the garage, and remember I will shoot if you do anything stupid."

Feeling the familiar thrum of the engine through the steering wheel, her mind calmed, churning over possible options. Stopping to put the validated parking ticket into the automated turn-style, she gritted her teeth, waiting for the gate to rise. Anger was slowly thawing the frost of shock. Being this close to Miles made her want to attack him in crazed fury.

The Vette smoothly negotiated the turn out of the garage exit and growled over the slow speed of the afternoon traffic. Miles was sweating buckets, mopping at his face with his free hand while waving the gun with his other. "At the next light, turn right again," he ordered.

Obeying his command, she negotiated the corner, thinking, *I've got to get him working with me...to let his guard down.* She glanced over; he was staring at her with a calculating look on his face.

"Where are we going?" she asked, hoping her voice sounded calm and relaxed. He looked straight ahead, not answering her. She tried a different tactic. "Thank you, for saving me."

He snorted and glared at her. "I didn't save you, and I'm not falling for that. You're just trying to work me. I did read your diary, remember? You hate me, remember? Can't stand me, wished I'd leave you alone. Well, I get it now."

A wave of resentment rolled through her. *Those were my most intimate thoughts, and he had no right to read them.*

"But," he said, turning to look at her, his voice softening. "But it's not your fault. We've just never had time together." Reaching over, he touched her hair. "Everyone interfered, told you I was no good. It's not true, you know. I love you. I'd do anything for you."

Anna froze, keeping her eyes on the shifting traffic. *I'll have to play along with him, gain time. I hate this.* Swallowing, she pleaded, "You're right. I know you care. Let's go somewhere and talk--just you and me."

Stopping at a red light, she listened as he spoke haltingly. "My sister died last night."

Miles stared out the passenger window. "I've got no one now." Looking at the people waiting to cross at the light, his voice rose in an angry whine. "It sucks, and I hate all of them. I'm not crazy. They're all crazy. I won't take crazy pills." He rolled down the window, waving the gun out the window. "Who's crazy? Who's stupid now? Look at you!" People scrambled back, scattering like wild birds. He laughed with a guttural, hollow sound.

273

Rolling up the window, she could see him slumping in the seat. "You wrote about God being fair and good, but I've never seen it. Why doesn't God love me? He's taken away everyone I've ever loved."

Tension rippled across her shoulders with each mood swing, sensing his mental instability. Hearing the tears and pain in his voice, she could see the broken, hurting child inside. Her anger shifted and for a brief moment, she pitied him.

While he was vulnerable, she tried again to connect with him. "Miles, where are your parents?"

"They were killed when I was three. Some drunk ran into them. All they were doing was coming home from Christmas shopping. I hate Christmas. Then my grandmother died, and we got sent to that piece-of-crap uncle. But my sister--she loved me, but she's gone…" A sob broke from him. "I'm alone."

It felt strange to feel sorry for him, but a cold, rational part of her continued to fight for survival. Forcing a smile, she kept her voice soft. "I am here with you, aren't I? I care. I want to be with you right now. Where are we going? Please, tell me."

He wiped at the tears, snuffling. Like a small child, he caught his breath in several, small, soft hiccups. Miles became quiet, watching her intently, and she could almost hear the wheels turning as he considered his next moves. He wiped his nose on his coat sleeve.

Obviously, Steve had messed with his plans. *How can I turn this to my advantage and give me some time?* She worked on keeping her face smooth, free of any emotion. Every time Steve slipped into her mind, she shied away from it, keeping focused on the moment. She needed to encourage Miles to talk so Chris, who, hopefully, was still listening, would have some clue where to find her.

"Miles, how about I head to the nature reserve? We can talk there about your family--feed the ducks, figure out what we're doing."

Miles lowered the revolver and rested it in his lap, with the barrel still aimed in her direction. She'd not even had time to worry about the gun, her thoughts staying centered on keeping alive.

Shifting again, his voice bright, he asked, "Do you remember our first date at the Dog Shack in the mall? I do. Let's go there again. Take a left on Harmony Lane and get on I-25 going south."

Raking through her memories, she struggled to remember what 'date' they'd ever been on. Then the flashback came in clear. Shopping at the mall with Carolyn--running into Miles at the Food Court--his offering to buy them hot dogs--her inability to say no--accepting, but feeling so uncomfortable.

"I do remember. You bought me lunch, and we chatted. That was very nice of you."

Again, she glanced at his face, watching the expression of hope, his smile. "I've fixed up a real nice place for you. You can live with me now. We can spend time getting to know each other. You have always been mine. I've known it from the first time you smiled at me."

Since Anna had felt sympathy for him, she reasoned maybe she could get him to do the same for her. "You know, I lost both of my parents too. Mom died in January. We are both orphans. I'm so sorry about your sister. I can't imagine how you are hurting. What was she like?"

He bent over the gun, and started to rock, another sob escaping. She probably understood this poor, wretched man better than anyone else in the world right now. Her throat constricted as she listened to him. He gasped for air, coming back to the moment, and waved the gun threateningly.

"S'not going to w-w-work. You are j-j-ust trying to sympathize with m-me to try and trick me into something." Out of the corner of her eye, she saw him straighten in the seat, his face slipping into an unemotional mask. "Keep driving, we have plenty of time now to be together."

She clenched her teeth; anger pushing away any sympathy. She'd never driven the Vette so slowly and carefully. The congested, downtown traffic gave her more time and opportunities. Like the chance to ram the car into something so she could bail. She checked the mirrors, and her heart leaped. It couldn't be! Was that Steve's truck three cars back? Or was it just wishful thinking?

Anna had focused so much on the traffic and her immediate surroundings that Miles's unexpected gasp made her flinch; then, she became lightheaded with adrenaline. Had he also seen the truck? She stole a quick glance in the rearview to see if the truck was still behind them, but Miles watched through the side window as a police cruiser came up alongside them.

Miles looked straight ahead and moved the gun down to rest in his lap again. "Move up in traffic. I've seen you cut and get ahead," he growled.

"Why don't you talk to me Miles, so that I can concentrate, okay? Tell me more about your sister...."

Miles shouted, "Just drive!" A string of curses rolled from his thick lips.

The police car had fallen in behind her. Turning left, she was now on a straight shot to I-25, the four-lane highway just as crowded as the main drag she'd come off. She purposely edged the Vette up over the speed limit, ducking around cars. Flashing red lights came alive on the police cruiser behind her.

"What did you do?" Miles screamed. "Keep driving; get it to the interstate, now!"

She could no longer see a truck behind her, only the police car and its lights. Miles brought the gun up to her head, looking back at the police, screaming, "I'll kill her! I'll kill her! She's mine!" Anna flinched away from the cold metal at her temple. She knew they couldn't hear him, but obviously able to see the gun; they pulled back.

Miles was so busy concentrating on the cruiser behind them that he missed the black sedan with the single flashing light on the driver's side come tearing up the opposite lane towards them.

As she picked up speed ever so slightly, the black sedan flipped into a U-turn, bumping over the median to fall in behind her. Miles smacked the gun into the side of her head. "Faster, damn it. I know you can go faster!"

The blow caused her to flinch away, the Vette swerving with her. Furious, she floored it, the Vette springing forward like a startled gazelle, the power throwing both of them deeper into their seats. The cruiser and sedan fell farther behind as Anna used every ounce of her skill to steer the snarling Vette while weaving and darting around the slower cars ahead.

Coming up on the last intersection before the exit onto I-25, she saw Steve's white truck on her left, speeding through the stop sign and barely missing a car coming down the overpass towards her. He seemed to be headed to the side street to the right of her. Miles was intent on cursing, waving his gun, looking out the back window at the pursuing police vehicles, which had fallen back. She glanced at the odometer, checking her speed, *too fast, too fast, God it's too fast!*

The truck came to a screeching stop about forty feet in front of her, its dented side panel filling her vision. Steve looked at her through the passenger window and for the quick second their eyes met. He nodded.

Her foot stomped the brake, no hesitation in destroying the beautiful car she had worked so hard for.

The long, low front end of the Vette slammed into the side of the truck, T-boning it, and wedging under its side. The impact of crushing metal roared, yet she still heard Miles scream and the ear-splitting report of a firing gun, a Nano-second before the airbag smacked into her face and chest with stinging agony.

Everything had stopped, and for a second all was quiet as the bag deflated, and then her car door wrenched open and strong fingers grasped her arm, pulling her out of the car.

She stumbled, but Steve's arm scooped her up against him. Her eyes quickly scanned his ashen face as they stumbled together around the moaning pickup. Helping her gently to the ground, she leaned up against the side of the truck. Still trying to focus on the events around her, Anna watched Steve grab his rifle from the front seat. She could see he was favoring his left arm and blood ran darkly down his leather coat and leg.

"Stay down, Anna!" he snarled. She watched as he used his uninjured hand to quickly bring up the rifle to rest on the side panel of the bed of the truck, cocking the hammer.

✿ ✿ ✿ ✿ ✿

The impact of the two vehicles locked them together, sliding both the truck and deceased Vette down over the side of the road at the intersection, into the barrow pit. A side road was to the left of them, and it gave access to a motel, convenience store, and gas station. Steve glanced over to see people who had been pumping gas now standing agape at the scene unfolding in front of them.

He waited, teeth clenched against the burning, gut-wrenching pain that lanced down his left side, making him feel slightly faint. He put it all aside as he steadied the rifle.

Sirens rent the air ahead of the approaching police as Miles crawled from the passenger side of the crumpled Vette. Standing, he looked around, dazed, and still gripping the gun. Looking stupidly at the car, he cursed. Steve watched him stumble around the back of the Vette to the open driver's door, foul language pouring out as he saw his prey had escaped. Standing in the corner created by the back end of the T-boned truck and the side of the Vette, his cursing rose in pitch.

Turning towards the truck, his eyes widened, suddenly cutting off the string of obscenities. Steve took a bit of pleasure in seeing Miles realize that he was staring at the barrel of a 30/30 with him on the other end of it, his finger ready to squeeze the trigger.

He ground out, "So now can you see why redneck cowboys have rifles in their trucks, Miles? To shoot low down, dirty vermin and snakes. That's why. Give me a reason to show you how good of a shot I am. Come on; every good hunter knows if you wound an animal, you always finish it off with a mercy shot."

"Go ahead, cowboy--how does it go?--oh yeah, make my day!" Steve could hear a hysterical note in Miles laughter.

As they talked, Chris's sedan skidded into the fray, the car lurching to a stop, the door flying open. Out of the corner of his eye, Steve saw him jump out, crouch behind it, revolver cocked. Chris called out, "Steve, stand down. I have it covered. Miles put it down. Put down the gun, now."

Miles's fishy eyes darted ever so slightly towards the new threat, and then back to glare at Steve.

Several more screaming police cars came to squealing stops on the pavement. Steve kept his eyes locked with Miles's cold, gray ones. Clicking metal on metal warned of guns being armed while authoritative voices cleared and directed people around the scene. All of this registered somewhere in Steve's mind but didn't deter his attention from Miles.

Chris called again quietly to him. "Don't shoot. Stand down, Steve. We have it under control. Let us handle this."

Miles, still watching Steve, copied Chris's voice in a whiny imitation. "Yeah, Stevie, be a good little boy. Put down your big scary rifle."

Without taking his eye off Miles, Steve eased off the trigger. Nope, *not letting him get to me. He's not worth it. But just in case, I'm not letting him out of my sight.* On the edge of his peripheral vision, he could see Chris watching as he put the hammer down on the rifle.

Chris stood up behind his car door now, his voice louder. "Miles, over here. Miles, let's talk. Come on, you can trust me. Remember me? We talked this out the last time; we can do it again. You did the right thing then. Do it now. Surrender and you won't get hurt. We can talk, Miles...."

Miles's crazed eyes swung to meet Chris's. "Yeah, we can talk again just like the last time, ole buddy, and I can go listen to those nice doctors telling me bullshit!"

Steve wavered, the blood loss now causing his sight to blur. With Miles's attention focused on Chris, he slowly eased the rifle to its side, to rest on the edge of the truck panel. Raising his hands slightly so all could see them, he stepped back slightly behind the cab, steadying his left shoulder up against the door-frame, watching the drama before him.

"Miles Rannet, put down your gun, show your hands and walk towards me," Chris demanded.

Steve noticed a rough edge of emotion break through Chris's normally smooth voice.

Anna pulled on his pant leg, whispering up at him. "Steve, sit down. You've lost so much blood. Please." Glancing down at her, he shook his head, finger to his lips.

Miles sneered, looking like a cornered animal. Steve watched him look out at the fan of police cruisers, his eyes livid with hatred, glaring at the guns pointed at him.

"All of you, all of you are crazy. Am I the only one that can see she's the problem? She's the one who brought us here. Think she wants you, Chris? Hell no! She used you like she's using that John Wayne cowboy over there. Like she used me!"

He was waving the gun in the air now, still ranting. Chris called again, voice stronger, authoritative. "Put the gun down, Miles, or we will shoot. Is this really the way you want to go out? Let us help you!"

"I don't need help! If you'd leave me alone, I could show her that I'm the one that loves her. She's mine. I can help her if you'd get the hell out of the way." Steve kept an eye on Miles as he sputtered and cursed.

Chris softened his voice, pleading. "Miles, your sister wouldn't want this. Let us help you. We don't want to shoot."

"Go to hell," were the last words Miles screamed on this earth, as he aimed the gun at Chris and shot. The gunfire was deafening, quickly leaving total silence in its wake.

Steve slid down beside Anna, gathering her against his chest, murmuring, "It's okay, it's okay, it's all over. Thank God, it's okay." He cradled her shaking frame, stroking her hair as she sobbed.

Beside the totaled Vette, Miles's body had fallen with a sickeningly soft thud. His lifeless eyes stared from under the twisted back end of the truck. Steve shielded Anna's face from the sight, whispering in her ear, "It's okay. I love you. You're safe now."

Chris ran around the truck, kneeling in front of Steve. "Where're you hit, Steve?"

The world was getting strangely dark around the edges. Steve mumbled, "Shoulder, but get Anna out of here."

"It's okay, buddy. We have an ambulance in route; you'll be okay. Anna, are you hurt?"

He heard her exhausted voice softly say, "I'm fine, but I think he's fainting."

Steve's arms fell away from her; he could no longer control them. He slid to the side; no strength left in his body, feeling as if he was underwater. The blackness was growing; he felt Anna grab

281

him, pulling him to her, cradling his head. She leaned over him, her face fuzzing around the edges.

"Steve Johnson, you hang in there. You can't leave me. I love you, Steve. I love you."

Steve grabbed on to the words he had waited so long to hear, before slipping away into the darkness.

Chapter 20 – Continuing

Anna flipped open the cell phone. *This is going to be the hardest call I've ever made.* Dialing Steve's parents' number, the ring sounding tinny in her ear, she held her breath, waiting.

"Hello?" Jack's voice came through strong.

"Hi, Jack, I'm so sorry--I've got bad news."

After a second of silence, he spoke, "What happened, Anna? Is everyone okay?"

"Jack, Miles came after us and Steve got shot. I'm here at the hospital. I think you need to come down." She took a big breath in the silence.

"How bad is he?" Jack's voice wavered.

Tears slid down Anna's face. "All they've said is he's lost a lot of blood, and the bullet did some damage to his shoulder blade. He's in surgery now."

"Okay. Everything is going to be okay. We'll be there as soon as we can. Call us if you find anything else out. Just keep praying." His tone was business-like as he went into emergency mode.

She snapped the phone closed, her right thigh burning. The lighting was muted in the surgery lounge, as if in this atmosphere of waiting, nothing wanted to disturb the possibility of hope. Flashes of scenes from the day popped up in her mind. Her last glimpse of Steve as the EMTs worked over him-- the ambulance taking off with siren screaming--Chris noticing she was bleeding from her right thigh--the crash and gunshot--the bullet grazing her.

The ringing phone broke the replays. Flipping it open, she answered. "Hey, thanks for calling back. No, everything isn't okay. Yeah, that newscast is about us. Miles is dead, and Steve…." Her voice cut out, her throat closing. Coughing, she continued, "He's been shot. Yeah, I'm at the hospital." She listened. "That would be great. I could use the support. Thanks, Carolyn."

Shifting on the stiff chair, she remembered her ambulance ride to the hospital had been uncomfortable. Chris's normally handsome features were drawn and tired. He told the EMTs he had to ride in with her to get her statement. She knew better but was grateful for his presence. After making sure she would be fine, Chris had apologized profusely for having to go back to the scene to handle the clean-up.

Anna had fibbed a little, telling the staff she was Steve's fiancée, desperately wanting to know his condition. But only after getting treatment for her bullet wound had the nurse filled Anna in on Steve. It had been an agonizing wait, testing her temper to the limits. That same nurse directed her to the waiting room, promising Anna news the minute there was any.

How had Steve handled this when he had been waiting for me?

More scenes played out in her mind. Steve's white face, Miles's inert body, covered with a sheet of plastic. Her mind still couldn't grasp that Miles was gone.

The odor of antiseptic cleaning agents lingered in the air as she limped along, no longer able to sit still. Anna wouldn't allow herself to think of what-ifs right now. Instead, she searched for the little chapel that had been a haven during her mother's struggle with cancer. Slipping past the stained glass doors, into the cool interior, eight pews of glowing, aged wood led up to a simple altar.

Walking up to the large Bible lying open on the ledge of the altar, she glanced down to see it was open to "The Book of Job." She choked on a little sob. *I don't need to read about the life of Job. I'm living it!* For the first time in her life, Anna felt totally overwhelmed and alone.

Falling to her knees, bowing her head, she sent her pleas heavenward.

❀ ❀ ❀ ❀ ❀

The sleet fell sporadically as if even nature couldn't quite muster tears for the deceased. Anna stood next to the headstone, the name freshly chiseled into the granite, wiping at tears. Chris put his arm around her shoulder, pulling her to him gently, holding the umbrella over them.

She looked up into his handsome face, tenderness in his intense, blue eyes.

"He couldn't get a break, could he? I feel sorry for him," Chris murmured.

Nodding wordlessly, she'd never seen this empathetic side of him before. Sometimes she imagined the childhood moments that drove adult motives. In this instance, she could see the little boy in Chris, fearing the monsters under the bed, donning the towel cape of a superhero and vanquishing them. The only way he knew how to cope with the injustice of the world was to catch the bad guys.

The minister, covered in the slick black of a raincoat, gave words of consolation after reading a brief Bible verse. They watched as the urn containing the ashes were lowered into the small hole.

Chris slid his arm under hers, helping her limp back to the car over the soggy turf.

"So when did you figure it out?" he asked, expertly merging into traffic.

"Not until he said something that day in the car; then, later at the hospital, I started putting it all together. I remembered Mom telling me, but I was little."

"With time, facts can get confused, or forgotten. You never had direct contact with the family, so it wouldn't have been something you'd recall."

"Yes, but my mom should've known. Why didn't she say something?"

He stared ahead into the traffic in front of them. "I don't know, Anna. I wasn't sure if you knew it had been your father who was responsible for the death of Miles's parents. But you already carried so much guilt over what you thought you did to bring this on yourself that I didn't want to add to it."

She leaned her head against the cold window, letting out a sigh. "I wish I'd known sooner. Maybe I could've helped him get into counseling, and it would've made a difference. If I had gotten to know Theresa, we could have talked, shared our experiences, and helped one another."

"I think what you did for both of them was very kind."

"I appreciate your help in getting them buried with their parents. I just don't know if it's enough, Chris."

"You're welcome. The cemetery owner owed me a favor of gratitude that he was most happy to repay." A rare grin lit up Chris's face at the memory of some inside joke.

She caught her breath at his shining smile. *No wonder Carolyn is head over heels for this guy.* During the intensity of the last few months, she'd been impervious to his good looks.

He sobered again. "You know, Anna, it's really not your fault. Knowing their parents were the ones killed by your father would've changed nothing. Maybe you could have been a support system, but Miles was doomed from the start. If it hadn't been you, it would have been some other woman. And you know that he made his own choices. You're not responsible for your parents' mistakes either."

She shrugged: these were her demons; she would have to conquer them herself.

"So how's Steve doing?"

Appreciating his change of subject, she said, "He is doing quite well now. It still scares me to think how close he came to bleeding out. Thank God he is still alive. What I can't understand is how he almost kills himself saving me without even thinking about the pain, yet he can be such a wimp when it comes to physical therapy."

Chris chuckled. "It's a man thing; you know-- the adrenaline rush to save the damsel in distress. Now he has to do the boring, painful stuff."

"You men all stick together, I see."

"Yes, ma'am, we do."

"And it's a good thing he got a medical emergency exception, so he hasn't lost his education grants. The tech school has agreed to let him catch up online while he's laid up. His AA group has been great too, helping him get to appointments when I can't."

"I'm glad things are working out. He's a great guy, Anna, and you deserve someone like him. But I'm going to miss our Friday night dinners. You know, I don't want to offend you, but--well, this is meant as a compliment: you're like the sister I've never had." A blush touched his cheeks.

287

Anna laughed, relief flooding her. "Oh, Chris, I feel exactly the same thing: I would love to count you like the brother I've never had!"

His phone interrupted them with an impatient ring as he pulled over to the side of the road to answer.

"Yeah, where? Okay, I can be there in twenty."

❀ ❀ ❀ ❀ ❀

A little Christmas tree in the corner flashed its lights; the smell of roasting turkey hung in the air. Holiday music added to the spirit of the celebration already alive and well in the house.

Delilah's barking and the thunder of little feet echoed in the loft above the adults gathered in the living room and kitchen.

"You kids quit roughhousing up there," Emily called out.

The thudding of multiple feet caused the stairway to squeak in protest.

Steve walked over to Anna, holding out her coat with his good hand. "So go for a walk with me up to the swing?"

"It's snowing, you know." She rolled her eyes at him.

"Yeah, well, it's beautiful out, and Delilah could use the walk."

At the sound of her name, the exuberant, yellow dog escaped from the embrace of Matthew to bound up to Anna, sweeping the floor with her feathered tail as she sat down.

Evelyn chided Anna. "You two need a good cooling off after all that smooching in the kitchen." Anna felt the heat of a growing blush.

Chelsea rounded the corner from the stairs. "What's smooching mean?"

Matthew giggled at her; Chelsea glared back.

"It means kissing, pipsqueak," Steve said, laughing, reaching out to tousle her hair.

Anna had invited Steve and his family over for Christmas Eve. Brad's two boys played with Matthew and John while Chelsea delighted in being the only girl, giving her the chance to rule. Aunt Evelyn and Uncle George had joined them at the last minute, filling the little house to the brim. All afternoon they had played card games and shared family stories.

Anna looked over the family scene in contentment. "Yeah, I think Delilah could use a break. Be right back, everyone."

She took the coat he'd laid over the back of the couch and slipped into it. Grabbing Steve's new leather coat, she helped him shrug his one good arm into the sleeve. Then, standing on her tiptoes, she pulled the side of the coat over his injured shoulder to let it fall over the sling on his arm.

"I don't know how you did this one-armed thing. It's a pain." Steve grumbled.

"Steve Johnson, you just be grateful to be alive and in one piece."

The new snow dampened all sound, creating an unnatural quiet as snowflakes fell from the gray skies in a leisurely way. Steve plowed through it up to the bare cottonwood, Anna following in his footsteps. She brushed off the swing and sat down to watch the winter show. Sticking out her tongue, she felt the soft landing of the cold flakes.

Watching Delilah, she giggled as the dog ran around in a frenzy, sending puffy clouds up as she burrowed here and there in the light snow.

Since it had been such a hectic year, Anna hadn't realized there had been many 'firsts' since her mother's death. The therapist warned her it would be hardest during the holidays. Thanksgiving had been the first holiday when it sunk in. She

289

decided the first Christmas without her mother would be spent elsewhere.

A squeak of a boot against fresh snow announced Steve's approach. Cloudy bursts framed his words.

"May I join you, lady?"

"Of course, right here." She patted the swing's bench.

The new leather coat tapered down to his slim hips, giving his shoulders a broad look, even with the sling evident. There was a green tint to his eyes in the gray afternoon light.

Noting her perusal he shyly looked away.

"Ever wonder why I asked you to marry me here?"

"Not really. I guess I was too panicked at the time."

He nodded towards the white lumps under the snow where headstones rested. "I wanted to include all of your family in the moment."

"Oh! I never thought about that. How sweet, Steve. So kind of you," she said, in a puff of white breath. "Remember, we had our first kiss here too."

"How could I forget that, lady? Do you think we're good together, Anna? Are you happy?" There was a probing intensity to his gaze.

Scooting across the frozen bench, she snuggled against him. Looking up, she heard his breath catch at the back of his throat. She didn't know how beautiful her jeweled blue eyes, framed in black lashes, looked in the gray light.

"I'm the happiest I've ever been in my life because I have you and love you. I think we are terrific together. Why?"

Slipping his arm around her shoulders, he bent in slowly, his sigh warming her cheek. His lips teased, lightly grazing hers, and then retreated. His cheek rested against her hair; his breath tickled her ear, causing goose bumps to slide down her arm. His lips nibbled as he moved up her cheek and kissed her closed eyes softly, her sigh answering him. Seeming satisfied in his conquest, he captured her mouth in a gentle, triumphant kiss. Willingly, she responded, her lips parting to join his.

Slowly breaking away, he brought his finger up to slide down her cheek. It had been hard keeping her promise to wait when she wanted all of him, the man she loved with all her heart.

He stared into her eyes, uncertainty in the depths of his. She held her breath as he tugged at her glove, finally getting it off. He pulled something out of his pocket, transferring it to the hand in the sling. Holding her gloveless hand in his right, he pulled it to his trapped left hand so he could gently slip a gleaming ring on her finger, the facets in the diamond rivaling the glittering snowflakes. It was snug, fitting perfectly. He bent his head and softly kissed the palm of her ring-adorned hand.

Looking into her wide eyes, he asked solemnly, "So Anna Marie Sanchez, I ask you again: do you want to spend the rest of your life with me? Will you marry me?

She took a quick breath, her eyes bright with unshed tears, flashing him an ethereal smile. Putting her hand on his cheek, she said, "I'd be very, very honored to marry you, be your partner in life, and have a lot of little ones who look just like you."

He laughed, little clouds of glee puffing into the air. He caught her hand to his chest.

"We're getting way ahead here. Let's plan a wedding first." He gathered her close, his lips warming hers in an ardent kiss filled with elation.

Delilah barked, warning them of company. Turning, Anna caught Chelsea watching them from behind the wide trunk of the cottonwood.

"You kissed her! You gave her a ring!" She turned and ran down the hill towards the house.

Steve chuckled. Anna raised an eyebrow, studying his flushed face. "And I think it's about time you did! I've been waiting and hoping since our first real date!"

"Yup," he said, smiling devilishly. "But it's all your fault. I wasn't taking any chances until you told me you loved me. Of course, you had to wait until I was practically dead to say it!"

"You know what they say, 'timing is everything,'" she flipped back at him.

"Let's get down there and tell them ourselves, shall we?"

As they walked in, excited faces and big smiles greeted them as the chorus of "Surprise" rang out. Anna gasped. In the short time they'd been gone, the family members had been quite busy decorating with brightly colored streamers. The food was out on the kitchen counters, several card tables pulled out and set up, and a punch bowl gleamed and beckoned.

She turned to Steve. "Pretty sure of yourself, eh, Sherlock?"

Steve raised an eyebrow. "Well, you did say you loved me--finally.

Anna lightly smacked his good arm, and Steve immediately feigned great pain.

George chuckled. "Well, she does take after her grandfather, you know. He had a hard time with sentiments as well. Congratulations, Son, and welcome to the family." He reached out to shake Steve's hand.

"And she smooches good, I saw," Chelsea said with pride.

Everyone laughed, jostling to get in to congratulate the glowing couple.

"Dinner is ready. Let's eat, everyone, and give these two lovebirds a break," Emily announced.

The odor of mouth-watering turkey filled the air as everyone scrambled for a place at the long, dining table with the add-on of various card tables. Steve pulled out a chair and motioned her over. Her heart tripped at the love shining in his eyes.

George bowed his head, and everyone grabbed a hand, following suit. At the end of the prayer, she looked up. Tears swam in her eyes as she gazed at George sitting at the head of the table where her grandfather used to sit. It was such a different dining scene than the one she used to dread because seated around it was what she now held most dear in the world: her family.

Robynn Gabel

Epilogue — New Start

The music stopped as the quiet breeze moved over bows and ribbons, tickling the leaves above the gathered crowd. In the quiet, the minister waited as George turned to give her a gentle kiss on the cheek before handing her off to Steve.

She gazed up into his face. Steve's slender fingers squeezed her hand and the world around her dissolved as she lost herself in the deep wells of his blue-tinted eyes.

Her voice, quiet and firm, acknowledged her promised vows. Steve gave strong and forceful replies. Then, at last, the words they both had waited for so long, making them man and wife.

Steve bent his head, his hand slipping to the small of her back to draw her in. He crushed her lips in fierce possession, not caring about what the crowd witnessed. Anna responded unrestrained, slipping her arms up around his neck. Time stood still as they kissed long and deep to hoots, hollers and clapping. Finally coming up for air, they turned to face the crowd, proudly Mr. and Mrs. Steve Johnson.

"Folks, we have pictures to do here. So if you want to go back down to the barn, there are refreshments there, and you can greet the bride and groom when they join you if you don't mind," Emily's strong voice directed.

The gangly photographer motioned them over to the swing where their wedding party had lined up.

"So do we want traditional or fun pictures, Watson?"

Anna laughed, looking down at her husband who sprawled out across the swing, his head in her lap, smiling back at her with the little crinkles she loved so much. "We need new traditions. Let's have some fun, Sherlock."

Emily snorted. "If you two don't hurry up, there's going to be nothing left of the potluck."

After several shots on the swing the photographer had them move to stand close to the big cottonwood tree.

"Did you ever think we'd make it to this day? I didn't," Steve murmured in her ear.

Anna smiled for the camera. After the click, she looked up at her husband. "No. If someone had told me a year ago we would be standing here as man and wife; I would've bet them hard cash it would never happen."

After the photo shoot, Anna and Steve, hand in hand, started down the path to the barn. She leaned into Steve as they walked. "Don't you think that would be the perfect place for the house?"

Steve stopped, looking at the wide shelf of land at the base of the hill across from them. "Yes, Mrs. Johnson, I do agree. We can add on as we have kids. All twelve of them."

"Mr. Johnson, I see that you've been missing your mirror sessions again," Anna stated flatly. An impish smile was at odds with her tone.

He gathered her into his arms, looking down at her upturned face. "If someone had told me you'd agree to move to Wyoming, I would've bet they were dead wrong."

"Ah, well, love does things to a girl, Mr. Johnson."

He threw his head back laughing. "You're going to wear out our last name, Mrs. Johnson."

In the barn, decorations brightened the long tables, and chairs sat on the right side, which formed a horseshoe, and on the other side was a dance floor; hay bales provided extra seating. A long table bowed under the weight of a sumptuous feast being supplied by the usual potluck.

Jim stood, calling for attention as he gave the Best Man toast. "I pray Anna can find the strength to put up with his pigheadedness." Laughter erupted. "But my prayers, as well as all of yours, I know, are that Steve and Anna will have a long, loving, wonderful, and sober marriage."

Clapping and acknowledgments were loudly mixed. Anna looked out over the crowd. Mary Beth was having a hard time handling the dirt floor of the barn in stiletto heels. Dressed in a fashionable sea-green that set off her upswept, raven hair, with makeup done in Hollywood perfection, she headed to the punch bowl with Rob hovering at her side.

Carolyn leaned into Anna. "Cake is ready. I know I've never seen one with a toy Corvette and a horse on the top of it before. Any special meaning to that?"

Anna giggled. "Chelsea wanted to make our wedding cake for us. We compromised and let her pick out our cake topper."

"Are you ready for dessert, lady?" Steve flashed an ornery smile.

Anna said archly, "That depends on who's serving it."

Evelyn finished setting out the plates for serving. "No cake fights today, okay you two?

Anna leaned into Steve; her eyes wicked with amusement. "So do you trust me to feed you?"

Steve snorted. "What do you think, lady?"

Her light laughter danced. The photographer readied his camera as Anna posed with a slice of cake, and Steve waited, his plate in hand.

A hush fell over the crowd, watching, waiting. Steve moved in, paused, and then, in a gentlemanly manner, slid a piece into her mouth.

She chuckled, eyes narrowed.

Steve watched her warily. "Lady, be nice," he murmured, backing up from her. The wall stopped him; he sighed, opening his mouth and closing his eyes. Anna took a larger chunk, squishing and cramming until he caught her hands, and swooped in to give her a cake-filled kiss.

Cheering erupted, and the fiddlers started tuning up.

Emily helped Anna wipe off the frosting. "Well, girl, that was the sweetest ceremony I've seen in years."

"Thank you, but you know it was all because of your organizational skills."

"I couldn't have done it without Carolyn. What a powerhouse of a girl."

Anna glanced around locating the bridesmaid in question and saw Carolyn leaning up against a support beam, Chris's intense gaze focused on her.

Emily saw where Anna was looking and gave a little laugh. "She's been a giggly mess over the attention of that detective. They make quite an odd combination."

Anna had been quite pleased her new, adopted brother had made good on his promise to be part of her life. He'd happily accepted her wedding invitation inviting Carolyn to carpool with him.

Mary Beth tottered to the table, Rob escorting her. "What a quaint wedding, Anna," she said tartly.

"Thank you both for coming. You both look wonderful. How has the calving gone this spring?" Anna asked, looking to Rob.

"We got a good crop this year," Rob enthused. "Had some nice late spring rains so we're going to be able to push out sooner this year. Hope you'll ride for us."

"Hey, Rob, thanks for coming." Steve walked up, holding out his hand. Rob responded with a firm shake.

As they moved off to chat, a bored-looking Mary Beth followed behind. Emily confided in a low voice, "Quaint is Mary Beth's way of saying how great hers was. It was the gaudiest affair I've ever seen. Old Rob has been acting like a nervous stallion protecting a mare in heat ever since."

Anna gave Emily a sad smile. She could see the insecure child inside of Mary Beth, the little girl who would forever chase after the things of the world, never feeling good enough, pretty enough or smart enough to be at peace within.

Emily interrupted her pensive thoughts. "Well, you got to get rid of that pretty bouquet now. Are you ready?"

Anna heaved the bouquet up over her head, turning to see Carolyn catch it and her ecstatic dance of joy at doing so.

Steve was drug over by his friends and urged to search for the garter they knew Anna had hidden. She lifted her hem, to expose a bright-white cowboy boot, causing hoots from those crowded around.

It was a quirky Hanson tradition that Anna's great-grandmother had started. Always frugal, down to earth and hardworking, she could only afford one pair of new shoes. So she chose to be married in cowboy boots, she would use them afterwards. No high heels: they were impractical to the life of a rancher's wife. Even Anna's mother, Jenny, had honored the tradition, borrowing a pair of boots for her wedding. Anna had embraced the idea, buying her first pair of cowboy boots.

Emily called out, "Well, I never thought I'd see the day when the city mouse would put on a pair of country mouse shoes!"

Anna stuck her tongue out, and everyone broke into laughter. With a wolfish grin, Steve lifted her gown higher to expose the dainty cowboy boot, and then took his time to slide his hand up to her knee and then above.

Anna blushed deeply, fanning herself as his lean fingers finally found the blue-colored, lacy garter. As he started slipping it down, she realized the boot would have to come off so he could slide it over her shapely foot. Laughter rolled out as he tugged at the boot and she struggled to keep her balance. Finally, he had the treasured garter and with a long pull on the elastic, he shot it into the air, everyone guffawing when it hit the back of an unaware Chris.

Evelyn was next, directing Anna into George's arms as they opened the dancing with the traditional father-daughter dance.

"Been some time since I dressed up and danced with a pretty girl," he beamed. "He's going to make a good rancher someday. You picked a good one, Anna."

Steve reclaimed Anna, sweeping her into his arms, leaning over to murmur, "Mine, all mine, my beautiful wife." She melted closer to him.

"I'm all yours, my handsome husband," she enthused. Hearing "wife" for the first time seemed proprietary yet intimately personal.

Several dances later, Anna was thankful for the practical cowboy boots, knowing her feet would never have survived in heels, even with the sheets of plywood they'd laid down to make a dance floor.

The time came for Anna and Steve to leave, everyone scrambling to line the pathway in front of the house that led down

300

to the brand new, metallic candy-apple red, Z06 Corvette. Its back window had been carefully painted with 'Just Married.'

Emily helped Anna slip out of her wedding dress, into the comfortable traditional wear of Wyoming: a blouse and blue jeans. "Girl, you're the only one I know who'd want to spend their honeymoon at a Corvette Rally!"

Anna gave her an adventuresome smile. "We got to try out our new wedding present, Emily!"

"Well, you were darn lucky the insurance company covered your suicidal Vette, and you had enough to cover the rest. But it sure is a nice ride. You two have fun. Love you, Anna." Emily buried her in a bear hug.

Anna was checking her hair in the antique mirror when Steve joined her, still looking slim and trim, despite having changed out of his wedding clothes.

"Well, lady, it's time to face the gauntlet. Are you ready?" She nodded.

Rice pelted them in sprays as Steve and Anna raced for the Vette. They waved and honked to the onlookers as they drove slowly down the dirt road.

"So, Sherlock, is this where we drive off into the sunset to live happily ever after?" She cocked her head to one side with a mischievous look.

"I can't promise 'happily ever after,' Lady. Only one day at a time," he answered gently, with her favorite eye-crinkling smile.

"That's all I can ask for, my love."

At the highway, before pulling out, Anna gripped the wheel of the purring Vette, looking over at him; her eyes alight with anticipation.

"Ready?"

Steve's daredevil smile answered her.

Robynn Gabel

About the Author

Though born in Columbus, Ohio, Robynn Gabel grew up in the western states of Colorado and Wyoming. Always an adventurer, she has traveled through or lived in forty-nine of fifty states. After trying her hand at several careers, which include movie theatre owner, convention manager and a certified nurse's aide, she retired. During the career years, she also helped raise a blended family of five children with her husband, Darrell. They have been blessed with 16 grandchildren. During retirement she took up learning how to play the piano, inspirational speaking, driving and auto-crossing Corvettes, and showing Missouri Fox Trotters. At last, she decided to work on her life-long dream of writing fictional stories.

Other Titles by this Author

The Heart of Elvis
Children books: Making Friends, I Know I Can Do It

Social Feeds:

www.robynngabel.com
http://www.dupler.org
https://www.facebook.com/AuthorRobynnGabel

Find more awesome reads at:

http://www.tri-swanpress.weebly.com

www.ingramcontent.com/pod-product-compliance
Lightning Source LLC
Chambersburg PA
CBHW061542170626
46811CB00001B/55